A Steal of a Deal

A NOVEL

Ginny Aiken

Revell

a division of Baker Publishing Group
Grand Rapids, Michigan

© 2008 by Ginny Aiken

Published by Revell
a division of Baker Publishing Group
P.O. Box 6287, Grand Rapids, MI 49516-6287
www.revellbooks.com

Printed in the United States of America

Library of Congress Cataloging-in-Publication Data
Aiken, Ginny
   A steal of a deal / Ginny Aiken
      p.   cm. — (The shop-til-u-drop collection ; bk. 2)
   ISBN 978-0-8007-3228-8 (pbk.)
      1. Home shopping television programs—Fiction. 2. Television personalities—Fiction. 3. Gemologists—Fiction. I. Title.
PS3551.I339S74 2008
813'.54—dc22   2007047491

This book is a work of fiction. Names, characters, places, and incidents are the product of the author's imagination or are used fictitiously. Any resemblance to actual events, locales, or persons, living or dead, is coincidental.

Scripture is taken from the New King James Version. Copyright © 1982 by Thomas Nelson, Inc. Used by permission. All rights reserved.

Published in association with the literary agency of Alive Communications, Inc., 7680 Goddard St., Suite 200, Colorado Springs, CO 80920.

"They shall be Mine,"
says the LORD of hosts,
"On the day that I make them My jewels.
And I will spare them
As a man spares his own son who serves him."

Malachi 3:17

1^{00}

I'm not feeling the love here. Of all the potential cohosts a girl can get stuck with, why did I wind up with a California surfer-boy gem-dunce? What's a California surfer-boy gem-dunce, you ask? Well, he's blond, blue-eyed, and gorgeous, but he knows nothing about . . . well, what really matters here—gems!

My boss, Miss Mona Latimer, who's known me since I was a tiny bulge in my mama's belly, should've known better. She should've known a co-anchoring gig would never work between a gemological dud and me in front of millions of money-waving, bling-bling crazed women wanting to know about the gemstones they buy.

The by-women, for-women, all-women Shop-Til-U-Drop television shopping channel was doing just fine without the issues testosterone poisoning brings. If Miss Mona, owner and genius extraordinaire behind the S.T.U.D.—what most

5

people call our shopping channel—really felt we needed a male to spice things up, don't you think she should've gone to the GIA (that's the Gemological Institute of America) to find herself said male? We're talking a gem and jewelry show here.

Fine, fine, fine! Max did ask me to share my knowledge. And I have been trying my best to work with him, but it's slow going. You'd think Miss Mona would be at least a little concerned about the situation.

What situation? Oh, the one where Max and I have . . . umm . . . disagreements while the cameras roll. Miss Mona calls it "Chemistry!" "Electricity!" She should be horrified to have that happening on her channel. Then again, I suppose I shouldn't expect her to be logical or reasonable. She is, after all, the queen of the "Huh?" factor.

What is the "Huh?" factor, you ask? That's when someone comes up with something so out of whack that your only possible response is, well, "Huh?"

My response exactly.

All right, I admit Max does have the rare redeeming quality. Like his killer great looks don't hurt the feminine eye. And he does think the world of Miss Mona and her best friend, my own great-aunt Weeby. But then again, everyone does, so that's no big deal.

Oh. You want to know who I am? Well. I really should introduce myself. I do it every single day at the start of my show. I'm Andrea Autumn Adams, master gemologist and host of the S.T.U.D.'s gem and jewelry shows.

My uninformed cohost is Max Matthews, a former Ohio State Buckeye football player. You know, he majored in football and minored in whatever. In Max's case, the whatever

6

was meteorology. So after a stint as a weatherman at a Middle America TV station, he's supposedly a pro at the on-camera thing. Which is how he wound up here.

And yeah, he knows nothing about gemstones.

Oh, okay. There was that moment when he did bring the cavalry to help me out of a tight spot a couple of months ago. And I am truly grateful. But, c'mon! That's as far as I'm going to let it go. After all, a fly knows as much as he does about gemstones and jewelry.

So now that you know all the details, please tell me why I'm such a patsy. Why, after everything I've just told you, am I sitting in my kitchen, the table spread far and wide with my treasured collection of rocks—some precious, some semi, and some plain old rocks—trying to get Max to understand and appreciate the beauty of God's genius?

Maybe it's got more to do with those killer blue eyes than with the show. How could I say no?

Yeah, I'm in trouble.

But he did ask for my help. Who am I to turn down someone in need? Plus Miss Mona, our boss, told me to play nice.

I'm sure you've figured out that playing nice with Max scares me. He has that oozing masculine appeal you can't ignore. At least I can't, no matter how hard I try.

And then he pulls out that endearing gentleness toward the Daunting Duo—Aunt Weeby and Miss Mona. Plus he hasn't been snarky about my faith—a major positive for any guy I meet. If I have to be squeaky-clean honest, Max has expressed interest in Aunt Weeby's and my approach to living out our love for Christ. Oh, he hasn't come out and said much of anything about it, but I can feel these things. I think he's told me he's a churchgoer, so maybe he's got that Christ-shaped hole in his heart ready for filling.

But I digress. We're in the Adams family home kitchen, engaged in one of my fave pastimes: playing with gems.

Max loops a magnificent three-carat kunzite. "It's very clean," he says, his voice rich and intent. "And the cut seems excellent. At least, it is according to the pictures you had me study." Then he looks up. "But give me a break, Andie. Who's going to know the difference between one of these and a super-washed-out orchid amethyst?"

See what I'm dealing with here?

I blow out a frustrated breath. "A gemologist is going to know. And care. A gem collector's going to care too." I raise a hand to stop his objection. "*And* any potential customer on our program is really going to care, especially since the price of gemmy kunzite is so many times higher than that of any amethyst."

He drops his tweezers on the Selvyt cloth I'd spread on the well-used pine farm table, kunzite still clamped between the steel prongs, then leans back in his Windsor chair. "So tell me, oh ye of massive gemological wisdom. Is there a lot of this kind of fraud going on?"

I'm not taking the bait, folks! "Amethyst for kunzite?"

He nods.

"Not much. How many gem geeks are out there who know kunzite exists? How many gem geeks d'you think would buy some from someone who's not up to speed on her gems?"

His iced tea must be warm by now, but he takes another swig. "I guess that's a good thing. But if no one really knows what this stuff is"—he gestures toward the gem still jailed by the tweezers—"then why is it so expensive? You know, the if-the-tree-falls-in-the-deserted-woods deal."

I sigh—again. I find myself sighing a lot around Max. Hmm . . . same thing as around Aunt Weeby and Miss Mona, my two most favorite people in the whole world. I'm not ready to nose around that random connection between the three most challenging humans I know.

"Because," I say, instead, "those who know their gems know how incredibly rare good spodumene really is. Let's face it, when anyone can get a top-quality amethyst for no more than fifty-sixty dollars per carat, you know you can find those anywhere. Well, sort of. But, to get a decent kunzite, you're going to have to pop about three hundred dollars a carat."

He scratches his blond head. "I'll stick to Titleist and cheap little wooden tees."

"How 'bout them pigskins?"

"A good football won't set you back a small fortune."

"It won't last practically forever, either."

"Nothing does."

I run my index finger over the garnet cross pendant I recently bought and haven't taken off yet. "That's where you're wrong. God lasts forever, and his creation does as long as he wills it to."

Max turns serious. "I've never known anyone who can flip the switch from dirt-covered rocks to heavenly heights so fast."

That catches me. I think about what he's said. "Maybe it's because I don't separate God or my faith from everything else. Or at least, I try not to."

He narrows his eyes. "Are you sure you're not just saying

that? You know, à la Andie the Super-Duper Christian Girl who wears her faith on her sleeve."

"Gross! Is that how you see me?" Boy, do I have a lot of work to do if that's the case.

As the minutes tick by without an answer on his part, I begin to squirm. Then I itch. "Aw, c'mon, Max! You can't see me like that. Not really. I'm just me. I mess up just like everyone else."

"Yeah, but there's something different about you."

"Gee, that sounds almost as nice as 'Oh, look! There's black gunk growing in your grout. Isn't that different?'"

He laughs, chokes, then clunks his not-so-iced-tea glass down on the tabletop, and that finally dislodges the kunzite from the clamp that held it in the tweezer's prongs. He ignores the bouncing gem as he recovers from my semi-lame crack.

I don't ignore it. I pick it up and place it back in its own little plastic gem jar.

Max says, "If that doesn't prove you're not like any other woman out there, then I don't know what does." He stands. "Anyway, I spent the afternoon working on my new old car. You've got to admit, Andie—that vintage Triumph is sweet."

"Dunno, Max. Ancient English sports car wrecks aren't my thing."

"Unenlightened!" He winks. "Anyway, I'm kind of tired, and I have an early tee time tomorrow morning. I need to catch some z's if I'm going to meet Tanya on time. She's the most punctuality-obsessed person I know."

I hoot as I stand. "You're playing Tanya?" I click the gem jar lid on the kunzite and follow him out of the kitchen. "As in our sports catalog host? As in our former college B-ball star and to-the-bitter-end competitor?"

A ruddy glow enhances Max's chiseled cheekbones. "Yes, well. I'm pretty new to town. She's the only other golfer I know."

For a moment, as I follow Max to the foyer, I feel a twinge. Don't ask me what kind of twinge it is, but I fight an irrational urge to say, "I'll play with you."

One problem: I don't know a thing about golf. I can just see me on the golf course, a death-grip on one of those lethal-weapon metal sticks. Then I'd have to figure out how to hit the hard, dimply ball with the metal stick, *and* get it to boing right into the little hole in the ground way out there somewhere. Right. Uh-huh.

". . . Earth to Andie!"

Screech, screech! The shriek punctuates Max's summons.

"Oh, hush up, Rio," I yell above the parrot's ruckus. The bird was a gift from a ruby vendor, and Aunt Weeby has taken to him as though they'd been born attached at the hip . . . or wing. Figures.

What had Max and I been talking about? "Oh! Well, I can just imagine the rout tomorrow."

He blows on his neat, blunt nails and then buffs them on his cream-colored polo shirt. "I do know my way around a golf course, you know."

"I kinda wish I could hitch a ride on that zippy golf cart you guys'll be riding. Then we'll see who routs who."

"Whom."

"Whatever."

Max opens the door and winks. "Good night, Andie."

I follow him to the porch and grin. "Good night, Max."

As he heads down the front walk, I shiver. It's scary. We've gotten into this routine, almost from the start. We could almost pass for George and Gracie—Burns, that is. Only about a century younger. You know.

Shiver number two . . . or twenty. He has that effect on me.

Even though I fight it with everything I have.

I shake off the spell he casts on me, spin on my heel, and head back indoors. Once the deadbolt's clicked into place, I lean back against the door. "What are you trying to tell me, Lord?"

I mean, I don't think Max's presence at the S.T.U.D. or in my life is a simple coincidence. I'm not so sure God does coincidence. Coward that I am, I don't let myself dig too deeply into that subject. I skim it and pray for God to keep me safe from the effects of good-looking, well-intentioned—I think—but ill-informed males.

Why couldn't Miss Mona just have let things go on the way they'd been? You know, the Shop-Til-U-Drop TV shopping channel, by women, for women, all women.

We didn't really need Max.

Really. We didn't.

As the final credits scroll up the movie screen in the East-side Christian Fellowship's basement media room, I wipe the tears from my cheeks. I turn to Peggy Ross, my closest friend from childhood, and see the matching tears in her brown eyes.

The speaker's voice draws our attention back to the lectern.

"Can you believe so little's been done to help those poor Kashmiri people?" she said. "True, after the earthquake, ministries sent a variety of forms of help and even missionaries. The problem is with Kashmir itself. Too many wars have been fought by China, India, and Pakistan over that small bit of land, and they've all played the battles to their individual advantages. That doesn't leave much to work with on the ground."

Our speaker slips a new transparency in place on the projector. "When I see pictures of children without even the basics . . . it's *my* kids' faces I see on those little bodies. And, after more than a couple of years' time, the destruction is still . . . well, there. No homes, no protection or heat for the winter. They also have very little food . . ."

The intense stare of the missionary passes from listener to listener. "Allow me to challenge you. What can you do?"

The gerbil on the exercise wheel of my brain starts on its daily workout. She has me. Even after she's done with her presentation. I don't know what I can do, but there has to be something . . .

I reach for Peggy's hand, and we bow down in private, silent prayer.

"Ahem . . ."

We turn to the owner of the cleared throat. At our side, the missionary—a tall, middle-aged woman, her clothes sensibly plain, her brown hair cut in practical, no-nonsense layers, her eyes bright with intelligence and determination—waits for our attention.

"I couldn't help but notice you were both still here, praying," she says.

I'll bet. "The movie hits harder than I imagined."

She nods. "That was my intention."

13

Hmm . . . "Are you the film's director?"

She laughs. "Thanks for the compliment, but I'm nowhere near that talented. May I join you?"

The chair at Peggy's side had sat empty through the presentation. "Sure," my pal says. "I'm sorry, though. I don't know you."

"Of course not," our new companion replies. "And at the beginning of tonight's program, your pastor ran through all the speakers' names so fast, I don't expect anyone to remember mine. I'm Laura Seward. My husband and I have served on the mission fields of India, Pakistan, and Kashmir for the last thirty-seven years. We're home on furlough now and have been using the time to reach out to others who might be willing and able to help us."

Peggy and I swap looks.

I square my shoulders. "Look. I won't act dumb here and pretend I don't know what you're up to—*and* I won't insult you and pretend you came to hit us up out of the blue. I suspect someone fingered us—me—as an easy mark. It won't take long for me to head down your road. What can we do to help?"

A grin brightens her plain features. "I have to admit, I didn't expect such directness."

"Ha!" Peggy elbows my ribs. "That's because you don't know our Andie here. She's got the subtlety and meandering talents of a heat-seeking missile."

"Aw, c'mon, Peg," I object. "I'm not that bad. I just don't like to waste time."

Laura laughs. "I like your style, Andie." She holds out her hand. "I think you can do a world of good."

Her hand is warm, dry, and muscular, clear evidence of years of doing the Lord's work under tough circumstances. I feel a twinge of nostalgia. "Thanks. You remind me of my mother, who can't figure out how the missionary zeal skipped me. It didn't really, but I haven't felt the Lord's call to the field."

She nods.

I go on. "I grew up in Africa. My parents have been missionaries for years."

Her smile says she knows she's got a live one on the hook. And she does. What can I say? It's bred in me. I kind of drank it in with Mom and Dad's hugs and kisses growing up. I'm just not full-time like them.

"Tell me more," she says.

"There's not much more. I grew up, went to college, graduated, got a Master Gemologist certificate from the Gemological Institute of America, and I now work for Mona Latimer, the owner of the Shop-Til-U-Drop network. How can I help you and your husband? Or maybe what I should ask is how I can help the Kashmiri."

Our conversation gallops from that point on. Before we know what's really hit us, Peggy and I agree to front our congregation's efforts on behalf of the Kashmiri earthquake victims, and a three-way friendship, as unlikely as it seems, is forged.

I glance at my watch and am stunned to see almost three hours have passed. Peggy and I hug Laura and head up the stairs.

"Who would've thought," Peggy murmurs.

"What? That a movie would affect us that much?"

She slants me a look. "No, you doofus. That sitting next to you would lead to chairing a missions committee project of almost astronomical proportions."

I sniff. "It's not that massive. We're just spearheading an effort to help those poor kids in Kashmir."

Peggy stops. "Are you forgetting the widows? And how about the doctors without meds, much less ER supplies or equipment? And that's before you take into account the reconstruction efforts that haven't gone anywhere in all this time."

My fluttery finger wave tries to dismiss her worries. "And you think you and I are going to fix all that? All we're doing is recruiting the talent and funds to do it. We're just the . . . oh, I don't know. The delegators, I guess."

She howls. "The delegators, huh? Boy, are you good. No wonder Miss Mona's got you selling rocks."

"Hey! I'm a master gemologist. I know what I'm talking about on-screen."

"And you know next to nothing about Kashmir, medical aid to disaster areas, construction, and third-world country cottage industries."

"What's that?" a familiar male voice asks. "Do you mean to say we've found the subject on which Andrea Autumn Adams isn't an expert? Will wonders never cease?"

I spin, smack my fists on my hips, and roll my eyes. "Me and my shadow . . ." I warble. Then I ask, "Whatcha doing here?"

He crosses his arms. "Are you claiming ownership of the church? It's Sunday, and I'm no heathen."

"Yeah, but the service ended hours ago."

"Yeah, but Mr. Seward spoke to the men's Bible study group for a couple of hours. The man's fascinating."

"And that sent you looking for me?"

That slow, maddening smile of his turns up his lips. "Wow!

16

What an ego, Miss Adams. Who says I came looking for you?"

A snicker at my side sends my elbow jabbing at Peggy's slender waist. "Whose side are you on?" I hiss at her. To him, I add, "I'm here, and suddenly you show up. What do you want me to think?"

Peggy laughs. "That you're both heading out the church door."

To my eternal mortification, I look up, and realize that, yep. She's right. We're standing right in front of the massive glass doors to the church. Anyone could've been there; anyone on their way out. It just happens that Max is the one who's chosen that moment to leave the building. Just like me.

Great. Proximity to Max the Magnificent has bred paranoia. Now what?

Before I have a chance to figure out what, Aunt Weeby marches up. "Hey, sugarplum! There you are. Mona and I were wondering if you'd like to go out for breakfast."

I blink. "Breakfast?"

When my great-aunt nods, I stick a finger in my ear and wiggle. Something must not be right with my hearing. "Are you sure? It's"—I glance at my watch—"two forty-five . . . P.M.! Who eats breakfast in the middle of the afternoon?"

An elderly chorus sings out, "We do!"

Aunt Weeby and Miss Mona nod like those dogs with bobbing heads in the back windows of big old cars. Then it registers. A rich male baritone had underscored their response.

"Oh no!" I shake my head. *Oh, Lord, please! More time with Max is too dangerous to me and my sanity!*

"What do you mean, no?" Max asks. "Breakfast is the

17

perfect food. There're whole restaurant chains devoted to serving breakfast 24/7."

The worst part about it is, he's right. And I know it. Not to mention I have my teeny, tiny weakness for the perfect pancake. Slathered in cholesterol-filled, calorie-heavy butter. Oh! And drowned in yummy maple syrup.

My stomach growls.

Yeah, that Benedict Arnold. It betrays me. Can you believe it? My body wants me to go to breakfast with a pair of world-class matchmakers, who'll have their beady eyes on me and their number one candidate for my match the whole time.

"Come on," Peggy says with a mischievous wink. "Admit it, Andie. You're dying to go munch on pancakes with this crowd."

"Pancakes?" I ask then grin. "Okay, you busted me. I love 'em. But the company?" I wink. "You guys are loony tunes."

Miss Mona pats her perfect silver bob. "That's right, honey! You couldn't ask for better partners than us."

I look from face to face and have to agree. I start to nod, but then my eyes land on Max.

Our gazes catch. Lock.

The unnerving electricity that every so often zings between us blazes back to life. Against my every effort otherwise.

"No . . ." Even to my oh-so-subjective ears, my objection lacks conviction. "Um . . . well, okay. I guess I'll join you guys."

Peggy, the traitor, giggles, hugs me goodbye, and saunters out the door.

Aunt Weeby and Miss Mona follow.

Max, however, doesn't move. The gleam in his eyes gets my dander going. I yank the door ajar.

18

"Look at it as an opportunity," he says, right on my heels. "We can talk gems."

I snort at the thought and hurry to catch up with the senior contingent. "Let's change the subject. How about we talk Kashmir?"

"Oooooh!" Miss Mona coos. "The loveliest sapphire I ever saw came from Kashmir. Long, long time ago. Can we get some for the show, Andie?"

Max looks even more interested. "Kashmir sapphires? I thought sapphires came from Myanmar . . . Burma—whatever. We bought a bunch of them when we went to the Mogok Valley, didn't we?"

A little bit of knowledge can be dangerous, you know. *I tried, Lord. I tried to turn the topic to where we could talk about serving you.*

"Well, yeah," I say. "We did buy sapphires in Myanmar—very, very good quality sapphires. But Miss Mona's right too. The finest sapphires in the world have come from Kashmir. The mines, though—"

"Don't tell me," he says, that glib look on his face. "The mines are mostly done producing stones, and the prices are out-of-this-world high. How'm I doing?"

At his singsong imitation of my teacherly efforts, I roll my eyes—I did tell you I do a lot of eye rolling around Max, right? "You did fine. You only got it a tiny bit off. The mines in Kashmir played out a long time ago. Like in the 1800s." I figure it's in my best interest not to mention the rumors of new finds in the last ten years.

"Phew!" he says, as he holds the door to the S.T.U.D. Network's limo for me. "And here I thought you were going

19

to try and drag us out there to film another rickety mine. Never mind start another international incident—"

"Max!" Miss Mona cries. "What an exceptional idea—"

"NO!" Max and I cry in unison.

Then we face each other. Max and I . . . in agreement? A wacko image crosses my mind again—pigs really do fly.

I squelch a nervous giggle. You bet I'm in trouble. What's my life coming to?

"Lord?" I whisper, almost whimper. "Please? Not again."

$2\underline{\underline{00}}$

A brief half hour later, I close my lips around another wedge of fluffy, gooey, scrumptious pancake. At the table, the conversation continues in bits and spurts without any help from me.

The pillowy texture and sweet comfort of the pancakes fill my mouth with happiness, and I chew, my every sense focused on the experience. Oh yeah. I do like my food.

". . . Andie?"

I bite my tongue. "Ow! Hey, what's that all about? Yelling at a woman who's busy enjoying her meal is not fair."

Three pairs of eyes stare.

"What?" There can't be spinach on my teeth. I'm not eating spinach. "What are you guys looking at?"

Max shakes his head. "No one yelled at you. You were way out in la-la land when Miss Mona asked you a question."

Choosing to ignore the la-la land comment, I turn to my boss. "What did I miss?"

"Not much," Aunt Weeby says.

"So much!" Miss Mona says. "I think you and Max have come up with a brilliant idea."

Aunt Weeby, generally allergic to business conversations, now pats my hand, points at a bilious painting on the wall, and murmurs, "That's a lovely picture."

My eyebrows fly hair-ward. "Hmm . . . ," I say before I turn back to Miss Mona. "You know I love you to pieces, but I'm scared of what you consider brilliant ideas. Especially those that have even the most remote connection to foreign countries."

"What I'm afraid of is losing any and all fabulous opportunities." Miss Mona purses her lips. "The network hasn't flourished by ignoring possibilities, you know."

"A really pretty picture," Aunt Weeby says, her voice determined and emphatic. "And the colors are great."

A glance at the orange, red, and acid green makes my eyes hurt. "Yep, it's colorful, all right." I turn back to Miss Mona. "We don't need to go to extraordinary extremes. I'm good at what I do. I know my gems, and my show adds to the network's bottom line."

Miss Mona smiles. "I'm the one who hired you, Andie. I know how good you are, and I know better than anyone else the bottom line. I also know a chance when I see one. It's all the way down in my marrow to grab it and run."

Aunt Weeby jabs her elbow into my side. "Doesn't it remind you of someone?"

Sore and unwilling to really comment on the hideous thing, I squirm and scoot my chair a fraction of an inch away from her.

She leans closer. "D'you think they had it painted special for them?"

Max snickers.

No doubt about it, I ignore him, but look from one senior citizen to the other. Usually, the two are in complete accord. But there are times, like now, when these two are enough to drive the sanest soul to the nearest shrink.

And there are those who question *my* sanity.

I take a deep, supposedly calming breath. "You know, Aunt Weeby? I'll bet it's one of those production-line paintings they sell out of the back of a rickety van parked in the corner at a gas station. I wouldn't confuse it with a VanGogh."

"I will admit," Miss Mona continues, oblivious of Aunt Weeby's diversionary tactics, "there were some queasy-making moments during our last trip, but the results? Why, Andie, honey, they were pure genius."

A quick glance reveals the green around Max's gills. It has to match the hue around mine. Neither one of us is about to forget anytime soon. "That trip, Miss Mona, was nothing short of a nightmare."

"VanGogh . . . that's the guy who whacked off his ear." Aunt Weeby gives an exaggerated sniff. "His stuff makes me think a' the nightmares that come after I get indigestion."

I smooth a hand over the skirt of my dress, ready to take the out she's giving me and run with it. "VanGogh painted marvelous, moody pieces, and his use of color was nothing short of brilliant. That"—I wave at the smears of primary colors—"is nothing short of . . . ah . . . well, colorful."

"Hmm . . ." Max grins.

I ignore him—again. "It's probably more Jackson Pollock than VanGogh."

"But how about the head? And the body?" Aunt Weeby prods.

I glance at the rectangle on the wall—head? Body? I don't see what she does. "Interesting." I snag another piece of pancake with my fork, and rejoice that the conversation has now traveled far afield of the Kashmir issue. "And the colors . . . they're very . . . primary."

"Don't forget we made an excellent profit from the stones we bought in Myanmar." Miss Mona raises her voice over Aunt Weeby's and mine, determined, as always. "You were there. And then you sold the stones."

I groan.

"Miss Mona has a point," Max says, his eyes sparkling with mischief—the rat. "We sold every last ruby, sapphire, and zircon you bought. Even those other weird things sold too. The ones no one had ever heard of."

I chow down more pancake.

"D'you think they'd sell it to me? I just have to have it." Aunt Weeby, true to form, is obviously not finished with our conversation but has now turned to glare at Miss Mona. "What's the matter with you people? Can't you see it? It's the spitting image of our darling little Rio."

I squint at the swipes of paint, and if I almost close my eyes, I can sort of make out the outline of what some might consider a curved beak. I'm no expert on van art, but I'm ever so grateful to the exotic breed right about now. "I suppose the painter made a bunch of them, but I don't know that you can track any of them down. And who knows? If you don't ask, you won't know if the owners of the restaurant will sell it to you."

Back to Max, who'd just murmured something about "weird purchases" again.

"Not fair! You know I never bought anything weird in Myanmar. Just because you don't know your gems doesn't mean kyanite, danburite, kornerupine, or peridot are weird."

He winks. "I love it when you talk rocks to me."

Aaaaargh! Even when he's driving me nuts, his mischievous grin melts my bones. What am I going to do with the guy—

Don't go there, Andie. You're doing nothing with or about the guy. You're as allergic to relationships as Aunt Weeby is to business chit-chat.

Since our party swells when two other S.T.U.D. employees come up on their way out of the restaurant, I'm definitely doing nothing . . . but scarfing another piece of pancake.

"Hi, all!" Hannah Stowe, my fave camerawoman says. "Food's great here, don't you think?"

Glory Cargill, Miss Mona's newest camerawoman, rubs her nonexistent belly. "Mmm . . . You southerners really know your eats. I'm stuffed with the most delicious pork chops, whipped mashed potatoes dripping with melted butter, and steamed-to-*the*-perfect-crisp broccoli almandine." Then she stares at my plate, the only one at our table with anything still on it. "Isn't it a little late for pancakes?"

Why me? "That's what I told this crew"—I jab my fork in the direction of my table companions—"but noooo. They wouldn't think of anything but breakfast at a time when most are getting ready for an early dinner. And they do a mean pancake here. You should try them next time you come."

"Isn't that painting of Andie's little parrot, Rio, absolutely fabulous?" Aunt Weeby asks.

Swallow me, earth!

Hannah winks. "I've always been crazy about brunch."

I steal another mouthful of my now cold, stiff pancakes. Yeah, I can agree with Hannah, even if my pancakes are past their prime. But then, who isn't? Past her prime, that is. Especially after a couple of hours spent in the company of the stars of the Cirque du Senior-elles. They do know how to push my frustration button better than anyone—except maybe Mr. Magnificent himself.

Who proceeds to scratch his chin. "Brunch? I think we left that back in the dust. How does 'linner' sound? If brunch comes between breakfast and lunch, then linner must be what comes between lunch and dinner."

I fight the grin; I don't want to encourage him. I mean, why?

Then Miss Mona throws me for even more of a loop. "See?" She points at Hannah and Glory, her words directed at me. "Here are the eyes of the shows. I think the Lord's working this one out for me." To the camerawomen, she says, "C'mon, girls. Grab yourself some seats. We have us some important decisions to make."

As the women scrounge for chairs, I drop my fork and scoot back. What are my chances for a timely escape?

"I know!" Aunt Weeby cries before I can flee. "I bet I have something like it up in the attic. Y'all know our family's never thrown any ol' thing out, and my uncle Zebediah was quite the bird fancier. Whoo-eee! Now, wouldn't it be super if I could find me my own original treasure hiding with them mothballs and trunks and old chairs?"

So there you have it. Miss Mona must have hired my foot-in-mouth-diseased cohost because she recognized in him the same malady from which her best friend suffers. I'm doomed.

I laugh in helpless surrender.

"What kind of decision are you talking about?" Glory asks Miss Mona, prolonging the nutty nature of the moment.

Hannah plunks her elbows on the last patch of available tabletop and props her chin on the heels of her hands. "I have to assume you're talking about work stuff, right?"

That's when it occurs to me. I stick my two pinkies into the corners of my mouth and give a shrill whistle. It works.

Too well.

The entire restaurant comes to a grinding halt.

"Ooops!" That really wasn't what I'd wanted. I turn to my fellow diners at other tables. "Sorry." Then I face my crew again. "You guys. It's Sunday. We just left church. How about if work and business and decisions wait until tomorrow?"

Miss Mona and Aunt Weeby both look stunned. "You're right," my aunt says, her tone apologetic.

"It is the Lord's Day," Miss Mona concurs, equally chagrined.

Max gives me a knowing look. "The Super-Duper—"

"Don't say it!" No, I wasn't rude. Well, maybe just a little.

But I had to cut him off. I did. Really. What he'd been about to say paints me in a very yucky light. One I don't want to see me in, even though I may have been the one to put myself in its glare. But I had to do something to derail the Miss Mona train. Otherwise she'd have had us chugging off to Kashmir.

And after our trip to the Mogok Valley in Myanmar not too many months ago, I'm not ready to repeat the madness.

"That, ladies and gentlemen," I tell my fellow worshipers a month later, my smile warm and inviting, "is why Eastside Christian Fellowship's putting together a number of missions teams to head out to help the victims of the October 2005 Kashmir earthquake." I point to the back of the room. "Peggy is at the table, waiting to take names, addresses, and phone numbers of all those who want to join me."

What's that? you ask. What's all that "join me in Kashmir" thing? And from the woman who didn't want Miss Mona to go nuts on the idea of a trip to . . . well, Kashmir?

Let's just say Laura Seward is one indomitable woman.

No matter what, I'm not going to let Miss Mona bamboozle me into any kind of gemstone shopping foray while I'm in the sapphire-depleted, politically embattled nation. I don't want to become acquainted with the Kashmiri authorities, not on the wrong side of their weaponry.

Or the Taliban, either.

Oh! You didn't know? Well, yeah. Those guys are buds with the mountain tribesmen up between Kashmir and Pakistan. Near the mines.

And you know, beyond a shadow of a doubt, that'd be my fate were I to succumb to Miss Mona's efforts. I find enough trouble on my own. I don't need her—or the Duo's—help.

Then there's the Max factor (pun intended) to consider. Once I had decided to go, I came in for more than my fair share of teasing at the hand of Mr. Magnificent.

"So you're abandoning me to Danni's tender mercies," he had said as we watched the lingerie host do her thing right before the start of one of our shows.

I smirked. "Serves you right."

"Why? Because I didn't major in rockology in college?"

"Maybe." I winked. "And it's gemology, you goof."

He scoffed. "I'm not that dumb, Andie. And you didn't major in footballology or golfology either, but you don't

28

see me sticking you with a blond piranha in silk and acrylic nails."

Even though the description of our fellow employee was somewhat accurate, and even though I've been on the receiving end of her attacks a time or twelve, that day my conscience reared up its head. "Um . . . how about if we try to find one—just one—of Danni's redeeming qualities?"

"How about if you find it and then let me in on the secret?"

I swatted his mile-wide shoulder. "Max! That's mean."

He crossed his arms. "And some of your snitty comments about me aren't?"

"I haven't been snitty—as you put it—in a loooong time." I tipped up my chin. "I promised Miss Mona I'd play nice, and I have kept my promise."

Well, I've tried. How hard? Hmm . . . I don't know. My success? Um . . . well, that's up for interpretation. But I have my reasons. You know.

Max made a major production of looking down his fine wool-clad legs, his arms and hands, twisting one of those arms around to pat his shoulders. "My puncture wounds argue otherwise."

The channel's theme song blared out over the airwaves, saving me from further embarrassment. I do have a smart mouth. It's my eternal downfall, and I try to work on it all the time. I pray about it, try to harness it, but don't always succeed. And Max has been at the receiving end ever since he showed up at the network.

He did come to his job unprepared. A meteorologist is no geologist, much less gemologist, so Max stepped in with no prior gemstone knowledge. But I did go overboard for a while. I'm reformed. Now.

I believe.

I trust.

I pray.

In any case, I hadn't been giving him a whole lot of chances to stick his size 12s in his mouth of late. Especially not on-screen. Just to make sure, I asked, "You remember everything we went over for today's show?"

He waved an index card. "See my crib sheet? I'm ready."

Danni wafted up in a pungent cloud of MauraLee, the ultra-spicy fragrance from the S.T.U.D. channel's signature cosmetics line. The smile she gave Max would've curled a lesser man's toes. The glare she gave me would've curled a lesser woman's lip.

She then turned her back on me and put a claw . . . er . . . hand on Max's chest. "I hear we'll be sharing airtime again," she cooed. "I just love it when Andie takes off on one of her vacations."

He stumbled back and hemmed and hawed inane nothings.

Whoa! From the way she'd said that, someone not in the know would have thought I made it a habit to miss work. In the almost year I've worked for Miss Mona, I've only taken a handful of days off. My advance trip to Kashmir for the mission groups will be my first real vacation.

But why cast pearls before swine? I stepped toward the set. "Let's get the show on the road," I told Max through clenched teeth. "It's cabochon day."

Our show went off well. Max only made one mistake . . . or two, but who was counting?

"See ya tomorrow," I told him as I walked out of the ladies' room, where I'd stored the gemstones we showed our viewers in the studio's vault. Yes, the ladies' room. Miss Mona, in her unique wisdom, had installed the vault's only door so that it opened from the ladies' room. "I'm off to church."

As we headed for the lobby, Max gave me one of those looks of his. You know, the ones that see too much. The longer I know him, the better he gets at them. "This trip means a lot to you, doesn't it?"

"There are lots of people who need just about everything out there. I want to do something. Someone has to go and set up the program. It might as well be me, since I do want to help."

His eyes narrowed.

I squirmed.

He said, "This wouldn't have anything to do with lingering guilt for not following in your parents' footsteps, would it?"

Did it? Nah . . . not really. "It's about the Kashmiri people, Max. Not me, not my parents."

"And how about your friend Peggy? Is she going to Asia too?"

"Didn't you know? She just learned she's pregnant again. She can't go to a country where the disaster has left a rich stew of disease just under the surface."

"So it really is all about you."

"No! It's not all about me. It's all about Kashmir."

"Then why argue with Miss Mona? Why can't she come with you? The two of you can take a side trip to check out the old mine sites, take some shots for the show, and she'll be happy. That won't stop you from doing your Mother Teresa thing."

Yuck! "What's gotten under your skin?"

He shrugged as he strode out of the building. "Maybe a zing or two from the expert. I do learn, you know. My college four-oh GPA wasn't a fluke, even though it wasn't in your vaunted gemology."

Ouch! I suppose I deserved that. I really was snotty when he first arrived. And he still sets my teeth on edge every once in a while. Especially when he's at his most appealing. That's when he wakes up all my self-preservation instincts. They, in turn, make me revert—

Nuh-uh! No way. I refused to examine what that said about me. Or my feelings for Mr. Magnificent.

All I knew was I really needed a vacation from Max. But I wouldn't say it out loud even if the Spanish Inquisition's master torturer got ahold of me.

I plastered on a cheerful grin. "Gotta move, gotta groove, my man! Go ahead and talk to Danni about your upcoming shows. I'm sure she can't wait to get you all to herself."

The look he gave me as I headed out the door didn't bear description. Then I went to my meeting.

Which is turning out to be a minefield of a different kind. I'm sure you've figured it out by now. The Daunting Duo are there, wacky minds made up.

"Of course we're coming," Aunt Weeby chirps once we say our amens at the end of our closing prayer.

"We wouldn't dream of abandoning the poor folk of Kashmir in their time of need," Miss Mona echoes.

"And I'm the real, the one and only Queen Nefertiti!" I counter, waggling a hank of my red hair. "See? It's jet black."

They give me pitying looks—the ones that tell me they're sure I've finally gone off the deep end.

"Good! You get the picture. That's how real you two sound. I'm not buying this story you've cooked up."

They swap guilty glances.

"Oh, all right." Aunt Weeby's pout could've caught rain. "I missed out on all the excitement all y'all had in Myanmar. I'm not letting this chance pass me by. Besides, I'm your auntie. I have to look out for you."

I snort. "I'm thirty years old, for goodness' sake. You'd think I'd be able to go around the world on my own when I want to, especially since that's exactly what I did for my job all those years I worked in New York. Why are you two so determined to tag along? It's not the easiest trip, you know. You're no spring—"

I see the error of my ways and cut off the comment before I plunge into even deeper waters. Good thing too, since arguing won't get me anywhere. At least not with the Duo.

"Why?" I ask again.

Aunt Weeby's eyes shoot off sparks. "For the adventure, of course. And see?" She raises her chartreuse-trousered leg. "It's not in a cast anymore. I'm not grounded, sugarplum. Plus I graduated from that there physical therapy two and a half months ago."

"Why, Andie!" Miss Mona clutches her chest. "You know me better than to question me." She points to Aunt Weeby. "I can't let Livvy go off to Asia . . . is it Major or Minor? Oh well, it doesn't matter, does it? What matters is I can't let my dearest friend here hare off to the back of beyond without a sensible soul to look out for her. I have to come along. Besides, you and I are business partners, of sorts. Oh, and in adventure too."

Of course, her outrageous statements detonate a disagreement of monumental proportions. And it ends with the predetermined conclusion. I don't know who argues more strenuously, Aunt Weeby against the idea of a cross-continental babysitter or me against any more Raiders-of-the-Lost-Sanity-type adventures.

"Oh, stop it right now, Andrea Autumn Adams!" Aunt Weeby says. "Who all died and made you queen? And don't go blathering about no Egyptian pyramid woman, either—isn't she the one with that funny black hair, all flat across the top like some peculiar hat?" She pauses and a quizzical glimmer strikes her eye. "How'd you think they got it to stay that way? Hair is hair, and it doesn't rightly grow all stiff, you know."

The off-the-wall question makes me think she might've derailed her streak. I roll my eyes. "Duct tape comes to mind."

She purses her lips. "Now, don't be silly. Besides, you can't keep us here."

I think and think, trying to find another reason, and come up with an off-the-wall argument. "Hey! How about Rio? He needs you. Who's going to take care of him if you leave?"

She gives me a vague wave. "I'm sure we can find someone who'll keep him, a friend, someone from church." Her brow furrows, and my hopes for derailment rise. Then she smiles. "I have it! We'll leave him with your friend Peggy. I'm sure her little ones will love having a parrot for a while. So there you have it, sugarplum."

Oh well. No derailment.

She rises to her full five foot three inches. "All the fussing and moaning you come up with won't change a thing. The Lord's work needs doing, and Mona and I have us two hands

34

apiece. We can pull up our sleeves and do our part. We're coming, and that's that."

Why did I even try?

Miss Mona's smile reeks of smugness. "I come armed with a nice, fat check too, honey."

I surrender to the inevitable and laugh. "You may be wacky, but you don't ever hold back, do you?"

"Hold back what?" Peggy says as she sails up, notebook in hand. "Did you see how many signed up? We have an army that wants to shuffle off to Kashmir with you, so you can lead the first group." She gives me a sassy salute. "Aye, aye, Cap'n Andie."

Do these things happen to anyone else?

At least I won't have to worry about the California gem-dunce surfer boy this time.

$3\underline{\,00}$

So much for Cap'n Andie and her missionary advance team. As soon as Miss Mona and Aunt Weeby bumped me off the mission team leader's spot by virtue of their powerful personalities and family pecking order (I'm not about to invoke their superior seniority, you understand), the number of folks on the first team dwindled—dramatically. All the way down to the S.T.U.D. folks they'd signed up the night of that fateful meeting. Something reeks of rotten fish en route to Kashmir.

Why, you ask? Let me tell you.

Our "team" consists of Aunt Weeby, Miss Mona, Glory Cargill, the newest camerawoman at the S.T.U.D., Allison Howard, our makeup artist, and moi. Yes, Glory has all her gadgets, and Allison her war paint. Get the picture?

Okay. So I don't have Mr. Magnificent with me. That's a bonus. When it comes to Aunt Weeby's and Miss Mona's crazy schemes, I have to take what I can get.

We ditch our plane at Srinagar's airport—after we survived delays, hours of turbulence, hopping in and out of

New Delhi, then Bombay—and make our way through immigration, customs, and finally reach the luggage pickup. Surprise, surprise! All our stuff's here.

"*Whoo-ee!*" Aunt Weeby says as we roll our suitcases to the sidewalk outside. "I wouldn't ever have guessed it'd be this hard getting just five women to this here Kashmir."

I wink. "What? You'd rather have done a *Star Trek* Scottie-beam-us-up?"

She returns my wink. "Wouldn't that be fun? The beaming up, that is."

"All kidding aside, my dear auntie, I'm with you!" Then I laugh. "Okay. Here's one for you. What day is it? Yesterday? Tomorrow?"

"Pfft!" She crosses her arms. "Ask one a' them foreigners, not me. Normal folks wouldn't go play with clocks like them time zone things. Tell me that's not the most turned-around foolishness you've ever heard."

Do *you* want to discuss the merits of time zones with her? Me neither.

I hitch my way-too-heavy backpack a little higher. "All I know is, we're finally in Srinagar, a whole lot of hours after we left New York. Too bad it's so late in the afternoon. The sun's setting."

Miss Mona comes to us. "Isn't it romantic? Dusk is my favorite time of day."

Romantic? Dunno about that.

When I look around, which I've tried not to do after the first time I laid eyes on them, I see the dark peaks of the Himalayas outlined in the red of sunset. It's one of the most breathtaking scenes I've ever seen, just not breathtaking as in "Oooooh! I want to move here!"

No way.

The mountains around the city, shadowed and foreboding, scream danger to me, especially in contrast to the russet-and-ink-stained evening sky. Those craggy sky-high barricades make me think of cell walls, and that thought crash-lands me right down to immediate reality.

As Dorothy woulda said, we're not in Kansas anymore.

Anything can, and very well might, happen here. As it did on our trip to Myanmar.

Shudders rip through me.

I silently pray for God's protection, and then, as I hit my "amen," Miss Mona lays an arm across my shoulders. "God is great, isn't he?"

"Mm-hm." Totally true. And since silence is a virtue—sometimes—there's no point infecting her with my wonky feeling until it's time. Or at least until I have a better reason to do so than a weird reaction to a bunch of spooky mountains.

"Wish I could draw like God," Aunt Weeby says. "He didn't go to no art school to make his perfect pictures. And, see? No black velvet, either. Isn't that blue sky with a red bottom plum perfect?"

That's one way of describing an Asian sunset.

While I wait for Glory and Allison to join us with their multitude of stuff, I check out the landscape again, but it still doesn't give me any warm fuzzies. It's exotic and beautiful, but with a heavy dose of *woo-woo* that makes me think of questions and riddles.

I prefer answers to questions.

The transportation Miss Mona had arranged beforehand hasn't shown up, so I soak in the sights at the airport terminal. A number of display cases throughout the cavernous

38

building hold a variety of crafts, anything from intricately carved wooden sculptures to gleaming brass bowls and urns. Other booths are filled with leather handbags and belts and sandals and shoes, gorgeous golden pieces that make this power shopper want to do her thing. But I can't stick another thread in my bags, much less shoes or belts. I'll have to wait till we're heading back.

Even our fellow travelers offer a feast for the eye. We denim- and khaki-clad Americans pale in comparison to the glamorous Asians in gorgeous red, gold, green, and cobalt silks, cottons, and chiffons.

Aunt Weeby doesn't let my visual feast last long. "Didn't you say some high muckety-muck from the Something-or-other a' Tourism was coming for us?" she asks Miss Mona.

Miss Mona shakes her head. "I told you more than that."

"Oh, I know you did." Aunt Weeby grins. "But it wasn't the most interesting stuff you ever said, so I didn't bother to remember a whole lot. I reckoned whatever I needed to know, you or Andie would tell me when I needed it. So are they coming or not?"

I shake my head too—happens a lot around the Duo.

"One of the deputy directors of tourism may be coming to meet us," Miss Mona tells her. "Someone from the TASK, the tourism agents group, told me they'd arrange for a director or one of the agents to take us to where we're staying while in Srinagar. The folks at the TASK are the ones who'll provide our guides for our whole trip."

That's when I ditch subtlety—and silence. "The tourism group, huh? From the government. Sounds like incoming goons to me."

Miss Mona gives me one of her more serious looks—I know when I'm being scolded as well as the next girl.

I hold my hands up, palm forward. "Hey! I object to that look. You know I'm right. You were there with me. You saw the Myanmar government goons' weapons. You've got to figure with directors and agents and all that, it'll be a gun-studded trip this time too."

"Now, Andie, dear," my boss says. "It's a different country, Kashmir is. You need to change your attitude. You don't know that we're going to have to have the same kind of supervision all the time—"

"Hello, ladies," says a dark-haired gentleman in an ill-fitting brown suit. "For you trip in Kashmir, I you escort, Robert."

If you're Robert, then I'm Bart Simpson. But I don't tell him. I've seen lumps like the one under his crooked side seam before. In Myanmar.

As Miss Mona steps forward to take the reins of the introductions, I step back and sigh. Here we go again.

The Daunting Duo doesn't need me to help land them in trouble. They're experts at sinking-ship scenarios. And my love, as well as my need to help and protect them, has dragged me into their chaotic escapades a time or two. Like when Aunt Weeby went stall-mucking and wound up with a broken leg, in traction, in a hospital—that's when I knew I had to come home and keep an eye on her. Then there was the time when a flea-market junket landed Miss Mona's new Jaguar in the junkyard and Miss Mona in the hospital.

You get the picture. I'll just chill and wait for the arrival of this latest sinking ship, and come to their rescue when they need me.

When "Robert" hails a waiting van, I'm thrilled to see it's one that stands a chance of getting us to where we're staying. Can't say the same about other vehicles we pass on the way through what he calls the Old Town.

We zip down a crooked spiderweb of roads in the deepening dark, where the ghosts of triple-decker buildings loom on either side of the street. The yellowed glow from scattered streetlights gives the ruddy brick walls an eerie blush. A bit farther along our route, the tables and booths in the abandoned bazaars wear shrouds for the night. Men and women in flowing traditional clothes scurry down the sidewalks. Goose bumps ripple my skin as I watch.

In spite of the relative safety of the van and the apparent normalcy of the intriguing sights, I can't shake the sense of danger that hit me the minute I set foot on this penthouse of the world.

"This, ladies," Robert says when we turn onto a road that runs along the bank of a wide river, "is the Jhelum. It very important for Srinagar. Once, commerce came and went on boats on this river, and this made Srinagar Kashmir's most important commerce town."

Lights on the opposite shore hide and flash in between the unusual, squat buildings we drive past on our side of the water. At first, the structures' proximity to the riverbank surprises me—I'd worry about erosion eating my backyard if I were the owner. But then, by the beam cast by a particularly bright streetlight, I recognize what I'm actually seeing.

"Look!" I cry. "They're houseboats. How cool is that?"

Miss Mona chuckles. "That's my surprise."

I tear my gaze away from the floating structures. "Your surprise?"

She nods. Her excitement says it all.

"Really?" I bite my tongue to keep from squealing—I'm more sophisticated than that. I think. "You mean we're staying in a houseboat?"

"Before I decided where we'd stay," Miss Mona says, "I did me a little research. That's how I learned that lots of tourists like to come to Srinagar and rent the houseboats. I've never stayed in one, so I made the reservation. Then I learned they come with all the conveniences of a luxury hotel."

I gape. Then I snap my mouth shut and peek out the window again. "Luxury? Here? I thought this country was war-torn and earthquake-rubbled."

"Yes, miss," Robert says, his voice somber. "Our country have much problems, but it also have much beauty. The houseboats is something very special of Srinagar. You will very much like yours, I'm sure."

"I agree," my canny boss says. "I was sent some lovely photos. Wait until you see the one where we're staying. It has four bedrooms, each with its own bathroom, a living room they call a lounge, a dining room, a kitchen and big ol' pantry—and it even comes with its own houseboy. Imagine that! I sure was surprised when I learned all this. Of course, I couldn't pass up the chance."

Of course she couldn't. She's Miss Mona Latimer. A woman with a keen sense of adventure. And I'm one with a keen sense of smell. Remember that stink I thought I smelled?

Well, I smell a rat too. Last I heard, this was supposed to be a mission trip, to check out an orphanage for kids who lost everything in the quake. Tourism agents and houseboats don't add up to missions to me. They make me think of, well, tourism.

Did Miss Mona lose her way?

Or is she mixing faith with pleasure?

And how about that keen business sense? Would she miss an opportunity?

Doubt it. Remember Glory and Allison? Uh-huh. They're in the van's rear seat, each sporting a *big* tote bag full of gear.

Miss Mona's never missed the chance to turn even a business trip into an experience in every sense of the word. Not that I'm questioning Glory's and Allison's urge to serve at the mission.

I knew going in who I was dealing with. I shouldn't be surprised.

At least the idea of staying in a floating house is a far cry from the reality of foreign government officials chasing us across a third-world country with weapons drawn. Yeah. Been there, done that. With Miss Mona, once was enough.

Fifteen minutes later, the van stops in front of one of the houseboats. Inside lights shine through detailed carved wood trim to give the vessel an ethereal, lacy appearance.

I'm charmed—what woman wouldn't be? Smiling, I slam the mental door on the spooky feeling I've had since we left the plane.

Dumb? Maybe.

Out of the van, I stare. Can't help myself. The houseboat is amazing. Then I catch sight of Aunt Weeby. She's staring too. Speechless.

Cool, huh? Aunt Weeby. Dumbstruck.

Maybe I misread the whole Kashmir experience back at the airport. Maybe Miss Mona and Aunt Weeby are right.

Maybe I do need to get myself an attitude adjustment when it comes to this glamorous place.

Oh, okay. Maybe. So a little bit of mystery isn't all bad. Right?

"Can we go inside?" The breathy sound of my voice catches me by surprise. After all my years in New York, it takes a lot to enchant me. Guess what? Kashmir's done it—and in the dark, no less. Can't wait until I take a look at this strange new world in the daylight.

"Yes, miss," Robert says. "We care for your luggage. Go. Go in. You will like it."

I do, I do! The houseboat's interior takes my breath away. A posh living room, its intricate walls made up of carved wooden panels, spreads out before me. It's much bigger than I would've expected from the outside, bigger than Aunt Weeby's parlor back home. Two half-moon sofas, overstuffed and cushy looking, wear ultrarich red wool upholstery and fill the two corners at the far end of the room, one on either side of the entrance to the dining room beyond. A cabriole-legged coffee table stands before each of the sofas, and all the furniture sits on a thick ivory carpet—no stains. Even on a boat.

Wow!

Then I look up. The ceiling is rich with more exquisite carvings that give it a texture like that of the quilted silk-satin bedding at Saks—out of my price range, that's for sure.

When I spot the pièce de résistance, I feel as though someone has just plunked me down into the set of *The King and I*. Suspended from that faboo ceiling hangs the most graceful chandelier I've ever seen—and I've lived in New York, *capisce*? Golden branches hold crystal lotus petals, lit from within, to form a cluster of perfect blossoms. Light dances over the delicate piece, but what most amazes me is how, in the heart of the flowers, tiny rainbows make the whole thing look like something out of a fairy tale.

Maybe everything's a fairy tale.

Maybe I'm dreaming.

I remember the times Max the Magnificent has caught me trying to convince myself crazy things really are as they appear. So I pinch myself again. Guess what? I don't wake up. It's not a dream, and the killer room doesn't change. My great-aunt and her best friend are both still beside me, each as awestruck as I feel.

And I miss Max.

Uh-oh!

Then my stomach growls—head-to-toe blush time.

Aunt Weeby and Miss Mona laugh.

"Hungry?" Robert asks.

Embarrassed, that's what. Can you imagine? I come to this incredible place, and my very mundane, lowbrow belly decides to tell everyone I'm dying to stuff my face. Good grief.

"Dinner should be ready," he adds, as though I hadn't broken every rule of etiquette known to mankind. "Go to dining room. You'll like."

I'll bet! So far, the only thing I haven't liked about Kashmir is the wonky feeling I got when we first landed. I guess I can chalk that up to past experiences of the not-so-cool kind.

I pause to take one more appreciative look at the lounge. Aunt Weeby marches up, stands square in front of me, sticks her fists on her still-slender hips, and sniffs.

"Oh, come on, now, Andie." She frowns from head to toe. "Don't just stand there like a big ol' stump. I'm hungry.

What's a woman got to do to get some food around you? You can come back out here after we've eaten and goggle around all you want. I want my dinner."

I stick a finger in my ear, wiggle, stare. Did I miss something? "What do you mean, Aunt Weeby? I'm starved. You know, wasn't it *my* stomach that growled?" But I wind up speaking to her rapidly disappearing back.

What can I say? She's wacky, but she's *my* wacky aunt, and I love her. She can change a mood at the blink of an eye. Or in the turn of a loony phrase.

We sit down to a meal that would make Rachael Ray weep. The large teak table is set for six, the Shop-Til-U-Drop contingent plus Robert. I wind up next to Glory on one side, and of course, Aunt Weeby on the other.

A twenty-something Asian man walks into the dining room, bows, and then points to his chest. "I Farooq."

We greet him, he disappears, then shows up again seconds later with platter after steaming platter of food. The mountains of Asian delicacies scent the room with rich and exotic spices. And Farooq bows. Every time he walks into the room, he bows. He bows before he leaves. He bows when he returns. He even bows before and after he refills our teacups.

Bet those bows keep his chiropractor in business.

After Miss Mona's blessing on the food, we pass dishes from one end of the table to the other, reviewing each morsel and bite.

"You have to take some of this chicken," Glory says. "I just snuck a little piece that fell off my fork, and it's to die for."

I take the dish. "Is that spinach stuffing inside the chicken? I love spinach."

46

"It is, and you are going to flip! This is *the* best."

"No, it's not," Miss Mona says. "This is. Here"—she reaches a deep bowl across the table to me—"the mutton is so tender it falls apart when you try and serve it."

I plunk down the chicken platter to take the lamb. When I take a bite, my taste buds throw a party—oh, yum! Then I scope out another bowl. "Are those white chunks potato?"

Miss Mona spears one on her fork, looks it over, then slips it into her mouth. "Nuh-uh," she says once she's swallowed. "I think it's something like . . . oh, maybe turnips? But it's good, very good, and cooked with some special spice. You're going to love it."

I do love every mouthful—and I take plenty. Even the pots and pots of light, fragrant green tea we down during the multicourse meal taste especially good.

"Okay," I say a short while later. "Not even Thanksgiving compares. I've eaten more tonight than I ever have before. Who wants to roll me to my bed?"

Everyone laughs, pats her middle, shakes her head.

"Oh, all right, you guys." I pretend to frown. "I'll walk myself there."

"Ooof!" Allison says. "I can't think of lying down right away. I'm too full."

"And too excited," Glory adds.

"Want to hang out with me in the lounge for a while?" our makeup guru asks our camera wizard.

Glory stands. "Sure. I have to check my stuff to make sure nothing got too rattled during the flights. I'd love the company."

They go one way, Aunt Weeby, Miss Mona, and I go the other.

Farooq bows and bows and bows. "Rooms ready," he adds, then bows again.

"Sugarplum?" Aunt Weeby says as we head out of the dining room, her voice dreamy. "D'you think the bedroom's gonna be something out of the *Arabian Nights* too?"

I chuckle. "Different continent." I take another peek over my shoulder at the posh table and chairs and beyond that, the movie-set living room. "Who knows? Maybe it's even more . . . *more*."

My aunt, better known for brashness than meekness, finally tears her gaze from the carved blossoms on the teak sideboard by the door. "Oh, Andie! I can't imagine much more."

When we reach our room, she doesn't have to imagine a thing. The room we share is luxurious almost to the point of too much. Gold silk draperies at the windows shield us from any possible chill. The same fabric, in a lighter shade of gold, covers a duvet on each of the two large beds, and a spectacular black-and-ivory Persian rug spreads out almost wall to wall. A huge dresser, topped by an equally vast mirror in an ornate carved frame, matches the two nightstands, and in a corner, a pair of slipper chairs in a warmer gold than the draperies flank a round side table. A lamp draped in sparkling crystal teardrops helps give the room its over-the-top appeal.

"I've never seen anything like it," my great-aunt whispers.

"Me neither."

That brings her back to the ground. "But you ain't lived half as long as I have."

"So there you go. You've got me beat fair and square, so there's nothing more to say. This is something else."

"That made no sense," says one of the queens of nonsense.

"That's because it's way past our bedtime—by maybe two or three time zones' worth of days." I plop onto the nearest bed. "I call this one!"

"I'm not picky. I'm so tired, I'm gonna sleep like a hibernating sloth. Oh! Do sloths hibernate?"

"Beats me. I know they're slow and sleep a lot . . ." I wrinkle my nose. "Wait! Can't you come up with something nicer than a sloth? Even Rip Van Winkle would do."

Aunt Weeby unzips her suitcase, her small, well-shaped nose high in the air. "I like me my sloths, sugarplum. And if you don't mind, I'll be brushing my teeth first."

Briefly, very briefly, I wonder if she even knows what a sloth looks like. Not exactly *GQ* cover material, get my drift?

Before long, we're both under the covers. We pray together, whisper our good nights. Then, in that same hushed tone, Aunt Weeby adds, "Glad you came back home, Andie?"

"I don't have to think about it. I was glad when I came home, and I'm gladder now. Good night."

"God bless you, sweet sugarplum."

"The Lord bless you too."

"Sweet dreams."

Nightmare . . .

I fight it.

A woman's scream . . . pounding footsteps.

Bad nightmare.

More screams . . . knocking on a door. Garbled voices, male and female.

"Andie! Wake up, sugarplum."

I roll to my right side, pull the pillow over my head.

". . . She sleeps like a rock, I tell ya," Aunt Weeby says, her voice shaky.

"But at a time like this!" Miss Mona counters, a hitch in her voice.

"How's she to know, Mona Latimer?"

Aunt Weeby? Wailing?

I fight the cobwebs of sleep but don't get too far. I'm beat.

"That, Livvy, is why you have to wake her up!"

I want to sleep. And they want to wake me up. This is no dream. Might be a nightmare. It is the Daunting Duo I hear.

Then it hits me: shaky voice, hiccuplike hitch, wailing—*a scream*? I bolt up. "Why'd you yell?"

"I didn't—"

"We didn't—"

"*Someone* screamed." I rub my sleep-foggy eyes, but nothing changes. Aunt Weeby's still in her rose silk pajamas, and Miss Mona's in a flowing, flowered nightgown. Trust me. You don't want to know about the hair situation.

When I look at the ladies again, I notice the fear in their eyes, the worry in their expressions, the lack of color in their cheeks.

I leap out of bed. "What happened? Are you okay? Is everyone else all right? Did the government goons with the guns come get us?"

Aunt Weeby gives a tight shake of the head. "Not yet."

Yet? My trouble-o-meter starts its deafening *wee-uh, wee-uh, wee-uh.* "Tell me what's going on. Now!"

Miss Mona reaches for my hand. "I'm afraid, honey, it's worse than government officials and all that. Glory and Allison stayed in the lounge for a while after we went to bed.

Then they went to their room. And that's . . . that's when they found . . . it. *Him*."

She sways, and for a moment, I'm afraid she's going to faint. I run to her side, wrap my arm around her waist. "It's okay, Miss Mona. Whatever they found, it's going to be okay. Just breathe, breathe slow and easy—"

"Sugarplum! A' course she can't breathe at a time like this. What are you thinking? Come on, now. Let's go. You gotta get to getting."

"But if she doesn't breathe, she'll pass out and won't get anywhere—" I catch myself. Why am I trying logic on Aunt Weeby in the middle of the night? "Okay. Let's go . . . wherever."

"To Glory and Allison's room."

Here we go again. I'm resigned to my fate. "Lead the way."

But Miss Mona's reluctance speaks volumes. Something's really wrong here. This isn't one of the Duo's usual escapades. My heartbeat speeds up. The chill I feel doesn't come from a breeze behind any silk draperies. I don't think Glory's found a mouse or a spider in her room.

With every step I take, I shiver more. That's when I start to pray. "Please, Lord . . . Father, help us. Keep us safe . . ."

The door to the bedroom is open, but neither Miss Mona nor Aunt Weeby will go in. I look from one to the other. Each shakes her head. I close my eyes, call out to the Lord again, and take that final step over the threshold.

"Oh, Andie!" Allison groans. "Look!"

There, on the floor between the two beds, is Farooq, motionless, his head twisted and lolling in an unnatural way.

I suck in a long, hard breath. "Not again . . ."

51

4 00

Remember those essays way back in grade school: "What I Did on My Summer Vacation"? Yeah, you know. Most kids go to Disney. Me? I go to jail. In Kashmir.

Trust me. Time in a Srinagar police holding pen is not something you want to do. Imagine five of us—plus Robert—in an eight-by-ten-foot cell: cozy.

Not.

Filth, stench, and nasty officers are about as good as it gets. It's worse, much worse than being chased by angry government goons with guns drawn through the wilds of Myanmar. That time, at least we had a vehicle around us, and it was moving. *Away* from our hunters.

Now, we're sitting ducks. And until someone comes out and confesses to whacking poor Farooq, we're stuck.

Let's face it; he had Allison's backpack in his clutches when we found him. Even the somewhat dim cop doesn't need too many mental lightbulbs to figure out Farooq got caught mid-theft and Allison took matters into her own hands—or broomstick, as the case may be. It looks like that's what the killer used to choke the guy.

Only problem is, Allison didn't kill Farooq.

She couldn't have. Wouldn't have.

I know Allison.

But how do you get foreign officials to listen when the evidence looks way clear?

Oh! You want to know why they've locked up the rest of us too? Accomplices, they say. One delicate little woman couldn't possibly have killed the "strong"—scrawny, if you ask me—male houseboy all by her weak self. We *all* took part in sticking a broomstick under his chin, pulling back, and asphyxiating him.

Yeah, right.

Hours float by.

We pray.

We try to lighten the mood with a couple of stories, tell jokes, but that goes nowhere. Even Aunt Weeby doesn't have much to say. My one question, of course, is why, if we were supposed to be short-term missionaries, did we wind up in a glam floating palace where some guy went and got himself choked?

You know I can't ask Miss Mona that. Not while she's scared, nervous, pale, and at times, green around the gills from the wretched stench. Instead, I put my arm around her, tell her I love her, pray with her, and remind both of us that even now our God is in control.

I check my watch, but every time I do, it seems to have stopped working. Then I look again, and I realize it's doing its thing, just way slower than I'd like. I'm dying to get out of this place. Time creeps by, hour after hour after hour . . .

Around dawn, Aunt Weeby and I lean against each other and manage to snooze for a very brief while. But Kashmiri jails don't exactly encourage rest and relaxation. Nor do they offer privacy for . . . ahem . . . bodily functions. At least not our sumptuous holding cell. The thought makes my skin crawl.

But God is good, you know? Are we still in jail?

Well, no. That was then. Now, midmorning, we're in a limo.

How'd we get out?

Let me tell you. Miss Mona's resourcefulness is a wondrous thing. Remember the political problems and all that stuff going on in this part of the world? Well, it's not so much against us as against each other, not like the unpleasantness between us and Myanmar. We have a good embassy in Srinagar, and all it takes is Miss Mona's call to get someone from the good old U.S. of A. to show up and plead our case.

I don't want to know if money changed hands.

Unfortunately, our freedom means bad news for poor old Robert. He's charged with Farooq's untimely demise and will be held for trial—if one can really call it that in this part of the world.

In the embassy limo, Allison shoves her brown curls from her forehead. "Could someone explain to me how things went from me killing Farooq because he was stealing my wallet to Robert killing him because they had a falling out over the loot?"

I blow out a gust of pent-up air, and with it goes a ton of stress. "Maybe they have some kind of evidence on the guy? If that's the case, he belongs in jail. If not . . .well, I don't know if there's anything anyone can do. We are where we are." I shudder. "But I will praise God we're not still there."

"D'y'all really think that nice Robert could've killed that poor little waiter?" Aunt Weeby asks, for about the fiftieth time since we got sprung. "And really, Allison, dear. Why'd you ever travel with all that loot in the first place?"

"Loot?" our makeup diva cries. "All I had was twenty bucks. I keep my traveler's checks in a pouch around my waist under my clothes."

"Isn't it so sad," Miss Mona says, her eyes tired and her face showing her age. "So many thieves lose their lives for so pitifully little. It just breaks your heart, you know?"

What else is there to say? Miss Mona's a pretty sharp cookie.

When we pull up before a tall, brightly lit building, I turn to my sharp-cookie boss. "Where are we?"

"The Hotel Broadway." She sighs. "I didn't think any of you would want to return to the houseboat after . . . well, after what happened. I sure didn't."

I scramble out of the limo and give her a hug. "You think of everything. I hadn't even considered that."

"Miss Andie, it scene of crime," Xheng Xhi, our new escort says with an alarming amount of relish—and an intense look for me. "Police investigate. A lot."

"How about our things?" Glory asks. "I had a ton of camera and video equipment."

"Mr. Moffett at the embassy is pretty sure we'll get everything back by the afternoon," Miss Mona answers as she enters the lush lobby. "I think we can all make do without our things for a few hours."

Aunt Weeby perks up for the first time since the shrieking

paddy-wagon-type van hauled us off to the pokey. "Betcha they have all those cute l'il soaps and lotions and shampoos at the front desk! And I'm gonna ask at the desk for a tooth-brush, toothpaste, razor, and shaving cream. Nice hotels hand 'em out like souvenirs."

My idea of souvenirs runs along the lines of the airport's luscious leather handbags.

We split up as before: Miss Mona in a single, Glory and Allison together, and Aunt Weeby and me, roomies again. I think of Robert's fate: somewhere he has his own single—with iron bars—and his own problems if he did kill Farooq.

I just don't buy it. But who am I to say?

The elevator spits us out on the tenth floor and we scatter down the hall. Aunt Weeby leads the way to our home away from home, her loot—as opposed to whatever loot Farooq imagined Allison had—clutched in her happy little fist. True, the rest of us asked for toothbrushes and paste too, but it didn't mean much to anyone but her. Home comforts have always been important to my aunt, and I know how much this night has rattled her. So if dinky sample toiletries make her smile, bring 'em on!

When we're both ready for sleep, me still in my wrinkled Tazmanian Devil pajama pants and blue tank top and Aunt Weeby in her rose silk jammies, slightly worse for the wear in a Kashmiri jail, we kneel between the queen-sized beds and pray, tears of gratitude wetting our faces, our love and trust in God almost palpable.

As the sun reaches the apex of the sky, we both crawl under the sheets, and in minutes, fall asleep.

After an uneventful if exhausting evening, and now a hotel breakfast of very American eggs and toast, we're treated to another Srinagar-style grilling by grim cops. When they finally give up on us, we head out to meet the missionaries who've been stationed here in Kashmir since a few weeks after the quake. The Sewards are still stateside, working to raise funds for and more interest in Kashmir's lingering disaster. Wow! So much has happened, it seems as though we met them in another century.

We meet our hosts, the Musgroves, outside the Anglican All Saints Church. Trevor Musgrove turns out to be a British man, tall, thin, and dressed in jeans and a short-sleeved, button-down plaid shirt. His wife, Emma, a tiny five feet— max—looks stunning in the most amazing green sari. She wears her blond hair coiled into a chignon at the base of her head, and her leather sandals peep out from under the swaths of fabric when she walks toward us.

After quick introductions, Emma holds out her hands in a gesture of welcome. "We're so happy to have you join us. Laura Seward has told us a great deal about you and your television network."

I take her hands and squeeze. "Laura told us about you and all you do for the kids." The memory leaves me feeling awkward and inadequate. "You know? I love what I do, but it seems so . . . so inconsequential here." I turn to Miss Mona. "Sorry."

She nods, a shadow of sadness in her eyes. "Don't apologize, honey. I understand how you feel."

I turn back to our new friends. "How can I—we—help you? What's the plan? I mean, I know we're heading for the orphanage, but I don't know any details."

"I'm glad you know about The Father's Lambs orphanage already." Trevor's British accent clips his words and seems to give them extra importance. I listen up. "The quake left these children with nothing, and they had precious little to start with. This country was—and still is, after all this time— more devastated than I can begin to tell."

The thought of the children's suffering makes my heart ache. "We're headed for the mountains, aren't we? That's where most of the destruction happened."

He shrugs. "It's quite hard to say what might be worse when we see ravaged villages and neighborhoods just about everywhere outside the few major cities."

I shudder. "Ouch. The Lord's laid on my heart a real hunger to help. Can't we get going?"

Emma holds out her hand. I take the slender fingers in my much larger paw again and let her draw me toward the church. "We're staying with the pastor. Let's go meet him, pray, and then talk action."

"I like your style."

She cocks her head and studies me for a minute . . . two. "I've heard I'm going to like yours too."

A ripple runs through me, but I'm not sure if it's from excitement, fear, or a motley mix of both. *Lord? You brought me here, and I'm so glad you did. Thanks. I want to help, to do something more real than sell bling-bling on TV. Oh yeah! And please keep trouble far away from us while we try to be your hands and feet. We've had way more than enough of that already. We sure don't need any more. And if Robert didn't do the deed, help the cops find the guy who did.*

Introductions are brief. Then, once the formalities are over, Trevor holds out his hands; Miss Mona takes the right and Glory the left. I snag Aunt Weeby, and still holding onto Emma, I bow my head with everyone else.

In his rich bass, Trevor says, "Father God . . ."

After an emotional handful of hours, during which I hear more tales of pain, misery, and courage than I ever thought possible, we leave the Musgroves until the next day, aware that our efforts will change little in the greater scheme of things. Still, not one of us is about to quit before we do our part.

"Sorry we came?" Miss Mona asks as we board our van.

"Me?" I glance at the nondescript brown car that's followed every step we've taken since Farooq's demise. What can I say? They do have a dead body.

Still . . . "Nuh-uh. I'm ready to get out there and do . . . whatever I can." I settle in next to Glory. "I'm surprised you ask. Are you? Sorry, that is?"

"No, honey. But I clocked in more than a few hours on the mission field in my day. I knew what to expect. But you . . . you're younger, and more a New York City kinda girl than me."

"Whoa!" I roll my eyes. "Forgetful all of a sudden, huh? I'm the missionary kid here. You know Mom and Dad never saw the needy African tribe they didn't want to help. And I was right there with them. I don't know that I actually helped, but I did share my toys and books with the little girls."

"You probably did more'n you know, sugarplum," Aunt Weeby says. "It's not always the big things what make the difference. It's more the loving and doing and being the bit a' Jesus someone else is gonna see that does the doing for you."

At my side, Glory wriggles, shifts the big red bag of electronic whatzits she always has at the ready, then tucks a lock of gleaming black hair behind her ear.

"Do you have enough room?" I ask.

"I'm fine."

And I'm the Big Bad Wolf; she looks anything but fine. I don't know for sure what's bugged her. I have to wonder whether it's the mission, the poverty, the tragedy, and the earthquake's devastation, or whether it's our faith talk that's got her so uncomfortable. I slant a look her way and notice her downcast eyes.

I know Miss Mona doesn't make faith a job requirement, but most S.T.U.D. employees are strong believers. "What did you think of the Musgroves?" I ask, my tone light and my expression—I hope—none too nosy.

Glory's eyes pop open wide. "Me?"

I nod.

"I . . . I thought they were fine. They're pretty committed to their work, aren't they?"

"I don't think it's their work they're so committed to," Aunt Weeby says. "They're just about some a' the most on-fire, obedient Christians I've ever met." She turns to me. "Kinda like your mama and daddy, sugarplum."

I nod but keep my eyes on Glory, who looks at me with what feels more like curiosity, or maybe questions, than before. She must be one of Miss Mona's rare nonbelievers.

Allison, our makeup genius extraordinaire, pipes up. "Miss Weeby, anyone would have to go a whole lot farther than Kashmir to find a more real Christian than you."

I can just about feel Glory's surprise. "Really?" she says. "Where've you been to . . ." She seems to want a word, a precise one. "To do the Musgroves' thing?"

Sadness fills my aunt's still pretty face. "Can't say I've ever been any too far from Louisville. I did go to Jamaica many, many years ago, and helped make clothes while my late husband worked to rebuild a church that burned down."

Allison pats Aunt Weeby's arm. "Foreign missions aren't all God calls people to, and you know it, Miss Weeby. You've been teaching and living it all out for us to see right back in Louisville. We needed you—still do, you know. Remember when you taught my Sunday school class? I was six years old, and I've never forgotten Joseph and his coat of many colors."

Aunt Weeby's laugh is full of mischief. "We sure did make us a good ol' mess with all that fabric and glue, didn't we?"

"But we made an awesome coat out of those bits and pieces of rags," Allison counters. "I thought it was the most beee-yoooo-teee-full thing I'd ever seen. Never forgot how Joseph lost his coat and everything else, thanks to his brothers' jealousy."

"Is that all you learned?" Aunt Weeby asks, her voice rich with dismay. "Well, phooey, girl! I went and blew it, then."

"No way." Allison shakes her brown mane for emphasis. "I got it all. The best part was when the drought came and Joseph had become the big man in town. His brothers knew who was who then."

Glory's eyes, which had bounced from woman to woman, land back on me. "Did you do the same class?"

"Nope. I'm too old. Allison's a baby compared to me."

"Give me a break," the baby says.

I wink.

Glory leans forward. "So Joseph's not just some old show."

Before I can stop them, my eyebrows meet my hairline. "You didn't know Joseph was real and lived in biblical times?"

"I knew he was an old guy Donny Osmond played in an old musical."

Yikes! Joseph, an old musical guy . . . and Donny Osmond?

Aunt Weeby beats me to the punch. "Well then, Glory-girl, let me tell you what all you've been missing about Joseph and his coat . . ."

By the time we get to the restaurant, a favorite with tourists (we'd rather skip Montezuma's revenge and don't check out the quaint but not-necessarily-compatible-with-American-digestive-systems local feeding spots), we've all learned more about Joseph than we thought possible. He's one of Aunt Weeby's Bible faves—understandably so.

But I digress. For dinner, we do some kind of banquet thing called a Wazawan—*waza* being what they call the chef. We have *yakhni*, a cream-colored meat dish with a curd base, and *munji-hakh*, kohlrabi—ever have kohlrabi?

Neither had I, until now. Anyway, the Kashmiri delicacies are delicious, and my ever-empty stomach is happy as I chow down with zest. But then, as I close my mouth around some *yakhni* and white rice, I hear a rumble of whispers behind me, a bit to the right.

I pick up my soupspoon, shine it on my napkin and, feeling rather Pink Panther-ish, if I do say so myself, use it to look over my shoulder.

Groan.

Aunt Weeby places her hand on my arm. "Sugarplum! Was that you? Are you feeling peckish all of a sudden? I bet it's that nasty ol' corroded gut a' yours again. I did bring me a bottle a' Great-Grandma Willetta's cod liver oil with me. It'll set you right in no time."

Perish the thought. As a kid, I was a victim of good ol' Willetta's favorite remedy many a time—gotta love my aunt Weeby. Don't want to go there again.

But Aunt Weeby's not too far out in left field, either. During my time as a New York gemologist in the famous—or infamous, you choose—diamond district, I achieved a teeny-tiny ulcer problem (times three, but who's counting?) that disappeared the minute I returned to Kentucky. Go figure. I wind up wrestling the mayhem wrought by two wacky seniors and a blundering cohost, and I heal.

Only me, you know?

Anyway, back to our exotic meal. I try to distract Aunt Weeby by shaking my head, smiling, and taking a bite of the *munji-hakh* that's grown cold on my plate. Cold kohlrabi? Who'd a thunk?

But eating foreign food does nothing to put a lid on the tide of murmurs to my rear. A tsunami's about to wallop us.

Thanks to my trusty spoon, I can see a slender woman in her late thirties elbow the older lady at her side. They put their heads together, and the older one points. The scene is repeated all around the eight people seated round the table. That's when I hear the dreaded words.

"It *is* her," the teenage girl at the far end of their group squeals. "I'm telling you, Mom. It's the S.T.U.D.'s Andrea Adams. I just looooove her."

Swallow me, earth. I eat with more single-minded diligence and attention than even a fire-eater at a circus midway show.

The older woman looks skeptical. "What would she be doing here? I've heard she's a Christian. She wouldn't come for Swami Devamundi's Eternal Growth gathering like everybody else here."

"Gramma!" the girl cries, exasperated. "Get real. She's probably on the hunt for treasure. I just told you. We're talking *the* Andi-ana Jones. Of gemology. You know."

Ugh. I hate that name. A gem thief thought she was so smart when she came up with it after what happened to us at a ruby mine little less than a year ago. I thought her just plain awful, and I still do, especially since she blabbed the stupid nickname during an early court appearance.

Ever hear anything dumber? I haven't raided any ark, lost or otherwise. But it's my latest cross to bear. Well, together with the cloud of nuttiness that follows my aunt and her best friend. And the gem-dunce cohost.

Oh, okay, okay. I'll say it. I may have my own problem with tromping into trouble just about every other time I take a step. All by my only-lonely self.

Unlike this time, when I'm minding my business: food.

But once I decide the teen's companions have chosen to ignore her, and I'm way more than ready to quit cringing, the girl lets out a disgusted-teen kind of sigh—yeah. *That* loud.

"You know," she says. "I told you. Margie says her older sister and the girls of Delta Epsilon Zeta say they heard people calling her Andi-ana Jones during that murder trial. Like, she goes all over the world, catches crooks, and brings back all those bling-bling treasures. She's just awe-*some!*"

I shovel the food faster than earthmoving equipment on steroids, but to no avail. Before I've washed down the last mammoth bite of the *yakhni*, the female neighbors make their way to my side.

My gulp is none too elegant, but it'd be so much worse to greet fans with a mouthful of mutton, no doubt.

"Excuse me," the girl says. "I know you're eating, and my dad said I'd be way rude to come and bug you, but I just had to prove it to my mom and grandmom. You *are* the Andi-ana Jones of gems, aren't you?"

I wince, nod, and give a weak smile.

She turns, crosses her arms, cocks out a hip, and smirks. "I told you so."

The mom shakes her head. "I'm sorry she disturbed your dinner. You're her favorite TV personality, and she wouldn't leave us alone until we came over. You are very good at what you do."

I stand, my on-screen smile at full-watt power. "It's okay. I'm starting to get used to it. I'm glad you like the show."

The teen pumps her fist. "*Woot, woot, woot!* Toldja."

"Stop it, Delia!" the mother scolds. "We're in a public place, and Miss Adams is being very gracious. That's just plain rude—your second episode in less than five minutes."

Delia gives her mother a prodigious glare.

In an effort to offset the oncoming mother-daughter brawl, I say, "So what's your favorite gemstone?"

"Gemstone?" Delia dons a look of total confusion. "Oh, sure. All that bling you sell."

Now *I'm* confused. "Isn't that what you watch me do?"

She laughs. "No way. That's why Gramma watches. I watch you and your stud! He's tooooo cute!"

And to think I spent all those years in and dollars on school. I could've saved myself, my parents, and Uncle Sam of the educational-grants-and-financial-aid fame a minor fortune and still come out the same.

"I . . . see." I turn to Gramma. "And which is your favorite gemstone?"

Gramma holds out a snap, crackle, and popping left hand. "Diamonds, honey. They'll never turn on you."

This is going south faster than the *yakhni* I scarfed before the conversation ever started. "And did you buy those . . ." I shove down my dislike of ostentatious glitz and glamour, and smile. "Did you buy those awesome pieces from Shop-Til-U-Drop?"

She beams. "Sure, I did. Well, all but this one."

Her right hand sports a goose-egg-sized pear-cut solitaire on her ring finger and a much lesser cluster on her index. She waggles the index at me. "This one's from the *other* place. See the difference?"

You bet. As much as I hate the gaudy pieces of jewelry, the diamond quality is undeniably outstanding—except for the piece she bought from one of our competitors.

I wisely go for nice. "I'm so glad you're happy with your purchases. Is there anything you'd like me to feature in the future?"

"Oh, honey!" Delia's mom purrs. "You bet. I'd be happy if all you showed was close-ups of Max. He's real eye candy, you know."

Heat rushes up my neck and into my cheeks. There's not much I can say to that. Max is one of the finest looking males I've ever seen, on-screen or off.

Aunt Weeby pounces on my momentary silence. "See,

sugarplum? Everyone loves you and Max together. Just like Miss Pig—"

"Aunt Weeby!"

"Actually," Delia's mom says, oblivious to my indignation—righteous, you know. "I'd just as soon see Max host his own shows. Don't ask me what he should sell, but I'll buy it. Whatever it is."

My stomach lurches. No one likes to hear she's chump change, as this woman seems to think I am. So I take my seat again and resume shoveling calories down the pipeline from gullet straight to hip. I want to avoid the question that's sure to follow at all costs.

"So where's your stud, Andi-ana?" Delia asks.

There's the question. Mercifully, my mouth's full. Otherwise, who knows what my defiant tongue might've blurted out?

Miss Mona's answer strikes fear in my heart. "Oh, here and there. You know. He's a busy boy. And they *do* make the most darling couple ever, don't they?"

That's not a good answer—it's a *rotten* one, in fact. I know Miss Mona way too well. She's formidable, in every way. My gut starts up a nervous rumble. Dread puts in an appearance. I glance at the Duo. And cringe at their canary-dined cat grins.

"He's not my anything!" I finally sputter.

"Too bad," Delia says. "That he's not here, that is. I woulda loved to have met him too, if he was. Just think. I coulda, like, waited to wash my hands until I got back home. I coulda gone to visit Margie's sister at school—you know, the sisters at Zeta would just about die to shake the hand that shook his."

That's too gross, but in the course of channel loyalty, I eat on. Soon, they've had their fill of us and rejoin the men at their table.

Phew! I'm as bloated as the next blimp. And happy to report that, not many minutes later, they stand, wave goodbye, and trot away. I relax.

But not for long. You know what's coming, don't you?

Not ten minutes later, the sound that fills me with the weirdest awareness I've ever known reaches my ears.

"There you all are!" Mr. Magnificent says.

I spin in my chair. "YOU!"

He smiles.

So does Miss Mona.

Aunt Weeby cheers.

There! *That's* the stinky-fish scheming I've been sniffing all along. You knew the Daunting Duo weren't about to take a vacation from their Cupid efforts, didn't you? My frustration with the meddlesome seniors steams to a head and then pops.

"How 'bout that vacation I'm supposed to be taking, Miss Mona?"

5.00

Max winks. "Yes, it's me. And this"—he waves—"is your vacation."

Fight it, Andie, fight it! I don't want to melt at that grin. I face Miss Mona. "Why? Why would you do this to me?"

Canary feathers float from hers and Aunt Weeby's mouths as they swap yet more looks. "Why not?" she chortles.

Yup. You know it. I've been had. A dull drumbeat starts up in my head—Max's presence does that to me. And the super-awareness thing too. It's a gift.

I grit my teeth. "Are you trying to tell me," I ask my boss, "that *he's* here to help the Musgroves?"

"I plan to pitch in with whatever's going on." Max pulls out the chair right across from mine. Rats! How'm I gonna avoid the blue, blue of those eyes now? "Who're the Musgroves?"

See what I mean? Rats! All of 'em. Lovable, yes, but rats, nonetheless. Well, the seniors among us are lovable. Dunno about the male.

Yet, whispers a mischievous imp in the cobwebs of my subconscious.

No! No way. There are not gonna be any "yets" around here. I can't deal with relationships—I'm a total zero at the boy-girl romance thing. And with a gorgeous guy like Max? Hah!

"Well?" That very same gorgeous Max guy asks. "Who are the Musgroves?"

I blink. "Ah . . . um . . ." *Get a grip, woman!* "The missionaries we came to help."

Under his dove-gray polo shirt, Max rolls his shoulders and flexes his biceps—very nice ones they are, too. "I can tote and fetch with the best of 'em. Just tell me what I need to do."

What's a girl to do? Even when I travel halfway around the world to help defenseless orphans and, to tell the truth, put some distance between me and Mr. Magnificent himself, I wind up with the man glued to my side. I hope he's better at toting and fetching, as he calls it, than he is at rocks.

I sigh. You know exactly how much trouble I'm in here, don't you? I don't get it—still. Why did nutty Miss Mona, in the worst moment of her nuttiness, ever get the random idea that the S.T.U.D. needed on-screen "chemistry"? She's known me since forever. Doesn't she—and Aunt Weeby too—remember how lousy I've been at "chemistry" for them to betray me and pull out all the matchmaking stops?

A great-looking guy + Andie Adams = disaster.

At the very least, bad idea.

As far as I'm concerned, it's their worst idea ever. I mean, until the dark day when Miss Mona suffered that particular brain burp, her flaky brand of wisdom had only led her to hire women. The Shop-Til-U-Drop Shopping Channel was the by-women, for-women, all-women network. And it worked. The channel was wildly successful. It made sense for her to hire me and for me to work for her.

You follow? Good.

So, if that's the case, then why, oh why, when she wanted on-screen "chemistry," did she go hire a man who could give a doofus a run for his money? And why, oh why did she then stick me with the gorgeous creature? Me! The relationship phobe. The dating dud. The chicken-hearted romance flop.

Just as I think this, my conscience, hitched at the hip to heaven as it is, puts in an appearance. It does that a lot.

Okay. So Max isn't a doofus. And he has made a sincere effort to learn about the gems we offer our customers. But he hasn't done a thing to shield me from his melt-me smile, his wow voice, or his oh-my baby blues.

Yeah, yeah, yeah. My problem, not his. I'm a coward.

And if I don't get a grip on myself, this up-and-down teeter-totter emotional mess is gonna be the end of me.

As the chatter flies around the table, my overactive conscience keeps up its efforts for a while longer. I study the swanky linen napkin on my lap to keep from peeking at Max.

It's time.

I have to quit dancing around the truth. I have to be honest and face what's bugged me most about Max from the very start. What's made me treat him like dirt a time or two . . . or ten.

There's way too much about Max Matthews I like.

There! I've admitted it.

71

Now what?

With my track record with men—or lack thereof—a guy like Max is way out of my reach. The last thing I need is to fall for him. If that happens, then, *BAM!* Soon enough, he'll find a princess, and there I'll sit with my broken heart.

At twelve, puppy love is cute.

At thirty, it isn't. It's not even puppy love anymore. It's unrequited love, hard and painful, and I don't want to go there.

Lord? What am I going to do about Max?

I glance up and notice the baby blues on me. Then the deafening silence hits me. Everyone at the table is staring at me.

Swell. "Ah . . . did I miss something?"

They fill me in. All at one time.

The result? A Tower of Babel replay.

I catch snippets about the Musgroves and their mission. I hear about the mountain village where they've built a school. I hear about Kashmiri sapphires and played-out mines.

"I knew it!" I cross my arms and stare at my boss.

Miss Mona clears her throat, smiles what I call her "Queen Liz" smile, and when she has everyone's attention, launches her speech. "As all y'all know," she says, posture regal, expression serious—have I mentioned the woman has star-quality flair?—"I was tickled by the results of our trip to Mogok."

When I croak, she has the decency to blush.

"True, Andrea." Her nod can make an emperor weep. "We did have us some unpleasantness, but we bought magnificent stones, and you and Hannah filmed wonderful video of the mining operations."

"I'm not into reruns," I mutter.

"I'm not into Muslim guerillas," Max adds.

"Oh, pshaw!" Aunt Weeby says. "Guerillas are people too. Why, I reckon they put on their trousers—well, those baggy things they wear like trousers—just like the rest of us do."

Her voice sets off the *beep, beep, beep* of my Aunt Weeby–alert system. *Patience, please*, I pray. "Have you lost your marbles?"

She frowns—something she rarely does, but when she does . . . watch out, world! "Andrea Autumn Adams!"

No question. I'm in deep, deep doggy-doo. And with Aunt Weeby among us, headed for a close encounter of the Muslim rebel kind.

I sigh in resignation. Remember the sinking ship? It's coming nearer. "Yes, Auntie?"

She sniffs—she's an expert. "You know perfectly well my daddy's marble collection is back home in his secretary in the parlor. I couldn't possibly lose all those precious marbles."

Trust me. The woman knows what I mean. Her brain just does curious things to her squishy logic when she wants to play fast and loose with it.

I waggle a finger. "Don't go there. You and Miss Mona are just plain dangerous to my hide—and yours!"

Miss Mona laughs. "Ah . . . but isn't it better to be . . . umm . . . unconventional and adventurous than to be boring and mindless ol' rocking chair residents?"

Can *you* see these two pushing rockers? Me neither.

I wave my white napkin in surrender. "Okay. You've got me there. Just give it to me straight." I square my shoulders. "And I don't want the ad campaign you've cooked up to sell me on this latest scheme."

In one of her hokiest and most theatrical moves, Aunt

Weeby does outrage. "Why, Andie! I've never in my life known you to be such a stubborn, contrary creature—"

"I have," Max says.

I glare.

He laughs, licks the tip of his index finger, and chalks one up.

I shake my head. "What's wrong with you? Do you want to play hide-and-seek with AK-47-toting Talibans and friends?"

"Oh, Andie," Miss Mona says. "That's not what we're here to do, dear. We're just short-term missionaries and part-time tourists. The Father's Lambs orphanage was built after the quake near the village of Soomjam in the Kudi Valley, not too far from the mines. Tourists take pictures. And videos. That's been the plan from the start. Nothing much, really."

See my point? There you have the Queen of Schemes, the researcher extraordinaire, the purveyor of rotten-fish-in-Denmark. No one ever said a word about the orphanage's proximity to the mines. Never. Ever.

True, I didn't take the time to do any research of my own, but you'd think logic—hmph! There I go again, hoping for logic when spontaneity and a sense of adventure are my aunt's and her best friend's overriding instincts.

So I make a winding gesture with my hand. "I suspected something like that when you insisted on dragging the crew with us instead of folks from church. But what's the appeal? Those mines stopped producing back in the eighteen hundreds—except for occasional minor strikes, and the last one of those was in the 1930s."

Aunt Weeby tsk-tsks. "That's the problem with you, sugarplum. You just try too hard to strip all the fun right outta life, what with all that there serious, practical stuff. What's wrong with a l'il ol' adventure every once in a while? Who knows what we'll find when we go poking in the mines?"

"Rocks and dirt is what we'll find," I answer. "If we're lucky and don't rattle the local tribesmen. They don't like outsiders." When the Daunting Duo's expressions don't change, resignation takes up residence. "All-righty, then. So what's the plan?"

"You know, it's a blessing we've come in August." Had the woman even heard me? Apparently not. She goes on. "The weather's about forty-five degrees below zero most of the year. But it's summer now. Lots, lots warmer. And we don't have to worry about snow and ice to get to the mines. Who knows? Maybe a miracle will happen, and someone will find a sapphire while we're there. Can you imagine the footage we'd get then?"

I can imagine Miss Piggy flapping plump, pink wings overhead too.

Aunt Weeby nods. "Miracles happen every day."

I believe in miracles: it'll be a miracle if we leave Kashmir alive. "But what about the mission? The Musgroves? We did tell them we had come to help."

Aunt Weeby clasps her hands together and brings them to her chest. "Isn't God great? He's put it all together for us. We're going to a ruined village on the way to the valley where your sapphires are. We can mine for souls and sapphires in one of the most un-Christianized places on earth."

We've got cops who aren't sure we're as innocent as the embassy says. We're about to trek through some of the world's most dangerous mountains. We'll have to dodge Taliban-friendly, gun-toting Muslim rebels to do it. And we're going to stay in a town that isn't so much a town as a trash heap these days.

Yeah, the thought of all that while working with abandoned babies *and* digging for sapphires is more than my stomach can take—especially now that I've eaten enough for a family of nine.

I push back my chair. "Excuse me!"

I pray every step of the way to the nearest john. What a time for my stomach issues to reappear.

When I walk out of the bathroom stall, I find Aunt Weeby sitting in an elegant cobalt silk-covered chair in the ladies' room, praying under her breath. Her relief tells me what a scare I've given her.

"I'm sorry," I say. "I didn't mean to worry you."

"Of course you didn't, sugarplum." She pats the arm of the matching chair at her side.

I sit.

She goes on. "You just urped. I came to pray for you in here on account of I couldn't shut off all that jibber-jabber going on out there." She weaves her fingers through mine. "Are you going to be okay? Let's see how you feel after I give you a good ol' dose of Great-Grandma Willetta's cod liver oil—you know how good that stuff is—"

"No!" Horrors.

She goes on. "How 'bout we go back home? To a good American doctor?"

"Of course we can't go back home—at least, not yet. I'll be fine."

"But you got sick—"

"Sure, I did. I ate too much and too fast. I know better than that. Don't worry. I won't do it again."

Aunt Weeby looks puzzled. "Did you like the meal *that* much?"

I shrug. "It was yum-oh, to quote Rachael Ray, but that's not why I ate like that. I just hated the whole 'Andi-ana Jones' deal, and it was easier to chow down than to deal with those people. My bad—and I *still* had to deal with them."

"Pshaw!" She stands. "Sugarplum, you just have to learn to . . . what does that there Dr. Phil guy say? That's it! *Embrace* your fame. It plumb won't do to run away from it. Or to eat yourself into a fat-fest frenzy, either."

"Now there's an image for ya."

"So's you running from . . ." She gives me what I call her evil eye, since it sees too much. "Well, y'aren't just running from the fame thing, you know. It's that dear boy Max what's really got you pigging out. Isn't it?"

I roll my eyes. "He drives me nuts, all right. It's no classified secret."

Her smile turns indulgent, and I realize the weapon I've given her. "You got it all wrong," I wail. "He's a pain in the butt—"

"They're the best kind, those pain-in-the-butt boys. Your uncle Harris was one of 'em. I like to have pulled my hair plumb out when we first met. I thought him the most mule-ornery male Creation'd ever seen. But he stuck to me like chewing gum to a summer sandal, and then . . . why, I loved him with all my heart."

Talk of love and ornery males makes my teeth itch. I don't want to go there, not about Max.

Not yet.

"Nope, Aunt Weeby. Please don't do this to me." I shake my head to where I hear a rushing sound in my ears. "That's *not* the kind of crazy he makes me. He makes me the kind of crazy that says he's going to sink our show if we don't watch out. I think Miss Mona really needs to find him a different catalog to sell our viewers."

She arches a brow. "And here I thought he was studying rocks with you. What? You reckon Danni's panties would be a better fit?"

Not even with the proverbial ten-foot pole.

I blush, rise, and slap open the swinging bathroom door. "I know I suggested it once before, but you know that's goofy. Maybe Miss Mona can start some kind of . . . ah . . . well, how about a motorcycle stuff program? He can sell that—gloves, sunglasses, helmets. You know."

As I stalk to the table, I notice how close Max and the gloriously gorgeous Glory have their heads. For some irrational reason, this irritates me.

"No!" I tell my aunt. "I have it. He should sell ladders and hoses and dead-bug-on-your-windshield cleaning goop—nice and studly stuff."

"Dead bugs?" Glory asks when I plop into my seat. "Did you find dead bugs in the bathroom?"

Figures she'd be the one who'd ask, right? It tweaks my irritation up a notch. "Yeah, bugs. But not in the ladies' room. Aunt Weeby and I were just trying to come up with a new program to feature Max. Like those women suggested."

"You want me to sell dead bugs?" Mr. Magnificent asks, disbelief all over his handsome mug.

Miss Mona looks thoughtful. "Well . . . it *is* odd, I'll grant you that, but you know? There are . . ." She waves in that vague way of hers. "Oh, whatever you call them. People who collect beetles and butterflies—dead bugs!"

The angry horror on Max's face makes me smile—and squirm, but I choose to ignore the squirm. For the moment. I'll pray about it tomorrow . . . later.

I dredge up a smile from . . . oh, somewhere deep and forgotten. "Who'd a thunk l'il ol' me would come up with the solution to Max's less-than-masterful gemological expertise?"

His eyes burn fiery blue. "You can't be serious."

I cross my arms. "Well, I'm not the boss."

He turns to Miss Mona. "I'm sure she was only joking. I know even less about entomology than I do gems. How many of your viewers are going to be interested in bugs? They like Danni's panties—er . . . lingerie, Wendy's girdles, Tanya's sports memorabilia—that I could go for, you know—Marcie's kitchen gadgets, *and* the gems and jewelry. I don't see where bugs fit in."

Before I can stop myself, I say, "How 'bout men's underwear with bug pictures? I'm sure *you'd* sell a ton—to the guys' wives, that is, and *if* you make the boxers cute."

Another of his glares comes my way. "Fine, Andie. If we're going to talk bugs, then let's talk about the one that seems to have flown up your nose. What's the deal? I haven't done anything to set you off this time. I thought we'd gotten beyond the snits."

Ouch! He's right.

My snit crash-lands, and I feel crummy.

I've let my insecurities get the best of me again. First, Delia and her mother's gushing about him hit me in the pride. Then his sudden arrival threw me for a loop. And finally his cozy little chat with Glory when I walked out of the ladies' room jabbed my old green-eyed monster up from its nap. What does it all say about me?

Ugly, ugly, ugly.

No way, no how am I going to examine my feelings right now.

"Okay. I'm sorry. Really, I am. Please forgive me. I was nasty for no reason, and I have to get a grip. Ah . . . umm . . . let's blame it on my rotten stomach."

It's Max's turn to cross his arms. "Rotten stomach? Is that a onetime deal? 'Cause if it is, I have plenty of Imodium— *mi casa es su casa* in the over-the-counter-meds world, that is—and I'd be happy to share. Or did you suddenly develop a new chronic condition?"

His sarcasm makes me wince, but I know I deserve whatever he sends my way. I did act like a snotty two-year-old. Not so hot, you know? "It's not sudden—"

"Now, Max, dear," Aunt Weeby says as she takes her seat. "Didn't Andie tell you all about her time in that Big Apple a' hers?"

When my cohost shakes his head—and I cringe—she continues. "Well, let me tell you all about it. She was so busy wheeling and dealing that she got holes in her belly, and her cat up and died. So, see? It's not new or nothing. She just has herself a corroded gut. Oh! She's pooped too. Uh-huh. She told me so herself. And bummed. She's pooped, bummed, and corroded on account of that nasty ol' Apple."

If that's not the loveliest description of my life in New York, then I don't know what is.

Yeah, right! Well, it's the main reason I came back home to Louisville, but little did I know I'd be facing wild escapades thanks to the Duo, and worse yet, their hyped-up forays into the world of matchmaking.

"Come on, Aunt Weeby. Let's not go there. That's not the best way to put it, and you know it." I turn to my nemesis. "I developed three ulcers during the years I spent in New York. My stomach still gets twitchy at times"—why tell him it's behaved ever since I left the city?—"and I suppose eating a lot of foreign foods too fast may have set it off."

I know, I know. Über-lame. What's worse, Max's skepticism tells me he knows it too. But what's a girl to do? Especially when the gorgeous brunette next to the guy in question leans closer and places her slender hand on his arm.

"You would be awesome in your own show," Glory says, her brown eyes glowing up at Max. "You are so photogenic. The camera loves you."

Not just the camera. The thought zips through my mind, but I have the sense to bite down on my tongue before the words pop out.

Max smiles at Glory. "Thanks." He turns to Miss Mona. "I wouldn't mind a sports show of some kind. Maybe something that features football memorabilia. I can do a good job when it comes to college teams. I could host players, coaches, even pros. I think interviews would work well to sell our products."

Even though this is what I've wanted since his first day, suddenly I don't want Miss Mona to agree. Especially since he and Glory would get a lot of together time. She usually works the kitchen and sports segments. Hannah, my regular camerawoman, is maid of honor at her younger sister's wedding this coming weekend. Therefore, Glory in Kashmir.

Oh, yuck! Yuck, yuck, *yuck*! I don't like how I'm feeling

right now. I don't want to be jealous. Not over Max. *Lord? Help me, please.*

Miss Mona purses her lips and narrows her eyes. "Hmm . . . I don't know, Max. I'd hate to bust up a good thing. And you do know we have a very good thing going with the gem and jewelry shows."

I breathe a little easier. And realize I need my crazy head fixed—help, please!

He tightens his lips into a thin line, then nods. "We can't argue against success. We rarely have any stock left at the end of our shows."

"I've kept track of every one of those lovely, fast-emptying shelves in the vault." Miss Mona's businesswoman's eyes sparkle. "But you can't deny something special happens when you and Andie take your seats and the cameras start to roll."

Special? Cat-and-dog snarls? Do people really want to watch us spat?

Okay. There's a lot to be said for the excitement in winning one of our verbal jousts. But would I like it better if he sold . . . thingamabobs with Tanya, Marcie, or all on his own?

A lot of zip would go out of the fun of doing my show.

Aaaargh! How can I be so mixed up? On the one hand, I can't stand that he doesn't know much about gems. On the other hand, I can't stand to think he'll go off into the shopping-channel sunset with Glory glommed onto his arm.

Am I bonkers or what?

Or what.

I exaggerate my yawn. "You know? I think we've overstayed our welcome. It'd be a good idea to head back to the hotel. We're going to need our sleep for tomorrow. I hope no one's forgotten we're meeting the Musgroves at eight o'clock."

"I'm looking forward to it," Miss Mona says. "I want to dig in and get something done for those poor children who've lost so much."

"Amen to that!" Aunt Weeby says. "I want to see for myself why no one else gets around to helping them any. Don't y'all think it's crazylike that we're the ones what have to come all the way from Kentucky to do it all here? Something's plumb wrongheaded with that picture. Where's everybody else what can help?"

Allison wraps an arm around my aunt as they head for the restaurant's door. "I'm sure that's not what's really happening," she says. "I'm sure lots of help has been sent and many others have tried to work with the Kashmiri. But I'll bet there's a whole lot of political roadblocking going on."

Miss Mona quietly pays for the meal, and our group heads out. I hang back, hoping to avoid Mr. Magnificent.

Mr. Magnificent, however, has my number. He hangs back too.

"Can we call a truce?" he asks.

"Oh, Max, it never broke," I answer. "Not really. I just . . . I don't know . . . but I do know I'm sorry for my snitty remarks. Just chalk it up to my not being in my right mind for a moment or two."

"Oh, so you have a right mind and a wrong one." He winks. "I wish you'd told me that the first day. It could've saved us both some grief."

"Don't get me started!" I ground the incoming smile. "What do you plan to do tomorrow while we work with the Musgroves?"

"I meant it when I said I wanted to pitch in."

Hmm . . . "It won't be a cakewalk—or in your case, a day on the green."

He holds the door open for me. "Do you think you could give me the benefit of the doubt? Just once?"

My hackles bounce right up to attention. "What do you mean? The benefit of what doubt—"

"I've spent a couple of summers on short-term mission projects abroad," he says.

"Missions . . . you?"

His expression turns indignant. "Yeah, me. I worked on a water project in Tanzania the summer after I graduated college, and three summers ago I went to Honduras for six weeks. We built three churches in that time."

Ouch! My pride poops out—as it should. How mean-spirited can a woman get?

I know better.

I do. Really, I do.

Max has said he's gone to church all his life. And I just assumed—yeah, don't tell me how dumb that is, okay?—he's gone as a what-you-do-on-a-Sunday-morning deal.

How many other ways have I underestimated him? All because of my pride . . . and my fear of relationships. Especially with a guy like him.

Worse yet: how would I feel if he'd done the same to me?

"I'm sorry, Max. I have no excuse. Beats me why I thought you'd resent working with the Musgroves. I deserve the crummy way I feel right now." I tuck a loose lock behind my ear. "I need to work a whole lot on . . . oh, let's just say my pride's first in line. I owe the Lord a bunch of knee time. It's going to be a long night for me."

To my shock, he drapes an arm over my shoulders. "Look, Andie. Everyone does and says stupid things." He gives me a mischievous wink. "Some of us just clock in more than others."

When I go to object, he holds up his hand. "Just listen to me, okay? I don't know why we got so far off on the wrong foot in the first place, but I do see where you felt I would ruin your show. Anyway, you can give your ruffled feathers a break now, since the show's a hit. And you can also rest easy: I forgive you. I'm not so frail and flimsy that a couple of zingers are going to do me much harm."

"But—"

"Shh!" He puts a finger on my lips, and my knees take a dive. I catch myself before I hit the pavement.

Uh-oh! He's at it again, doing that good-looking, nice-guy thing he does every once in a while. Of course I can't work out a word, the way he's turned me to mush.

He goes on. "I don't get why you're so hard on yourself—and everyone else. One good thing. You don't discriminate."

I chuckle—no humor there. "One redeeming quality, then."

He puts his other hand on my free shoulder and makes me face him. "Oh, I've found a couple more here and there. But you are the tightest wound person I've ever met. How about you do us both a favor and let the spring go sprung?"

Before he really gets me under his spell, which is what scares me most about him, I ease away. "How about I hit the sack and get some z's? Jet lag's not helping my niceness quotient any."

He looks about to object—to what, I don't know. Does he

want to keep on holding me? Or is he about to call me on blaming my sniping on jet lag?

Then he shrugs. "If you say so. Let's go. Everyone's waiting for us."

With every step I take, I cry out to the Lord. I can't stand the emotional seesaw I've been on since the day I first met Max. I need help to get my feet back on level ground.

But when I'm almost at the van, I look up and groan. We're the center of everyone's attention. Miss Mona and Aunt Weeby look as though it's their birthday and Valentine's Day all in one.

I wince. "Sorry about that—them—too."

He looks embarrassed. "They would have been a hit in small-town America about 110 years or so ago."

"What makes you think they don't get away with matchmaking these days?"

Alarm widens his baby blues. "You're not their only victim? I thought it was because they love you so much."

I laugh. "Not hardly. And because they know me so well, they really should know better, but I guess they don't. Let me tell you. There's a scary number of families they take credit for, and they take their inspiration from their record of success. They see themselves as wise Cupids. I thought they'd drop that side job with the channel's success, but only God can move mountains."

He winks. "Then maybe our on-screen routine will help off-screen. To keep them off our backs."

Huh? "You think? It hasn't done a thing so far."

"Hey, you know them better than I do. Would it disappoint them enough to go on to more likely victims, or would it make them twice as determined?"

I look at the Daunting Duo, both members of which are now busy whispering to each other, smirks on their lips. Double trouble, for sure. "Beats me, but it's worth a try. Put it this way. It's better than having them buy china patterns and toaster ovens because we ended the war."

He gives a dramatic shudder. Then, with another wink, adds, "Since you have such a smart mouth to begin with—"

I plunk my fists on my hips. "And here I thought the truce was on!"

He tips his head Daunting Duo–ward. "Not as far as they're concerned."

I slant them a glance, catch their expectant stares, and come to the only possible decision. "You have a point."

"So you're ready to beard the wild matchmaking beasts again?"

"As ready as you are."

We laugh.

"Hey! Put a cork in it!" I add in a whisper. "They're watching."

He snorts. "Give it up already, Andi-ana Jones!"

I glare.

He stalks to the van.

Aunt Weeby and Miss Mona join us, together with their living, breathing dismay. We drive away.

The nondescript brown car follows.

Oh well. Have government goons, will travel.

6<u>00</u>

We return to the hotel in silence, most of us too tired to do more than fight off the yawns. Once we reach our home away from home, we scatter in seconds, but no one closes their door until chivalrous Max has checked out closets, behind curtains, under beds, and in tubs.

No corpses tonight—*thank you, Lord Jesus!*

I don't forget my earlier offenses; after I remove my minimal makeup, brush my teeth, and don my PJs, I reach for my Bible. I hit God up for wisdom—yeah, yeah, I'm lacking there; guidance—okay, so I tend toward a wee bit of blindness; and his awesome love—I'll never get enough of that, and he's got plenty to give.

After a while, I sigh. *Will I ever learn to think—and pray!— first, then talk, Father? And what's with my reactions to Max? I'm seasick here from the up-and-down of it all, Lord!*

In the velvety silent night, I turn to the Proverbs, so full of advice for emotionally messy blurters like moi. Once I've soaked a good long while in God's Word, I turn off the bedside lamp and fall into a rock-solid sleep.

It takes us days to get to the Kudi Valley. Let's just say the Himalayan concept of road doesn't match mine. Their preferred mode of travel doesn't, either.

"The fine print never said I'd have to ride a mule," I mutter as the earthy-smelling animal plods along the narrow lane. Too many days on this critter's behind has not best friends us made.

Turning in his saddle, Xheng Xhi gives me another of those too-bright looks of his. "You mule like you, Miss Andie."

Right behind me, Max chuckles. "Where's your sense of adventure, Andi-ana Jones?"

"Back in Filene's Basement, where it belongs. I'm an expert hunter of *bargainus extraordinarius*, not a fan of extreme encounters with massively haired mountain goats."

"Goats?" Aunt Weeby warbles ahead of me. "I haven't seen a single one a' them. Unless we call them yak things a kind of goat. Are they goats? Or maybe they're deer? Elk? Buffalo? Cows?" She falls silent for a moment. "D'ya think we could do like with sheep and angora goats, and shear them yaks? Then . . . I reckon we could get some a' them ol' hippies out there in California or Oregon to spin the fur into thread—no, no! It's yarn, I mean . . ."

Max's choked-off laugh lets me in on what he thinks of that idea. I'm so glad I can't see him; right about now I'd be howling too. That, of course, is the kind of fuel that feeds Aunt Weeby's extreme wackiness.

"Oh, it's the best idea, Mona!" she says. "We can sell yak sweaters on the S.T.U.D."

Huh? The fur of the shaggy beasties I've seen speaks of

hedgehogs in need of lawn mowers rather than future warm fuzzies. "Hey, Aunt Weeby! I feel a major itch coming on! We'd have to sell Gold Bond lotion with those woolies you're talking about."

"Yaks have two kinds of fur, Andie," Glory says, her voice faint. Her mule is behind Max's. "The outside stuff is tough and harsh, but the inside layer is soft and super warm. That's what the people of the Himalayas have used for winter clothes for centuries."

Smarty pants! I make sure my voice comes out nice and pleasant. "How do you know so much about yaks, Glory?"

"I'm not sure. I must have read it somewhere. My memory's kind of weird. It picks up info and stores it in random bits and pieces. I never know what's going to pop out when I least expect it."

Her answer is just a hair away from total airhead. But since no one's perfect, least of all me, I give her the benefit of the doubt. I do, however, want to thwap her for the wacky idea her answer gives Aunt Weeby.

"Ooooh!" my aunt cries. "I got it! Better'n sweaters too. That *other* channel has some woman selling sweaters with all kinds a' crazy pictures all over 'em. Let's sell us some yaks!"

Shock makes me clench my knees. Bad idea. In mule-speak, that means STOP, which my mule does. Immediately.

Max yells.

His mount ignores him. They crash into mine—mules aren't the brightest diamonds in the gem-jar trays. "What do you think you're doing?" he gripes.

At me! Not the mules. What's up with that?

"Miss Andie?" Xheng Xhi asks from up ahead past my aunt and my boss. "You fine?"

90

"Whoa!" Glory yelps from farther behind.

"Hey!" Allison joins the chorus. "What's going on up there? This is no six-lane highway, you guys."

I blush. Then, the clatter of metal adds to the commotion.

Nope. It's not Santa's reindeer on the roof. "Uh . . . ," Max says, "I have to pick up some of my things that fell."

I snicker and turn at the waist. "Aren't you sorry you dragged all that with you? It's a lot to lug around on the back of a beast."

He dismounts, squeezes between the animal and the sheer rock wall, then reaches, *very* respectfully, below the animal's snout.

Xheng Xhi leads his mule back past Aunt Weeby and Miss Mona to my side, anxiety on his features. "Mister Max hurt you, Miss Andie?"

When Max straightens, he sends us one of his icy blue glares. "If Andie hadn't just stopped like that, I wouldn't have dropped my club." He shakes the dumb thing for emphasis.

Yes, ladies and gentlemen. The gemology-challenged cohost has carted his golf club, a little packet of golf balls, and even his football on our trek.

"Sorry, pal," I say. "You're not giving me the guilties. No one in his right mind goes trekking the Himalayas with a bunch of sports gear on top of a mule. Maybe you can use the long ride to ponder more important things—like those bugs you'll soon be selling."

Xheng Xhi resumes his lead of our ragtag army.

Max grabs the reins in his left hand, puts his right foot in the mule's stirrup, plops the right fist—clutching the golf club—on

91

the pommel, then pushes up and swings his left leg over the animal's rump. Gotta give the guy credit; his athleticism has a masculine grace that impresses me every time it shows up.

". . . And I suppose that serious pondering," he bites off, "is why you just *had* to lug that designer bag with all the brown Cs all over it with you."

I blush—again. What can I say? It's shallow, but I love my Coach bag. "Ah . . . I just need to keep all my documents in one handy spot, so it makes sense to keep the bag with me." True. Sorta. In the most basic of ways.

He laughs. I'm so happy I can afford Max so much merriment.

Not.

"Don't even try, Andie. You love that dumb bag with some chi-chi design company's name woven into plain old canvas because some style guru has anointed it as the height of fashionistas' desire. Tell me how that figures into the purpose of *your* life."

That's my Coach bag on which a jock is casting aspersions. Ahem!

Well . . . okay. So his question has a ton of merit. Not that I'm about to tell him that. It is something for me to ponder—I'm starting to seriously dislike that word—later.

I try to coax my mule to forward motion. "How would you know it's canvas?"

"Canvas is canvas. It's what teachers used for art class 'masterpieces' back in school, the same stuff on my old Keds sneakers, and it's the same thing you paid a small fortune for, just for the sake of your goofy Cs."

"What are you slowpokes doing back there?" Aunt Weeby hollers from way ahead.

"Not to worry," Glory yells back. "It's just the latest battle in the Max and Andie war. We'll be right there."

Thank you, Glory, for the serving of humble pie. After that, I don't make a peep. We plod on and I pray. I pray for control, for wisdom, for help with my pride, and for the Lord to get us in and out of Kashmir's mine country without any Muslim guerilla sightings.

Sure, sure. Some, like Aunt Weeby, might see it as a cultural experience. Not me. It doesn't thrill me that elements of the Taliban and their tribal buddies like to hide out from the good guys—read "our side"—with villagers in the area.

Let's hope Soomjam, the village nearest the mines *and* the orphanage, isn't their latest choice for home sweet home. I don't think they'll like to see Americans anywhere near their sapphires.

The sooner we get there—and out—the better. With that in mind, I catch up to Aunt Weeby and the Musgroves, and follow in silence for the next three, maybe four hours. Finally, we plod into a valley, striking in its austere, treeless beauty.

I'm excited. We're here . . . almost.

We head toward a cluster of homes at the right side of the flat valley bottom. I soak in everything I see with curiosity and a hunger that surprises me.

But guess what? Even here, at this rocky top of the world, we have to clear one more military checkpoint. Yes. Another one. In spite of Xheng Xhi, our guide, and the "other party" of travelers that's had the same itinerary we have. Yeah, right, travelers. More like guys with gun-shaped lumps under their clothes.

"I thought we were done with this when we left Myanmar,"

I grumble. "So now we come to Kashmir, and it's all the same old thing all over again."

"Now, Andie, dear," Miss Mona says. "The government's just being cautious."

And I'm Obi-Wan Kenobi.

Our herd approaches the wooden booth. I knee my steed closer to Aunt Weeby. I don't want an international incident. We already did the dead-houseboy gig back in Srinagar. And one of her funny and innocent but off-the-wall comments might do worse than launch a thousand-year war.

As I reach her side, I notice the cross-legged, uniformed Asian man on the rough stone slab that passes for a front step.

I risk alerting the guy. *"Psst!"*

Aunt Weeby glances over her shoulder. "You okay, sugarplum?"

"I'm fine," I whisper. "Just don't say anything. We do better at these when we let our guides do the talking."

"You calling me a blabbermouth?"

"Um-huh-hum-hum . . ."

She winks. "I've been known to say a thing or two!"

I laugh. Who can resist?

When the guard spots our crew, he leaps up, gawps, takes a couple of steps forward, stops, stares some more, then whirls, runs into the booth, slams the flimsy door, and watches us go by from inside.

I shake my head. "Do we make an entrance or what?"

Aunt Weeby giggles.

Don't ask me what kind of checkpoint guy the more . . . intense, shall we say, elements of the government would prefer to replace this one with, but I'm okay with him myself.

Xheng Xhi, who replaced potential killer Robert as our guide, leads us to a fairly new brick structure. Without knocking, he opens one of the double wooden doors into what looks like a courtyard from where I'm sitting—yeah, I'm still on my stinky mount.

"Xncsent tspher owxaki shuyz!" he yells—that's how I "hear" it.

A petite, older woman dressed in a gorgeous russet *salwar kameez*, the traditional Indian and Pakistani outfit of tunic and loose trousers, runs out, bows deeply, and smiles a welcome. She shoots back more garbled chatter at Xheng Xhi, punctuating her words with birdlike hands. He then throws open the other courtyard door, they stand aside, and Xheng Xhi waves us through. We all troop in—yep, people and mules and junk, oh my!

In the Himalayan dusk, the shadowed courtyard of the three-story building looks exotic, intriguing, and very much like a barnyard. Smells like one too. Once I get my bearings, I identify the source of the . . . um . . . scent. Stable-like cubbyholes line three sides of the ground floor; the fourth side being the massive doors Xheng Xhi has now barred shut. From one far corner, a fast flutter and a ruffle of clucking tells me the family keeps chickens—in their home!—as well as the snuffly beasties in the stalls. Fast and furious yapping alerts us to the watchdog.

Watchdog—hah! As soon as we slump, slither, or crash down off our mounts, the lean brown pooch rolls over on her back at my feet. Who am I to deprive a lovable canine of a belly scratch?

"Aren't you the sweetest?" I croon and rub.

She wriggles in ecstasy. Can she ever smell a sucker!

I rub some more. "Have you been working too hard, girl? Don't you have a little friend to tickle and cuddle you?" Of course, the dog responds with a fresh burst of excited, ecstatic yips. "Tell you what, then. While we're here, I'm going to have fun spoiling you."

Max laughs. "She's got you where she wants you."

I give him a wry grin. "I'm a sucker for a pooch. But I'm also hungry, and don't have a clue where we're bunking down for the night. How about we figure out what we're supposed to do?"

As harrowing as our trip to the Burmese ruby mines was (imagine a collapsing mine shaft and a chase by armed goons—didn't bother to check whether they were government types or not), we did stay at a plain, clean hotel while there. This looks like a huge farmhouse, maybe for multiple generations—of fowl, humans, and other mammals too.

Glory sidles up to Max, then flashes him her widest smile. "Is there anything I can do to help you with some of your gear?"

Ick! Ptooey! Yuck! All that sweetness and light is enough to give a woman cavities. Max? Well, he's not a woman and has the typical male sweet tooth. He eats it up with a spoon.

Xheng Xhi hurries to my side. "Nice here, Miss Andie. You no more ride. Okay?"

I give the man a weak smile. "Not for a while, but we still have to go back to Srinagar soon enough. But thank you for your help."

He beams, then bustles off after the mules.

The dog nuzzles my knee. "C'mon, girl." To my surprise, or maybe not so much, since she strikes me as a kindred soul, she follows. "Let's go find some chow. Your ribs didn't feel too well padded, so I'm sure you can use a scrap or two . . ."

Fifteen minutes later, Glory, Allison, and I walk into a room with three wooden bed platforms, a folded fur at the foot of each, but no mattress or pillows in sight. "Phew! I'm glad we brought our gear."

Glory runs her fingers through the animal skin on one of the beds. "I bet this is yak."

I shudder. "Thanks, but no thanks. I'll stick with my sleeping bag."

Since we're about to become roomies, I make sure to "please" and "thank you" Glory to pieces as we make our beds. I dislike the . . . oh, phooey! I might as well admit it—again. I don't like the jealousy I'm feeling. It's not her fault she's pretty and likes Max. I have no claim on the guy.

Then we head downstairs for our evening meal. Far from the lavish feast we enjoyed in Srinagar, this family's dinner consists of rice, curry-scented veggies, flat bread, and—get this—yak butter! The spread has an earthy undertone, but it's not so bad.

I eat in silence. I'd rather keep my loose tongue occupied with food than talk, since it gets me in trouble too often when it flaps. As I munch, I take a discreet survey of the room we're in.

We must be in the original great room of all great rooms. Living, dining, and cooking all happen here. The area's main feature is the huge clay oven at the center; a round mouth in the front lets me watch the raging flames. As hot as it must be, the oven's walls look thick enough to contain all that heat, since I'd felt little warmth when I walked past on my way to the long, low table. Smoke puffs out around the bottom of two pots that simmer on holes along the oven's top. The sooty clouds rise to escape through a small vent opening in the ceiling. There's no chimney in the place.

Don't think of smoke inhalation, carbon monoxide poisoning, or five-alarm fires, Andie. Don't. Just don't.

But I can't help myself. I don't want to wind up as a shish kebab. Which reminds me of the two little goats that greet everyone with a nudge of their knobby heads.

"Can you believe they live with their *animals*? Inside the house," Glory whispers as we take another flatbread.

"Looks that way," I say. "But it's probably not that much different than living with cats, dogs, or pot-bellied pigs."

She scoots away from me on the bench to give me a "you-gotta-be-kidding" look. "I've *never* known anyone who lives with a pig."

There's a million mouthy ways I could answer, but I remember my many prayers for control. "Me neither, but I hear they're popular."

During the meal, I tear chunks of the yummy flatbread slathered with yak butter, and slip it to my furry friend. She returns the favor by plunking her warm butt on my frozen toes—have I mentioned the Himalayas have the iciest summer *ever*?

"So what's the plan for tomorrow?" I ask, once I'm done with my last cup of fragrant green tea.

Trevor Musgrove, who must think we're the weirdest bunch on earth, clears his throat. "They're expecting us at the orphanage tomorrow morning. There are a number of projects waiting for us."

Miss Mona stands. "I suggest everyone get a good night's sleep so we're all good and ready to pitch in."

A quick glance around the table shows no resistance to

her suggestion. Then I hear Aunt Weeby. Since I can't make out what she's saying, I stand to look for her. I find her at the far left of the room, where she's cornered our host beneath a high shelf that holds three cooking pots.

". . . Is that your best price?" she asks the wizened gentleman with a complexion reminiscent of a prune.

To my amazement, he shrugs. "Best price."

Who'd a thunk we'd find someone out here who speaks English? Then again, there have been a bunch of crews who've come out this way to survey the sapphire mines' potential over the years. It's not too far-fetched that someone who once dealt with the assayers would have picked up a working knowledge of the language.

"Whoa!" What am I thinking! Who cares if the man speaks English or Martian? They're talking price over there. I hurry across the room. "What are you buying, Aunt Weeby? Your mule can't carry a whole lot out of here—not if you want to come home too."

She gives me that smile that sends terror down my spine.

Uh-oh. Here we go again. See the ship about to take a dive? *Help us, Father!*

"Aw, sugarplum, you don't have nothing to worry yourself about. Mr. Xi La here will take care a' sending 'em to me."

"Them" implies multiples. I slip an arm around her waist. I love the dear woman, even though her trouble quotient is astronomical. "What 'them' is he sending? And where is he sending 'them'?"

"Why, Andie!" Exaggerated surprise widens her eyes. "Louisville, remember? You moved back. That's where."

I cross my arms and tap my toe, more worried by the second. "And the what?"

99

"Why, I'm doing my part to help my dearest friend."

My boss—her dearest friend—makes a choked sound, and charges up, abject fear on her face. "What are you up to?"

See? I'm not the only one. "That's right, Aunt Weeby. What *are* you up to?"

"All y'all were on that donkey ride too, sugarplum. Let me tell you, I don't *ever* plan to do that again! Been praying up a storm the good Lord doesn't have another a' them treks in my future once I'm off this mountain." She shudders for emphasis.

She's hedging; never a good sign. "Can we get back to the point, please? What's Mr. Xi La sending you?" Let me tell ya, I'm scared. I know the woman. Really well. "And no more beating around that beaten-up infamous old bush."

Miss Mona drags in a toe-deep breath.

"Hmph!" Aunt Weeby offers. "We talked about it on that nasty ride, dear." She turns to Miss Mona. "It's the only Christian thing to do. We have to bring business to the Kashmiri, and this is the best way."

The vibes I'm getting here are worse than bad.

Miss Mona frowns. "What way?"

"The yaks, dear."

My boss shrieks, "The *whats*?!"

I thought she'd forgotten. I really did. But Aunt Weeby's got a mind like a trap, I tell ya.

She smiles. "A' course, Mona, dear. We're going into the yak business."

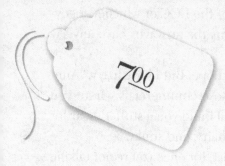

7<u>00</u>

I gape at my favorite relative. "Please! Please, please, please tell me you're not trying to buy yaks. You can't still be on that selling-yaks-on-TV kick."

She tsk-tsks. "What's wrong with you people? A' course, I want to sell yaks. We'll make a nice business with it, since we have that there TV channel of Mona's all set up already."

Miss Mona starts waving a hand in front of her face, her tomato-colored face. "Wha—how . . . *why*?"

I pat my boss's arm to offer her the comfort I'm not feeling right now. "Don't give it another thought, Miss Mona. She can't sell yaks on TV. No one sells livestock on the airwaves."

Aunt Weeby crosses her arms and gives us her smuggest smile. "That just goes to show, sugarplum, you don't know everything, after all."

I ignore Max's snort of laughter. And Glory's giggle too.

I really thought Aunt Weeby'd forgotten her yak woollies after the mule ride. Boy, was I wrong! "You *can't* sell livestock on TV."

Her chin tips up higher. "Says who?"

Hmm . . . is there such a law? I know you can't sell live stuff on eBay. Does the FTC or the FCC or whichever government alphabet soup governs the airwaves have any say in this kind of madness?

I try reason—without much hope. But I have to try. "Aunt Weeby, a yak is hardly like those commercials where you call the 800 number and they'll build you a stuffed bear for Valentine's Day. Yaks are big, hairy, and stinky."

Max sidles up to me. "At least, for once you're not talking about me."

"Oh, please. I've never called you stinky." I turn back to my aunt, try to reason with her. "Please tell the nice man you can't buy his yaks. Or sell them for him—whatever. There's no such thing as selling big beasts on TV."

My contrary relative gives an exceptional sniff. "That, Andrea Autumn Adams, is where you're plumb wrong. All that time I was stuck in the hospital after my leg problems, with nothing to do but watch that big ol' TV, I got to know me all the channels ever—there's one for just about anything. And, let me tell you, there *is* such a thing as selling livestock on TV. Why, honey! They sell cows and bulls all day long, sometimes."

"Huh?" And here I always thought Miss Mona the queen of the "Huh?" factor, while Aunt Weeby's the one who's held the title all along. Learn something new every day.

I blow a strand of hair off my forehead. "I'm so sorry, Aunt Weeby. It must've really been rough, the surgery and all that. Those pain meds must've done a number on you. I'm sure the movie you watched—"

"That weren't no movie, Andie. Not mooing and pooing all

over some corral, what with the auctioneers, and the cowboys, and the straw hats, and all."

Cows and bulls and straw hats. Hallucinations, don't you think? But there's no way I can say that without making a scene, so I scramble through my mush-for-brain to try and come up with something to derail Aunt Weeby's latest lunacy. But before I come up with anything, her partner in crime opens up.

"Actually," Miss Mona says, her voice just dreamy enough to tell me she's had another brainstorm. That trouble-o-meter of mine is getting a workout.

"No way." I have to derail whatever's coming. "I can't—*won't*. It's not in my job description. I'm not auctioning off hairy, pooping beasts. No matter what."

"But, sugarplum—"

"Why, Andie, dear—"

"I won't film them—"

"No makeup—"

A shrill whistle pierces the cacophony. I cover my still-ringing right ear, the one next to Max, the source of the deafening sound.

"What'd you do that for?" I ask.

"Because none of you is making any sense." He looks at Aunt Weeby. "You know and I know we can't sell Kashmiri yaks because import/export laws, customs officials, quarantines, and all that make it a nightmare."

"But—"

"And"—he turns to me, as if she hadn't spoken—"I'm with you on this one. We're not chasing yaks on-screen."

I grin. "You see the light! You agree with me—"

"But I'd like to know," he says, ignoring my victory cheer,

"what Miss Mona thinks. Her ideas are usually pretty solid."

"You'll see." I shrug, pretending a confidence I don't feel. "She'll agree with me sooner or later. Who'd want a yak?"

Miss Mona humphs. We turn.

She pats Aunt Weeby's shoulder. "They're right, you know. We can't auction off wild and woolly beasts, but we can latch on to the exotic woolens craze. You know what they're getting for llama and alpaca scarves, sweaters, and shawls? *Whoo-ee!* My word, they're pricey."

At first, Aunt Weeby looks disappointed—why she would ever want to deal with a yak, I'll never know—but then a satisfied smile curves her lips.

"See? I told all y'all it was a good idea. We will be selling yaks, after all. Just not the whole yak."

Miss Mona nods. "Yak woolens can certainly keep Maine lobstermen, Minnesotans, and Michiga—what *do* they call themselves in Michigan? Michiganians? Michigonians?" She shrugs. "Anyway, all those who live in cold places will have something special to keep them warm all winter long now. And the S.T.U.D.'s going to see to it."

"Plus the Kashmiri will make a living," Aunt Weeby adds.

Max drapes that long arm over my shoulders. "If we play our cards right, we'll never have anything to do with the scratchy things. Maybe Danni can come up with some selling gimmick. Yak woolens and spandex Capris. All the rage."

I swat at him, laughing at the thought. "I suggest we all sleep on this idea. It's going to take some mountain moving to get it to happen."

As we head off toward our respective rooms, I pray for

the Lord's mercy. Again. But then, outside our room, when Aunt Weeby hugs me, I realize my relief may have come prematurely.

"You know," she says. "That there yak butter's pretty tasty. Maybe there's some way for me to get it shipped to the S.T.U.D. . . ."

I close the door firmly on her ramblings. Only Aunt Weeby would think about importing gamey yak butter for American palates. Not in a million years—

That's when it hits me. The yaks will, soon enough, be a nonissue. And we—I—have better things to think about. Tomorrow we'll be working at the orphanage, helping little kids who know nothing but sadness and loneliness. I pray I can make a difference for at least one of them.

There's also the possibility that, if we don't rattle any un- friendly natives, we might get to film the played-out sapphire mines. I am excited; just don't tell the Daunting Duo—it might give them more ideas.

Of course, we plan to film in this open, treeless land, a disputed territory, over which numerous wars have been fought, where Taliban forces are said to hide.

They have weapons.

We have Aunt Weeby.

Trouble?

Oh yeah!

Who cares about yak butter at a time like this?

The next morning, I make a personal discovery. I've de- veloped an addiction. Oh, come on. You know it's going to be harmless! At least, it's only bad for my hips and waistline.

Sheermal are sweet Kashmiri breads eaten for breakfast. Chased down with cups of hot green tea, they have now become my greatest weakness.

Too bad I'm nearly hopeless in the kitchen. I'd love the recipe. If I could really cook. You can't get *sheermal* by nuking.

Now you know why everyone's staring at me. They're ready to roll. I'm still at the table, sipping and munching.

The thought of the kids at the orphanage is the only thing that gets me moving. Well, that and the end of the stack of *sheermal*. Let's face it. I like my creature comforts. And it's cold out here on the mountain peaks. I don't want to move from the relative warmth of this room. Trust me, this trip is not for the faint of heart.

But, armed with backpacks full of what we consider crucial for our day, we head out to The Father's Lambs with the Musgroves. Once we leave the farmhouse, it hits me again. Few people have ever seen this place. And I'm really here.

The steep Himalayan peaks, sliced by rocky crags, inspire my greatest respect. This must be one of the most wildly beautiful places God has created. On our way here to Soomjam, we saw enormous contrasts. On the one hand, Srinagar and other small cities closer to the Indian border seem to have been spared by the earthquake. As we climbed into the higher elevations, however, that changed.

I'd read that the villagers in the mountains usually use flimsy construction methods, but I wasn't prepared for the devastation I saw. The worst of the rubble had been moved from the center of some of the villages, and tent cities were set up where the vulnerable homes once stood. The Musgroves described the tents as weatherized, but let me tell you, no one wants to spend a Himalayan winter in any kind of tent.

I don't want to spend a Himalayan winter. At all. It's cold here. And yeah, it's summer. In August—*August*—I'm forced to pull on fleece outerwear. Hey! The temperature's hovering around a balmy forty-five degrees Fahrenheit.

Uh-huh.

I'll take Kentucky's hot, sticky summers any day!

Then we reach the orphanage. We meet the children. Beautiful little faces peer at us, the eyes huge and filled with hope. That they've seen things they never should have is without question. What is also unquestionable is their strength and courage. How can I not help?

The orphanage is getting a new wing, and that's where most of us are needed. We set up shop at the far west end of the building, find hammers, nails, saws, and boards, and get to work.

Aunt Weeby and Miss Mona head indoors to spend their time cuddling beautiful, lonely babies and working on less strenuous jobs. Every time I get a break—from work and Xheng Xhi's constant presence at my side—I chase them down; can't stay away from the kids. This time, I find Aunt Weeby in the laundry, two little girls at her side. The three of them are having the funniest conversation; no way can they understand each other.

But with Aunt Weeby, it's the love that carries the day.

". . . And that's the kind of horses we have in Kentucky," she says as she holds out a stack of snow-white towels. "Kentucky. Say 'Kentucky.'"

The girl giggles, whispers something that sounds like "Khaki," then scurries from the room. The other one waits for Aunt Weeby to finish another pile of towels.

"Hey, Aunt Weeby. Sounds like they find Kentucky as hard to say as we find the names of their towns."

"Nuh-uh, sugarplum. She's just little. Can't be so hard. Don't see how it could be. Kentucky's easy. We just need to teach them English. It's not so hard."

"You really think they'd find it easier than . . . Kashmiri? Is that what they speak?"

Emma Musgrove rolls in a massive laundry cart piled high with what looks like clean sheets. She launches into über-convoluted descriptions of the zillion-and-one different dialects spoken in the Indian peninsula and this stark region so close to Pakistan. None of it registers with me, since the sweet children claim every bit of my attention.

The little girl waiting on my aunt steals my heart. She stands at Aunt Weeby's side, her big, brown eyes taking in every move she makes.

"Who is she?" I ask.

"This is our Devi," Emma answers. "She lived with her grandmother about fifty miles northwest of here. The quake destroyed their shack and . . . well, it took her grandmother too."

I blink angry tears from my eyes. "Why hasn't anyone built decent housing in this country? In the villages we went through, I saw nothing more than lean-tos built from junk. Oh yeah! The lucky ones had a tin roof."

Emma rubs Devi's glossy black hair; Devi gives her a shy smile. "Poverty and politics make it impossible. That's why we're here. 'Whatever you did for one of the least of these . . .'"

Something squeezes deep inside me. *Oh, Lord Jesus! Father God, help us help them.*

As my heart breaks, I go back outside to do my part to improve the children's livelihood, my resolve reaffirmed.

They might no longer have homes of their own, and they might no longer have families of their own, but they do have God's love. We, his children, will be their new family, care for them any way we can. As I stack wood and bricks, the image of Devi fills my mind. Over and over again, my eyes overflow, which in turn makes me work that much harder. I want to give Devi a decent place to live, and sadly, there are dozens of Devis, some of whom come watch us, fascinated by what we're doing.

Not that all of it is productive, you know. Xheng Xhi's on a new kick. Every chance he gets, he plies me with questions about all things American. The guy has way more questions than I have answers.

Why me, Lord? Why not Allison? Or Glory? They're both out here too. But noooo. He picks me.

And his latest kick is fast food; I'm so not a fan. "Miss Andie?" he says. "McDonald's, right?"

"What's that?"

He draws arches in the air. "McDonald's. Good, right?"

A Kashmiri guide and Micky Dee's? I shrug. "McDonald's is fast food. It's okay. Not the best."

He droops with disappointment. "No good? *McDonald's?* I hear it very good."

What can I say? "It's chopped up meat, mushy bread, soaked dried onions, with ketchup, mustard, and a pickle on top. What's so great about that?"

"Chop tup meat?" He scratches his long beard. "What is 'tup'?"

I mime chopping. "I meant chopped—cut into tiny little pieces."

"Ah! Like *rista?*"

Rista. That sounds like something I've eaten in Kashmir . . . aha! At the restaurant. "No. *Rista* is round, a meatball. McDonald's are flat meatballs." I pantomime squashing the meatball. "McDonald's."

Alarm widens his eyes. "Dead? McDonald's die?"

"No! Flat."

Where's our translator when we need him? I look around, and spot him with the "other party" that traveled up the mountains behind us. Like the rest of them, he sports the familiar gun-shaped lump under his clothes.

Oooops! Not calling him.

So I try pantomime again. I cup my hands as though forming meatballs. "Ball of meat. *Rista*, right?"

He nods.

I smush the pretend meatball. "Flat *rista* inside bread. That's McDonald's."

"Okay," he says, but doesn't look convinced. "Not dead."

"No, not dead." If I have trouble explaining a beef patty, I won't even try to explain the health of corporate America, with a burger joint on every street. I go back to work.

An hour later, Xheng Xhi is back. He points at Max. "Golf, yes?"

Figures. "Yes."

He then swings an imaginary golf club. "You golf?"

"Ah . . . no." His whole body droops with disappointment. I smile gently and point at the jock—I'll kill two birds with one stone. Max can answer questions I can't, and Xheng Xhi can bug someone else. "Ask him."

He jabbers at me in his dialect while I stare in horrified fascination. If he thinks I get even a fraction of that, he's wackier than Aunt Weeby. But once he's done and smiles, he does head over to my cohost.

Peace. For a while. But it turns out I'm not the best carpenter, not when you compare me to Glory or Allison. They're smokin', while I'm still trying to get the hang of holding wood, hammer, and nail all at the same time with only two hands.

Yes, my heart's in my work, but my talent isn't. Every other swing of the hammer misses and dents wood. The saw is beyond me; I chew wood into useless chunks of oversize sawdust. Trevor Musgrove, who I decide must be the world's most patient man, tries to improve my hammer-and-nails technique again.

So I focus on construction for another hour. Then I smash a thumb.

While I suck on my injured digit, I realize the sun's begun to drop in the sky. It's time to call it a day. I want to live to try again tomorrow. I look around and notice that, aside from the diligent and silent Trevor, who's still whacking away about fifteen feet from me, everyone else has already quit. At least I gave it all my effort.

The only ones still outside are the crowd of our former observers, none over the age of . . . oh, about twelve. But they're not watching anymore. And I now enter a parallel universe. Go ahead. Pipe in the theme song to *The Twilight Zone*. It won't faze me. There's no other way to explain what I see.

There, in the packed-dirt front yard of the orphanage, are Max and about two-dozen kids. But it's not the random assortment of humans that's surprising. It's what the humans are doing that knocks my socks off.

Xheng Xhi sidles up to me again. "Miss Andie?"

"Mm-hm." My thumb throbs.

"American football good, right?"

Oh, buddy, you asked the wrong girl. I give him a wishy-washy shrug and nod toward the good-looking guy in the cluster of kids. "Go ask Max. I'm sure he'll teach you too."

That's when weird gets even weirder. After the two men talk—with words and hands—for about five minutes, they part ways and divide the kids into two groups.

One of the groups, under the direction of our chatty Kashmiri guide, launches into a bizarre game of football. Yeah, you got it. Quarterback, passes, huddles, and tackles in yak country . . . sorta. Let's put it this way. The NFL wouldn't recognize this. Xheng Xhi's version of the All-American game consists of a pass—by Xheng Xhi himself—followed by a free-for-all to see who knocks everyone else out of the way to come up with the pigskin. No touchdowns.

Go figure.

The other bunch is lined up behind Pied Piper Max as he tries to turn a lanky Kashmiri boy into—get this—the next Tiger Woods. Yep. Golf club, little wood thingy stuck in the dry dirt, and white, dimpled ball.

Glory comes outside and gets a load of Max and company. "Oh, good grief!" She turns and heads back the way she came.

Where'd all her interest in helping Max go?

I shiver in the cooling winds but can't stop watching. Why? I don't know. I could leave; I could also go join them, but I don't. I just watch . . . and enjoy. There's something way charming and totally cool about the big, strong American playing with a bunch of Kashmiri kids.

Just don't tell him I think that. I'm not ready to face the consequences.

When the football bonks one of the girls, I run over to help. "Is she okay?"

Max, now sitting cross-legged in the dust, the sobbing child in his arms, looks up. "I think so."

I sit at his side, then smooth a lock of blue-black hair off her cheek. "It hit her head."

He nods, checks her eyes. "I don't think it had a whole lot of oomph behind it. The boy who threw it is even smaller than her."

"Anything I can do?"

Max's warm smile gives me goose bumps. "I think you've done it already."

I glance down, notice the deep, dark eyes glued to my hair. The goose bumps fly south. "Great! The carrot-top strikes again."

But when the child reaches out, I lower my head and let her run gentle fingers through my work-wild locks—last time they faced a brush was hours before my frustrating efforts in carpentry. She grins, scampers out of Max's lap, and runs to her friends, chattering every step of the way.

"Get ready!" Max says, mischief on his face.

"Attack of the Curious Kashmiri?"

He laughs. "You betcha, Red. Here they come."

What can I say? He organizes the small army, and one grubby paw after another checks out my hair. Ah . . . yes. The glamorous life of a TV personality.

But they have no consideration for my ego; I don't prove all that interesting. As soon as they realize there's nothing to the hair but the different color, they drag Mr. Magnificent back to play. And he proves himself . . . well, pretty magnificent.

He again divides the kids into two teams, and starts a new football game. The non-jock in me fights it kicking and screaming, but I follow the game. When the little girl who got hit by the ball catches a pass, I cheer for all I'm worth.

"That's it!" Max yells. "Run! Yeah, yeah! That's it!"

The kids answer with a chorus of "Yah, yahs." And then she's tackled.

A little boy now lobs the ball, the players scatter. One makes a catch, then runs to Max, who's standing in what he's termed the end zone. The little guy crashes into Max's long legs, drops the ball, and wails in dismay, his eyes huge and dark and heartbroken. Max throws up his arms in the universal—well, even I know what it means—sign for success.

"Touchdown!"

His excitement infects the little guy, who picks up the ball again and starts a victory wriggle. After a couple more "touchdowns," a bell inside the orphanage clangs out, and the kids hurry off. In the silence, I head over to Max, who's dropped the football in favor of gently swinging his golf club inches away from the hard white ball.

As I walk, the stark reality of the world his little playmates live in hits me again, especially in contrast to the relative frivolity of sports. I shake my head and chuckle. "I still can't believe you really insisted on carting that stuff all the way out here."

"A guy's entitled to a break after working all day."

"Yeah, but football? Golf? *Here*?" I take another look at the barren landscape. "I wouldn't have thought of it."

He shrugs, wiggles like Tiger Woods, and fusses around with his shiny steel club. "Why not here? Kids need to play."

"You're right, of course. But there's something so gut-wrenching about their lives. Golf . . . football"—I shake my head—"it's almost obscene."

The club connects with the ball with an earsplitting CRACK! There's no sound pollution here at cloud level.

He glares when the ball seems to go astray. "What happened with the truce?"

"I didn't break it."

"What about calling me obscene?"

"I didn't call you obscene, Max. Sorry if it sounded like that. I'm seeing the silliness of sports as obscene. I can't help it, especially when I contrast them to the reality of these kids' lives."

He crosses his hands on the handle of his steel club, leans forward, and stares. "Just because I want to, have helped, and will help even more, do I also have to become a Kashmiri quake victim? I'm blessed with American citizenship and get to go back to Louisville. Besides, those kids had fun today for a change. That means something."

I sigh. "You do have a point. It's just that the contrast really hits hard. It makes everything I've known seem so trivial." I shoot him a glance. "I've been struggling with that."

He lets the club drop, and looks off in the direction of his lost ball. "I'd agree with you if I didn't know you, Aunt Weeby, and Miss Mona better. True, American lives are cushy compared to life in other parts of the world, but it's not our fault where we're born. God plants us there for a reason."

I pick up the club—hey! The thing's heavy—but I don't

let it distract me. "Okay. And that reason may be to recognize how much more we have than we need, and then go share with those who don't have a thing. I understand all that. Still . . ."

Max curves a finger under my chin. *Oooooh!* A shimmy of energy rushes through me. I'll never get used to how his touch makes me feel. I shiver, and not from the chilly Himalayan breeze.

"Isn't that what we're doing here?" he asks.

Get a grip, woman! "So far. I do have to wonder about Miss Mona's determination to film sapphire mines that haven't belched up more than an odd stone or two since the 1930s."

"Indulge her. She's got a great heart, and she does so much for so many."

The woman with the great heart saunters out of the orphanage with Aunt Weeby, both smiling and chattering as always. "She's why we're here in the first place. You do know she's financed the whole series of trips out here, don't you?"

His brows arch. "For everyone at the church?"

"Everyone who signed up—about fifteen."

"Wow!"

I watch the best friends argue, laugh, and then argue some more. Love for them warms me—as it always does. "She's a pretty wow woman."

Then another wow woman—different kind of wow—walks up.

"There you are, Max!" Glory says. "I've been looking for you. Did you forget you promised to teach me to putt?"

Now she wants to putt? After she "good griefed" not

116

twenty minutes ago? I drop the club. It lands on Max's toe—accidentally. Really.

"Yeow!" He glares.

That's when my hate for the game of golf really takes shape. The thought of Max spending hours with his arms around the pretty brunette, pretending to teach her to golf, is more than my green-eyed-monster can take. Hey! I've watched the TV shows and movies, you know. It's a Hollywood cliché. I know what happens next.

Petty? Yes.

Human? That too.

Christian? Not so much—I'm imperfect.

I hustle off, unwilling to watch, irritated, but well aware of my need for prayer.

What does this say about me?

That I want Max's attention. That I don't want him to touch Glory the way he touched my chin and made me quiver in response.

Aaaargh! No way. I don't want to go there. Oh, I know what's going on. But I really, *really* don't want to deal with it. Not right now.

I'm going to have to go there sooner or later. But I want time and space to face my fears and my feelings for Max.

As I head toward Aunt Weeby and Miss Mona, I cast a glance over my shoulder. Max takes Glory's hand and curves her fingers around the golf club's grip. A wince zings right through me.

Okay. It's true, and it's real. And I'm not going to get to choose when I face some things. I like Max—too much—even if he is a jock and not a gemologist. Glory's too pretty for my liking, and she's done nothing wrong, other than just plain *be*. So I shouldn't be so irritated with her, but I'm jealous, and I am. Irritated, that is. By Glory and how pretty she is. By how much she seems to like Max.

And by how Max seems to revel in her crush.

There you have it, in all its ugly high-def clarity.

So since I have nothing better to do with myself, I join the group heading back to the farmhouse. I may as well prepare the script for the show Miss Mona wants us to film. The sooner we're done, the better. While half of me wants to stay in Kashmir and help the sweet, sad children, the other half of me wants to hurry home, where I don't need to see Glory laughing up at Max every single, solitary day. I can hunker down at Aunt Weeby's house and only see him at work. How mature of me, don't you think?

Oh, ick.

8⁰⁰

"... The rich, velvety blue and exceptional clarity of Kashmiri sapphires—"

"Cut!" I stomp past Glory, who's holding her camera as close to Max as possible and still film, to where her irritating subject is standing in front of a hole in a rock—an old mine shaft. "I can't believe you just said that."

His chiseled jaw juts out and he narrows his blue eyes. "What do you mean? Sapphires are blue, the Kashmiri ones are always described as velvety, and the greater the clarity, the more valuable a gemstone."

I make a cross with my hands. "Cut! Cut, cut, cut! That's not right, Max." I turn to Glory. "Okay. Let's start again. I have to fix this part now."

Glory backs up, her expression not the happiest I've ever seen. "Ladies and gentlemen," I say once she refocuses, "as I'm sure you've learned by now, gemstones with greater clarity are generally the more valuable ones. Kashmiri sapphires are just a little different."

Max's expression takes a turn toward the intrigued.

Good. Maybe we can turn his blooper to a bonus for the viewers.

I continue. "The stones from Kashmir's Old Mine get their legendary velvety texture from a slight haziness that, under magnification, is seen as many fine particles oriented in three directions in the basal plane. The actual composition of these particles hasn't yet been determined, but most experts agree they're made up of exsolved rutile."

Max brings palms together, closes his eyes, and lays his head on the back of one hand to mimic a snooze. "Boh-ring," he mouths.

Glory shrugs.

I have a point to make. "Many of you have bought rutile quartz stones from us in the past. You know: those crystal-clear pieces of quartz with gold needles running through them. Gorgeous, remember?"

My cohost nods and, with his right hand, makes the universal get-on-with-it sign. I try again. "The really cool thing about these stones is that the rutile of Kashmir sapphires differs from that of Burmese or Sri Lankan stones because the crystals are so tiny, and they show up in snowflake patterns. The very fine size makes the light scatter in a super-subtle way, and this is what creates the velvet glow of Kashmir sapphire."

Max steps up in front of the camera. "If these rutiles—whatever they are—are so fine, then do they really affect the clarity?"

My cheeks heat up. "Well, if I have to be absolutely technically precise, then I have to say they don't affect it much, just enough to create that unique velvet quality that's not evident in any other sapphire."

He arches a brow. "So I wasn't wrong to say their clarity counts."

"I suppose." My teeth begin their familiar Max-induced itch. "If one goes by that particular criteria, then you weren't completely wrong in that most technical way."

His smile gets smug.

My teeth itch some more. "*But* that microscopic velvet haze has to be present, or the value goes way down." I wave at Glory. "That's enough for now. I'll take a look at the footage after lunch. We can decide then what to cut and what we might want to redo."

Once I flee the wicked embrace of all the audio widgets and wires needed for filming, I head back to the tent we've set up as S.T.U.D. Central.

The last thing I want is more Mr. Magnificent smugness— he really is no dummy.

Our hostess in Soomjam packed us a meal before we left, and my stomach has decided to make its noisy presence known at just the perfect, ego-rescuing moment. As I duck under the tent flap, I cast a glance over my shoulder to catch a glimpse of the animated chat Max and Glory are having as they approach.

Fine. I have better things to do. "Hey, Aunt Weeby! What do you think of the mines?"

She sniffs. "Not much. That's why I came back to the tent to nap. Why, there's hardly anything to look at out here. There's mountains, dirt, some scruffy shrubs . . . not even one single, solitary yak! I reckon your show's bound to be one great big ol' sleeping pill. Maybe you and Mona here oughta sell it as better and cheaper'n that there Ambien and Lunesta stuff."

I roll my eyes. "Oh goody! That's what I went to school for—to replace counting sheep."

A corner of the carpet provided by our hosts is clear and looks inviting, so I help myself to a cup of green tea and then crash—figuratively, you understand. Our hostess has sent a huge jug of the beverage, and I glug down the tasty drink. I could get addicted to the stuff.

"Hungry and grumpy, are you?" Aunt Weeby grins, reaches into a number of baskets, and then hands me a plate. One of the excellent Kashmiri flatbreads covers the whole circle, and Aunt Weeby's piled it with a fragrant mixture of potatoes, peppers, and meatballs, all smothered in rich gravy.

I grin. "Wow!"

My aunt winks. "Just you wait until you taste it, sugarplum. Those little ol' taste buds a' yours are gonna have them a real humdinger of a hoedown when they taste that . . . that I don't-know-what-it-is."

And they do. My taste buds a' happy, all right. Kashmiri food is delicious, well seasoned with onions, garlic, turmeric, and other spices I can't identify. Soon, my stomach's happy again, and I lean back against my backpack to think.

But my Kashmiri shadow doesn't give me a chance to put together more than a fleeting thought.

"Miss Andie?" Xheng Xhi says.

I sigh. "Yes?"

"Tell Xheng Xhi of Wal-Mart."

Oh. My. Goodness. If I struggled with something as simple as fast food, how do I go for the gluttonous extravaganza that is Wally World?

Max! I'll send him . . .

But my cohost—and our camerawoman—is nowhere to

be seen. I'm in this one all by myself. "Okay. Wal-Mart. It's a store. You understand stores, right?"

Xheng Xhi nods. "Buy things."

"Yes. But at Wal-Mart you can buy *every*thing."

His brows crash over the bridge of his nose. "E-ve-ry thing?"

"Sure. Clothes, food, soap, car tires and batteries, toilet paper—everything."

"Wal-Mart sell *rista*?"

"Well, no. But they sell chopped meat."

He scratches his long beard. "No *rista*." After a second or two, he smiles. "McDonald's. Wal-Mart sell McDonald's, yes?"

"No. McDonald's sells McDonald's."

His confusion grows. "Wal-Mart sell e-ve-ry thing, but no *rista* and no McDonald's."

This isn't working. "That's right."

"E-ve-ry thing." A short silence follows. Then, "Wal-Mart sell food, yes?"

I nod.

"Good! Wal-Mart is good. Sell good yak, yes?"

I blow the hair from my eyes. "No, Xheng Xhi. Wal-Mart doesn't sell yak. They sell cow, chicken, fish, lamb, and pig. But no yak. Okay?"

"Okay." But I can see from his expression that not much I've said is okay to him. Where's the surfer boy when I need him?

Enter Glory, followed by said surfer boy. Laughing. Together.

I see green again. And feel pettier than ever.

"Miss Andie?"

123

Not again! Not when I really should be dealing with my conscience. "Yes, Xheng Xhi."

"Yankees win World Series?"

I squeeze my eyes shut. Hard. Then I point at Mr. Magnificent. "Ask him. He's all about sports." And a certain camerawoman right about now.

Oh, yay! My inquisitor follows my suggestion. And I'm free once again. I head outside for fresh air and the chance to think of something other than a blond head right up against a brunette one. And try to deal with my petty jealousy. Even though I don't want to.

I find a big rock and take a seat. *Work, Andie. Think about work.* It's less daunting than the other stuff. And I do have a job to do.

With every bit of discipline I can dredge up, I make myself focus on the show Miss Mona wants. How much airtime should we really spend on depleted mines? Should I try to get access to the collection of stones at the Kashmir State Treasury Chambers instead of wasting film on—let's face it—boring rocks? Am I setting myself up for a snoozer of a show with what we've filmed? Who should I ask? I know what Miss Mona says she wants.

Aunt Weeby? *Nah.* She's already given us her opinion. She's bored.

And Glory? I'm not so sure I want to go there.

That leaves me with the one and only person who has as much at stake in my show as I do: Max.

Oh, joy. Maybe after we wrap up a few more shots, once we're back in Soomjam, once Glory's busy doing . . . whatever. Maybe then I'll hit him up for his opinion.

We return to the film site, and again, Aunt Weeby and Miss

Mona come along. After about an hour of work, though, my aunt squeals right into my explanation.

"Ooooh, look, Andie! You have fans even out here."

Groan.

"Cut!" I turn to see what Aunt Weeby's talking about and almost swallow my tongue.

Seven men stand in a cluster at the crest of a nearby rocky ridge, no more than four or five miles away from us. Their shaggy, loose garments, turbans, and long, ragged beards identify them as native tribesmen. Their weapons label them dangerous.

They look like Muslim extremists on the evening news to me.

"Ah . . . guys?" My forced smile threatens a downward flip. "Let's not make any sudden movements. I know, I know. I sound like a bad B movie, but work with me here." I swipe a hand across my sweaty brow. "And let's not stare at them either, okay? They're no welcoming committee. Trust me."

Max's Adam's apple jerks up and down. "Show's over, right?"

I stroll toward Glory and make a big deal of checking the camera, a forced smile smeared all over my face. "You betcha. We're outta here. But casually, okay?"

Yeah, right.

Tell me: how does one go about running from armed guerillas casually? I don't know how we did it, but we hustled off in the quietest, calmest way I've ever seen people—scared people—flee the scene of a future crime.

Come to think of it, I've never seen the scene of a future crime. At least, not live. Who'd a thunk that working live TV would turn my life into a TV drama? With a script-as-you-go format, no less.

"Miss Mona?" I say five minutes later. "This wasn't in my job description, you know."

"Not in mine, either," she murmurs, her lips edged in white, her normal peaches-and-cream complexion less peach and more cream. "This is scary, honey, and I'm real sorry I dragged you into it—"

Oh, great. I didn't want to make her feel bad. "Don't give it another thought. I promise I won't." I flash her a grin. "I bet you once we're back in Kentucky, we'll all agree we wouldn't've missed it for . . . well, for just about anything. Now, if they start shooting, I might change my mind."

"Oh, pshaw!" Aunt Weeby says, her excitement practically crackling around her. "They're not in the shooting mood, sugar. They just came to watch the show, is all. The 'Watch the Crazy American Tourists' show. It happens everywhere I travel, you know. Foreign folks are just plumb curious about all us Americans."

I bite my tongue—hard—to keep from identifying our particularly loony tourist. You know we have one. Yep. The one with the newfound affection for yaks. Off to my right side, I feel Max's silent laughter, and behind us, Allison chuckles.

Everyone knows Aunt Weeby.

From the front pocket of my backpack, I pull out a compact mirror. You got it. I'm about to reprise my shiny soupspoon gig. I just *have* to know what those scary guys are doing while we do like the rats in the sinking ship.

What I see doesn't exactly reassure me. They've come partway down the ridge and haven't taken their beady peepers off us. "Uh . . . guys?"

Aunt Weeby trots up to my left, a worried look on her still-beautiful face. "You okay, sugarplum? Is that nasty ol' gut a' yours acting up again?"

"I'm okay. My gut's not acting up, but those guys with the guns are. They're on their way down the hill, and I'm definitely not feeling the love here."

"Do you really think they're terrorists?" Allison asks.

I check out my mirror again. "Beats me. Wanna ask Xheng Xhi?"

"Sure," she says. "Where is he?"

I stop. "What do you mean, where is he? Wasn't he with you and Glory, leading the mule with the tent and stuff?"

"He was. But he's not anymore."

"D'you think we should go back for him?" Miss Mona asks, worry in her voice.

I take another look via my trusty mirror, but there's no chatty guide in sight. What is in my sights is the group of seven, closer every time I check. "I hate to do it," I say, my heart racing, "but these guys don't look happy. Maybe Xheng Xhi popped into a cave or something. At least, I hope he did. We can't wait for him or take the time to search."

Max lays his arm across my shoulders, leans closer to my mirror, and gives me a gentle squeeze. "Houston? We *do* have a problem."

To my surprise, the warmth in his touch comforts me—at a time I most need comfort. I shoot him a grateful smile, touched perhaps with a hint of regret, and pick up my speed. "Not if we don't hang around."

And we don't. Hang around, that is.

We reach the farmhouse a good while later. Don't ask me how long it took us to get here; I can't tell you a thing about that part of our adventure. I prayed the whole way.

Every last one of us runs the last few yards as fast as our feet can carry us. Once inside the huge wooden doors, I collapse onto the courtyard's dirt floor, my knees jelly, my nerves shot. "I don't ever want to do that again."

Allison plops down next to me. "I'm with you, sister." She closes her eyes—tight—and shudders. "They didn't look civilized."

Max rushes in, Miss Mona on one arm, Aunt Weeby on the other. "Civilized enough to carry sophisticated weapons."

"Oh, I'm so sorry I ever had the idea to go film those fool mines," Miss Mona moans, her usually smooth bob ruffled and wind-tossed. "I should have just let you lead your mission trip and be done with it. Now we've had terrorists chase us down, and we've lost our guide—our second guide. See what comes of wanting to do something for yourself rather than just what the Lord calls you to?"

Aunt Weeby shakes her head and pokes her friend's shoulder. "Why, that weren't so bad at all, Mona Latimer. It was plumb the most exciting thing I've done in all my born days! I kinda like living the Andi-ana Jones life. I'm so happy ya'll didn't give me heartburn about coming with all ya'll. You just can't go traipsing the globe again without me, you hear?"

We stare, shocked silent.

My certifiable relative goes on. "Just think of all the stories we'll have to tell at Bible study, Mona." Then she turns to me. "And imagine your viewers, sugarplum. They'll be lime green with envy. We saw our very own Talibans with our very own eyes!"

"But what about Xheng Xhi?" I ask. Sure, the man drives me nuts with his questions, but he's somewhere out there with gun-toting terrorists on the horizon.

"Oh, sugarplum, I'm sure he's fine." When I arch my brow, she continues. "He knows the area, and he might even know those Talibans. If not, I'm sure he has a hidey-hole"—she waves—"somewhere. And I don't think he's scared at all. He probably thinks it's normal. Maybe he does think it's an adventure, something to remember. That's what you should do."

Before she gets any more carried away, I stand. "It's way past time for a nap, a snack, a cup of tea, and *prayer*."

Aunt Weeby swipes the dust off her sturdy walking shoes on the backs of her trouser legs. "Why, sure!" She holds out her hand. No one takes hold. "C'mon, now. Let's thank our Lord for such an exciting opportunity. He brings us here, shows us things we can't never even imagine back home, and then he keeps us safe. He is such an awesome, awesome God."

Gulp. She's right—yet another reason to love her, wackiness and all. But who's counting reasons?

I take her right hand. "You're pretty awesome, yourself, Aunt Weeby. I've been so busy being terrorized, that I've forgotten who's watching out for us."

But before we begin to pray . . . . "Ahem!"

I turn toward the stairs to the upper family floors of the farmhouse—as opposed to where we are on the ground floor, domain of the grunting, snuffling, clucking, and lowing beasties in the stalls. A stranger, a tall, handsome Westerner, is staring at our little group, a mystified expression on his weathered face.

"Hi" is all I can manage.

He smiles. "I would know you anywhere, Ms. Adams," he says in a deep, bass voice. "My sister and mother own the television whenever you and Mr. Matthews are on."

Miss Mona coos.

"Oh, my!" Aunt Weeby says in a breathy voice.

I'm almost as impressed as the more mature ladies among us. The stranger's dark brown hair is sprinkled with attractive silver at the temples. He wears the ubiquitous khaki pants and long-sleeved knit shirt of the world traveler with casual elegance, and his warm chocolate eyes sparkle with humor and intelligence.

"You've got us at a disadvantage," I say. "You know at least some of us, but we have no idea who you might be. Were we expecting you? Are you with the Musgroves?"

He lopes over, his movements graceful and athletic. "Sorry about that. I've heard a great deal about the Musgroves and The Father's Lambs." He extends his right hand. "Rich Dunn, senior pastor at the Riverside Chapel in Mount Cheer, Pennsylvania. I'm here with Oxfam to deliver supplies to earthquake victims."

Aunt Weeby gets her Perry Mason look in place. "But they weren't hit too hard around these parts by that there earthquake. There aren't many *earthquake* victims here in this here Soupjam town."

She's had her issues with the town's name. "Soomjam, Aunt Weeby."

Her hand draws a lofty wave. "Fine. But I don't see a whole lot a' ruination and destruction out here. Oh sure, they aren't rich or nothing, but they're not desperate either."

Rich approaches my outspoken aunt. "And you would be . . . ?"

Aunt Weeby pats her upswept do. "I'm Andrea's auntie." She holds out her hand. "Olivia Adams Miller. Pleased to meet you."

"The pleasure's all mine," the reverend says, a genuine smile on his lips. "And, you're right. This area was spared the worst of the quake. I'm on my way farther northwest, toward the Pakistani part of Kashmir. That's where the worst devastation happened."

Max steps forward. "Good to meet you, sir." After they shake hands, he adds, "Is this a convenient stop on the way?"

"Mr. Xi La and his family are well known for their hospitality."

"Rich, son!" a woman calls from upstairs. "Did you find my shawl?"

"Not yet, Mother. I've just met the other Americans."

Footsteps clatter down the stairs. The woman who rushes out is a surprise—to say the least. Tall, close to or maybe even taller than my five foot ten, she's slender and dressed in Madison Avenue–worthy garb. Her camel-colored trousers—probably custom-tailored—emphasize her long, slender legs, and the ivory turtleneck under the long-sleeved sage-colored silk blouse is cashmere. Trust me. I know these things.

Her gray-blond hair is in a short, spiky cut, mussed to chic perfection, and her exquisitely made-up face is youthful and radiant. My careful scrutiny reveals no telltale tugging of a face-lift or the freeze-factor of Botox. She's not beautiful, but she's not the kind that goes under the radar, either.

"How wonderful!" Her scarlet lipsticked smile lights up the courtyard. "It's such a treat to meet fellow Yanks so far from home."

She freezes in front of me. "Oh!" She spins to her son. "Why didn't you tell me?" She whirls back. "I can't believe it's you!"

Her hug throws me for a loop. "I'm tickled to meet you, Andrea. Eleanor Dunn here, but please call me Nori. Everyone does."

Yikes! Nori Dunn, Miss Mona, and Aunt Weeby on the same continent. Look out, world!

I ease away. "I'm afraid I've got dust all over you. But it is a pleasure to find fans even out here."

"Fans?" she asks, then winks. "Friends, Andrea. Friends."

How do you answer that?

Fortunately for me, the three ladies and Pastor Rich yammer away, no interest in whatever I might've said. I take the chance to head up to my shared bedroom, my knees still wobbly from our hasty retreat. I lie down on my sleeping bag, close my eyes, take deep, slow breaths. Was that insane trip to the mine area worth the danger?

Father God? Did we storm up here by mistake? All I really wanted was to help the Musgroves, The Father's Lambs, and any quake victims you led me to.

In the dim, quiet room, I bask in the wonder of a God who has blessed his children with the gift of prayer. Whether his answer comes later rather than sooner, I know he's there, listening, loving, leading. I pray for the patience to wait and listen, for the grace to keep from bumbling and stumbling and getting in his way.

Again.

9:00

The next morning, after a simple breakfast of *stot*—a small, round bread studded with poppy seeds—and all the hot green tea we can drink, I come to a rotten decision.

Now I have to break the news to everybody else—fun.

Not.

"Hey, guys. I checked out the footage we shot yesterday, and I hate to say it, but we have to either do a couple more takes or scrap the whole thing."

The S.T.U.D. people, seated down one side of the table, while Pastor Rich, Nori, and the Musgroves line the other, don't take my news well. They offer their opinions—all at once. And loudly.

Those on the pastor's side stare.

While everyone yaps, movement at the top of the stairs catches my eye. Xheng Xhi slinks in, but instead of joining us, or even greeting us, he scoots across the room in the shadows and up the stairs to the top floor. Strange, but then he is a strange guy. At least he's safe.

My fellow travelers, oblivious to his return, gripe away.

I'll tell them of Xheng Xhi's return later, when they're done objecting to my statement.

Finally, the chaos dies down. "Okay. That wasn't the response I'd hoped for." I turn to Glory. "What did you think of the film?"

She wrinkles her nose. "We have a couple of good bits, but . . . I don't know if it was the rapid retreat that caused the problem or if the tape itself was bad, but a large part of what we shot taped grainy. You can't tell what's going on. And that's if we don't count all of you and Max arguing over . . ." She shakes her head. "Whatever. But since that's what you guys do anyway, we need to think about the grainy video."

I blush at the mention of Max's and my ongoing on-screen skirmishes. "So you think I'm right. We either scrap or redo."

"Oh no," Miss Mona says, shaking her head. "We're not going back out there. We're done with this project."

Half of me cheers; the other half protests. "Oh, Miss Mona, I know I wasn't very positive yesterday, but that's probably because I was so tired." And freaked by our close-enough encounter of the Taliban kind. "Those men only showed up after we'd been out there filming for hours. I think we might be able to get away with a quick reshoot and then hurry back without rousing them. And no tents and picnics this time."

Max sends me his trademark glare. "You are nuts, you know."

I glare right back. "Do I take that to mean you're not interested in another chance in the spotlight?"

"I'd rather live another day to do another spot."

Aunt Weeby slaps both hands on the table and stands. "Aw . . . sugarplum! Don't you worry yourself none. I'll go

134

with you. I'm sure our Glory-girl here can show me how to make her camera work. A camera's a camera, right? Hers is just bigger'n mine. You'n I can get the job done."

Aunt Weeby and the Taliban . . . the Taliban and Aunt Weeby. Hmm . . .

I'm no dummy. "Miss Mona's right. I'm sure we can make do with what we have."

"I don't have a problem going back to the mine site," Glory says. "But I don't think we should all go."

"You won't get an argument from me," Allison says. "I'll even give you my war paint, Andie. Knock yourself out."

"I'm with Allison," Max says—to my surprise. I would've thought he'd Gorilla Glue himself to the very appreciative Glory.

Miss Mona shakes her head. "I can't let you girls do that. Just think about it, Andie. Two of you against seven armed tribesmen. You won't even be able to explain yourself, since they don't speak much English in these parts."

"I'm sure you're not going to believe me," Max says with a wink and a smile, "but I'm not ready to lose my cohost to a bunch of crazed rebels. I don't think this is your best idea, Andie."

"Oh, *pshaw!*" Aunt Weeby's eyes sparkle with excitement. "I think Andie's plan is great. We just do like in the movies— get in, get out. Oh, and we have to have faith."

Faith I have, but I also have a dangerously adventuresome aunt. My resolve wavers, but then I realize there won't be any point to a show on Kashmir sapphires if we don't even show the mines. And I do have faith.

"I think Glory and I can carry this off, but only if we go lean and mean." When Aunt Weeby's frown ruffles her brow, I

135

give her my unperfected version of the evil eye. "That means only Glory and I go. The fewer of us, the less likely we are to catch the tribal folks' attention."

"Like I said before," Allison murmurs, "you can count me out. I'll stay here and spend time with the kids."

Max shakes his head. "Count me out. The kids are more my speed."

The Dunns ally themselves with Allison and Max, and in the end, everyone comes down like a ton of bricks on Aunt Weeby to keep her from going. Let me tell you. Persuading Aunt Weeby isn't for the faint of heart.

Glory and I take off, minus my shadow. Who knows where Xheng Xhi is now? But I don't complain. Without his zillion questions to deal with, we might get enough good material to call it a wrap. Then I can get back to what I really want to do: help at the orphanage.

We do get the job done, and only as we're about to head back do Glory and I spot the armed tribesmen again, but this time there are fewer members of their posse, and they stay farther away. Doesn't matter; we break speed records hustling to the farmhouse anyway.

About fifty feet from the large building, Glory pulls up short. "Hang on! I need to breathe . . . This camera weighs a ton . . . We've practically run . . . the whole time."

I stop too. "Your bag of goodies . . . is no lightweight either."

As we gulp in air, and I think calm, peaceful thoughts to try and slow my racing heart, Glory pokes me in the shoulder.

"Look."

When I do, a familiar Kashmiri figure dodges around the

corner of the farmhouse, away from us. "What a kook! What do you think Xheng Xhi's up to?"

She laughs in breathless chuckles. "Don't ask me. I'm not the one he's got a crush on."

"Huh?"

"Come on. You have to have noticed. The guy's nuts about you."

"No way! He just wants to know all about America. You know, McDonald's, football, golf, and Wal-Mart. He's got a list of questions longer than the run of the average daytime soap. I'm just the one he figured would let him chatter on and on and on."

Her look carries a truckload of pity. "You can't even tell when a guy's interested, can you? You're all about your rocks and God."

"I'm not that bad." I think. "Sure, I love God, and I'm a serious gemologist, but I'm not . . ."

I let my words dry up. She might be right. I might have a tiny problem with tunnel vision. Is there such a thing as tunnel life?

"Mm-hm," Glory says. "You're clueless. Totally clueless. In every way." She whirls and stalks off away from the farmhouse.

"Gee, thanks, Glory. So nice to know how you feel." I hoist her sack of gear back up on my shoulder and march toward our lodgings. I'm irritated—okay, I'm mad, but who's counting?

Just what am I clueless about? But since she's not around to ask, I stomp up to our room, dump Glory's junk on her bed, and go look for the rest of our group. Turns out they're still at the orphanage, and since I'm running out of afternoon, it doesn't make much sense for me to go meet up with them. I stop in the main living room, grab a drink of water, then head back outside. I don't see Glory on my way, nor do I want to right now.

I pull my green fleece jacket closer and head toward Soomjam. I may as well visit the town, do the tourist thing, while I'm here. I wouldn't want to be accused of cluelessness about that too.

But I don't get too far. I find Max and his golf club and balls behind a row of neighboring homes. As I approach, the now-familiar CRAAAACK! of club hitting ball rings out.

"I thought you were all still at the orphanage. Did you quit working early?" I ask.

"Xheng Xhi and Pastor Rick needed help carting Oxfam supplies to a little town about five miles west of us after lunch."

"How'd that go?"

He takes a deep breath. "Humbling. I remembered what you said yesterday when I saw the people's faces. Rice and protein meal really mean something around here. There's so much hunger, so much need in this country. It felt great to do something about it."

I cross my arms and lean back, pretend to study him, analyze his words. With a wink, I say, "You're not just a pretty face, then."

He rolls his baby blues. "Give me a break."

"Can't you take a joke?"

"Not when you've spent months telling me what a washout I am."

I hold my hands up, palms outward. "Okay, okay. We're supposed to have a truce going. I didn't mean to insult you. That was just my lame stab at a joke."

"Ooookay." He returns to his golf.

His response is less than encouraging. But in all honesty, I can't blame him. I've been less than welcoming—hah! I've been a total pain to him. And even now that I know how rotten I've been, my frustration with his lack of gemological knowledge, combined with my unwanted but very real attraction, can still get the better of me.

Yeah, I can't blame him for turning away. I've done far worse to him.

Forgive me, Father.

I realize I have to ask Max's forgiveness too. *Gulp.*

"Umm . . . Max?"

He looks over his shoulder. "Yeah?"

"I . . . ah . . . really owe you an apology. I've been rotten to you since you came to work for the S.T.U.D., and it's wrong of me."

He turns slowly to face me, a bemused look on his face. But he doesn't say a thing, so I'm still on the hot plate here.

"I may mess up again—actually, I'm sure I will, out of bad habit—but I ask you to forgive me, for my past nastiness, and for future failures too."

With his club in one fist, he crosses his arms, his eyes narrowed. "What's brought about this epiphany?"

My blush almost hurts—like my conscience. "I'm not stupid, just stubborn and sometimes blind. You've made more efforts than I have, and you haven't laid into me, no matter how nasty my comments got. And—" I hesitate, weighing my next words "—you've smashed a bunch of my assumptions about you."

The more I say, the narrower his eyes get, and the tighter

his lips clamp. In desperation, I point at his mouth. "See? That's what I need to learn to do—what I'm trying to learn to do. Shut my mouth before I blurt out dumb stuff."

At that, the corner of his mouth gives a twitch, as if he's trying to keep from smiling.

"I'm serious! I do want to change, and I really am sorry I've been a pill."

As his mouth curves into a real smile, he nods slowly. "That you have been, Andi-ana Jones. A pain, a pill, and nasty-mouthed. I have forgiven you—it hasn't been easy, since you've never really seemed to repent of your—" he waves toward me "—your attitude. But maybe you do mean it. And since we're going to be working together indefinitely, I'd rather move forward than stay stuck in the nasty past."

My eyes burn; tears well up. All this time I've been so hard on him, he's been quietly living what I have been talking. How humbling is that?

"Thanks," I whisper.

"You're welcome."

And then, as if nothing had ever happened, he leans over, plunks another ball on his tee, then does the golfer's wiggle again. He swings and whacks the ball . . . right at the nearest house's back door, from where it boings off into the Kashmiri sunset.

In spite of the turmoil inside me, I grin. "Uh-oh!"

With a grimace, he yanks the tee from the ground, and his graceful lope takes him in the direction both balls disappeared. That's why he's not here when a bearded, turbaned gentleman throws open the door the ball just hit.

A blitz of angry Kashmiri dialect slaps me in the face. The home owner shakes a fist inches from the tip of my nose.

Two more men, similarly haired and clothed, come out of neighboring houses and join the attack.

I step back.

They step forward.

"Sorry, but I didn't do it!" I show them my empty hands.

One of the men mimics Max's golf style.

I take another step back.

They follow.

"Look, no golf club. No balls!" Where's Xheng Xhi when I need him? For that matter, where's Max to take responsibility for his jockiness?

The men complain some more. Then they come closer, surround me, and take turns getting in my face. Fear chills me.

Two of the men shake their fists. The third grabs my arm and squeezes—hard. I'll probably have a bruise to go with my raging red panic. What can I do? How can I get away from them? What are they going to do to me?

I don't want to find out, so I apologize even more.

Finally, they shake their heads in obvious, cross-lingual disgust, and go back home.

My feet can't get me to the farmhouse fast enough. And I'm scared. Really scared. Which makes me mad.

Of course, the first person I see in the courtyard is Max. "Where'd you disappear to? I just had to face down an army of angry villagers back there because of your golf!"

Mr. Magnificent looks at me as though I've morphed into a yak. "What are you talking about?"

My hearbeat begins to slow—but not by much. The image of the angry men makes me shudder. "Don't you remember? You whacked that ball against someone's home."

141

Red blooms on his cheeks. "Someone got mad?"

"Someone?" I may never be able to get rid of the memory of those scary men. "It was a *bunch* of someones! And they weren't mad, they were *furious*! I feared for my life."

Well, that might be stretching the truth a bit. I try to corral my off-kilter emotions, without much success.

"You're nuts, Andie."

Upset? Sure. But nuts? "No, I'm not. You hit someone's house, and then you ran off to get the ball. I was stuck having to try and pacify the angry natives—and I don't speak their language! Trust me, I was scared."

He studies me for a second . . . two. "You're not kidding, are you?"

"No, Max, I'm not. Three Kashmiri men ran out of their houses, all yelling who-knows-what at me. One even grabbed and shook me. I don't speak Kashmiri or Indian or . . . or whatever. I had no way to give them a decent apology—for you."

"I'm sorry. I didn't leave you in the lurch on purpose."

His apology drains the oomph from my fear. Still, his gear has been a pain—even though yesterday's games with the kids did bless the little ones. "Did you ever check with Xheng Xhi? Maybe he could have come up with a better place to use as a golf course."

Max starts up the stairs. "As soon as we delivered the supplies, he disappeared. I couldn't find him for a friendly putting challenge."

I follow him. "What's up with the guy? First, I can't get him to stop with his questions—his inquiring mind just *has* to know. Now no one can find him. Maybe he's up here waiting for us to come back."

"Maybe." But Max doesn't sound convinced.

I peek around him and, aside from our hostess who's dressed in another glorious *salwar kameez*, this one a regal purple, the room is empty. "I think yesterday's encounter with the gun-toting tribesmen spooked him. He's gone."

"Not much of a guide, is he?"

I give him a wry grin. "He's better than one in jail."

Max nods. "Or the dead houseboy."

I shudder. "Did you have to remind me?"

He sits on the corner of the table, a foot on one of the benches. "How could you forget? Your four goons—your word, not mine—haven't let us out of their sights since we left Srinagar."

"They didn't follow Glory and me today."

He smirks. "That's what you think. One of them did."

"We never saw him."

"I think that was the plan. They probably think they're being subtle."

"I guess even runaway rhinos can pull it off every once in a while."

Surprise, surprise! The runaway rhinos march in. They nod at us, chat with our hostess, then take their places down one side of the table. Yes, the same table where Max has plopped his . . . umm . . . behind. He scrambles up, and Mrs. Xi La sets out a major spread of platters piled high with fragrant food.

My stomach growls on cue.

The oldest goon grins and rattles off a string of jibberish.

Great. Now I'm providing not just Max but also the goons with their entertainment. As I'm about to escape to my room, my hostess calls out my name. "Yes?"

She brings me one of those wonderful *sheermals* and a cup of green tea, a sweet smile on her lined face.

"Oh! Thank you. Thank you so much."

She bows. "Wel-come."

"You speak English!"

Mrs. Xi La shakes her head. "Thank you. Wel-come." She shrugs.

My stomach growls again, so I take a bite of my sweet bread, and then, since it's so delicious and she's so sweet, and my day's been so rotten until she made it better, I throw my arms around her. To my amazement, she hugs me back and smiles again. I've made a friend. Too cool.

Munching happily, I head for my room.

"That," Max says when I find him still in the hall, "was a really nice thing."

"Isn't she a sweetheart?"

"Yes, but I meant you. I don't think you saw it, but she had tears in her eyes when you hugged her. I'll bet everyone takes her for granted, even though she works nonstop all day."

"Really? Tears?"

He nods.

I shake my head. "That's so wrong. She's great, and I should make sure she knows."

His eyes twinkle with mischief and something else. Could it be . . . approval? Certainly not admiration—I haven't done much to admire. But I'll take what I can get, and go with the approval.

He opens the door to his room. "See ya at dinner, Andiana Jones."

"See ya, Mr. Ma—" I catch myself. There's no way I'm letting him know I secretly call him Mr. Magnificent. No way. No how.

144

Nuh-uh.

"Mr. Matthews. You've got your moments too."

My dreams hum with the luscious notes of "Stranger in Paradise" . . .

"*. . . The sweetest thing . . . ,*" *Mr. Magnificent whispers.* "*You're the sweetest thing . . .*"

A coy smile on her rosy lips, the lovely young woman with red hair flutters her lashes. "*And you're the handsomest golfer.*"

The brazen black-haired siren slithers up and separates the happy couple. "*Can I please collect your old tees, Mr. Magnificent? Just as a marvelous memory of your magnificence. Please?*"

"*No, ma'am.*" *Mr. Magnificent lays a strong, manly arm around the lovely young woman with red hair.* "*My tees belong to my lovely headache—*"

"*Mr. Magnificent!*" *the lovely young woman with the red hair objects.* "*How could you?*"

True remorse makes his handsome features droop. "*Forgive me, dear lady with the red hair. I meant my heart's delight—*"

A scream of joy bursts from the lovely young lady, and runaway rhinos stampede across the mountains, their hooves pounding and pounding and pounding—

I bolt up into a sitting position, my heart beating hard against my ribs, my breathing sharp and shallow. No more *Stranger in Paradise* for me.

The pounding resumes. It's a lot closer than the nearest Himalayan peak. A sense of déjà vu hits me. I shake my head. "No," I whisper. "No, please. Not again, Lord."

I clutch my green fleece jacket tight across my chest. It's too cold to sleep in only my cotton tank and cartoon pajama pants. Every millimeter of my body shrieks in protest, but I still get up. A faint spill of moonlight slices in through our small, high window. At my right and my left, Glory and Allison look confused, scared, and as disoriented as I feel.

More pounding assaults our door. "Andie!" Trevor Musgrove calls out. "Allison, Glory! Ladies, there's been . . . an incident. Please wake up."

I start to cross the room, but Allison reaches out, grabs my hand, and scrambles to her feet. We walk to the door, Glory right on our heels.

"Don't leave me behind," she cries, her voice high-pitched and shaky.

When I meet Trevor's gaze, fear tightens my gut, and nausea hits me hard. "Who?" I ask.

"Follow me."

Once in the great room, I count familiar faces. Max, Miss Mona, Aunt Weeby, and Emma Musgrove are all there. So are Rich and Nori, Mr. and Mrs. Xi La, and the four goons. There are also two grim-faced, uniformed strangers, their weapons very much in plain sight.

Mrs. Xi La's heartrending sobs break the silence in the room. Her husband holds her close, his hand gently patting her back, while he looks devastated.

Bad. The vibes I get are wicked bad.

When I scan the faces again, I know what's wrong. I know who's missing. And I no longer want to ask. I don't want to hear.

But it doesn't matter what I want.

One of the armed soldiers nods at Trevor. He clears his

throat. "Andie, I'm sorry to say, but Xheng Xhi is no longer with us. Mrs. Xi La found him in the courtyard when she went to feed the chickens a short while ago. Because Xheng Xhi was . . . fond of you, these gentlemen will want to speak with you."

Shivers turn to shudders, and a vise of pain tightens across my forehead. The two soldiers stare, and one takes a step closer.

To my surprise, Max comes to my side. "Are you going to be okay?"

I snort—oh yeah. How elegant of me. "I'm not okay, and I don't know when I'll ever be okay again. I can't believe this is happening again." I stop myself before I lose control. That tiny pause gives me some perspective. "But I'm way better off than poor—"

"Hush! Don't say another word!" he hisses. "You don't know how they'll interpret whatever you say."

The soldiers spit out a series of commands—I don't need a translator to get their tone of voice. Trevor nods.

"Officer Mustafa wants everyone packed and ready to head back to Srinagar in fifteen minutes. Because of the—" he pauses, takes a deep breath "—earlier incident in the capital, the investigation will be handled by the Srinagar police."

I gulp. "Investigation?"

"Yes, of course," the Brit answers. "The investigation into—"

"Into the untimely death of Mr. Xheng Xhi," I finish.

Allison's hand spasms around mine. "First me, now you. This can't be for real."

Glory grips my shoulder. "I'm sure it'll work out okay like before."

Miss Mona sighs, shakes her head, but doesn't speak.

Aunt Weeby says, "Oh, dear. Another one turns up dead. What's the problem with this here Kashmir place? Don't their guides know how to stay friends with folks? Everyone has to have enemies or something? No wonder they have themselves so many a' them crazy wars."

I turn to Max. "She's the one you should keep quiet. Stuff like that could launch another skirmish."

He shakes his head. "She can say anything she wants. She's not the one in trouble."

I have a bad feeling about this. I also have a good idea why the soldiers haven't quit staring at me, but I want to hear it. Out loud. So everything's out in the open. I plant my fists on my hips. "And I'm in trouble because . . . ?"

"Because everybody saw Mr. Xheng Xhi glued to your side. Because everyone knows he got on your nerves. Because he was last seen alive and kicking right around the time when you and Glory returned from the mine site. And because, for some reason, the guy had a death grip on your stupid Coach bag when they found his body in the chicken's space. That's why these gentlemen think you may have had something to do with Xheng Xhi's death."

I hear the clang of jailhouse doors come down around me. I'd much rather hear "Stranger in Paradise" as backdrop to my too-weird dream.

Why do these things happen to me?

"There was no reason for me to hurt Xheng Xhi. Yeah, sure. He almost drove me crazy with all his questions, but we needed him to translate so we could get to know the kids at the orphanage. Now we have to go back to Srinagar to answer more questions, and we won't have the chance to do what we came here for. Common sense says he's more valuable to me alive and bugging me than silent and dead."

"First Myanmar," Allison murmurs. "Now Kashmir. You've got some kind of luck, Andie."

"She's lucky enough," Trevor says through tight lips, "that the soldiers find it quite conclusive that Xheng Xhi died hugging her Coach bag. They found signs of a struggle and feel an argument led to the death. Someone used the wooden handle of one of the barnyard rakes to choke him from behind."

Sound familiar? Remember Farooq?

That splash you just heard was the key to my jail cell plunking down into a deep, deep ocean. I think I'm sunk.

10<u>00</u>

Back on the mules again, after we've said our hurried good-byes to the Dunns, the Musgroves, and the little ones at the orphanage, my mind turns over and over the scraps of all that's happened. What else can I do? I'm stuck in the mountains of a strange country not known for its legal fairness, and with no rights for the common woman. The bunch of official-type lunatics escorting us back to Srinagar thinks I had something to do with the murder of our native guide. Oh, and the houseboy too.

You know I had nothing to do with either death.

I may not know what happened, but I can connect some dots. "Did anybody else notice that Xheng Xhi's murder sounds a lot like Farooq's?"

For the span of about ten seconds, all I hear is our beasts plod down the mountain we climbed only days before. Then Miss Mona sighs loud enough for everyone to hear.

"Andie, dear," she says. "I don't think it's wise to talk about this right now." She bobs her head toward the goons and soldiers. "You might be misunderstood."

The six men have arranged themselves between us, and that makes it tough to talk, but hey! I'm going nuts here. I can't just ride a mule to my funeral. Know what I mean?

"On TV," Aunt Weeby says, "lawyers always say suspects should keep their mouths shut. That way you can't say anything the cops can use against you. You'd best not talk so much, sugarplum."

Aunt Weeby's telling me not to blab. How's that for irony?

I sigh. No one has to tell me my situation's grim, but it's not *that* grim. I did nothing wrong. I will not take the blame for those two dead Kashmiri.

I sit up tall on the back of my beast. "What do you think they're going to do? Shoot me because I ask a question? Right here, right now? I don't think so."

"Andie!" Aunt Weeby frowns. "You don't listen so good, do you?"

I ignore Max's burst of laughter.

So does Aunt Weeby. She dishes out more advice. "Don't you go giving 'em any a' those ideas. I'm sure they can come up with plenty a' their own. Why, I'm sure they know all about tortures, and all that kinda thing."

Fear rumbles around my stomach, but I refuse to let it do its thing. God is greater than any Kashmiri threat. "Don't even go there. You know I didn't do a thing to Xheng Xhi. I'm going back home to Louisville. It might take some fast talking from embassy types, but that's what they get paid to do."

"Of course, we know you didn't hurt that man," Miss Mona says. "But folks here in Kashmir don't know you like we do. Even your fans know you better than that. But dear Trevor here says it's best not to say anything until we've met with

151

the folks at the embassy. They'll know how to deal with the authorities. Besides, I'm sure someone there will speak their language so they don't misunderstand what's what."

Frustration is fast becoming my permanent state of residence. "Doesn't anybody else think it's weird that both these guys were killed while they were around us? Don't you think something's going on? Don't y'all want to know what it's all about?"

"I just want to go home," Allison says. "And I want to stay there. Don't ever ask me to come on another one of your crazy trips, Andie, you hear? I won't go."

"Oh, so it's *my* crazy trip." I sniff. "Mine was a missionary trip to help earthquake victims. Miss Mona's the one who hijacked it into something else, something sapphire-related, something crazy."

"Umm . . . Andie?" Glory says. "I don't want to upset anyone, but I just looked back. Do you still have your mirror? You might want to use it."

"Forget the mirror." I glance over my shoulder and almost fall from the mule. "Oh, swell. Remember the folks Aunt Weeby called my native fans out by the mines? The ones with the handy-dandy weaponry? Well, they're with us again."

"You don't think they plan to follow us all the way down to the city, do you?" Allison asks.

A tsunami of exhaustion hits me. "Who knows? Who cares? You guys don't want to help me figure this out, so I don't want to do all the thinking anymore. I don't even want to talk—and don't say anything smart about that, Max. I just want to crawl into bed, pray, and sleep until I can't sleep anymore, and then pray some more. But I don't think I'm going to get what I want anytime soon."

No one says a word. I suspect they think a wholesale melt-down's around the corner. And it might be. Do you blame me?

But a meltdown won't change much. Two men are dead. Our party's right in the thick of the investigation, even though we had nothing to do with the killings.

I blink away sudden tears. Once I can see again, I notice a familiar cluster of homes up ahead. We stayed in this tiny village on our way to Soomjam. I might catch some z's sooner than I thought.

"Look!" Glory says, beating me to the punch. "We're almost to our overnight location."

"Progress," I murmur with only a touch of sarcasm in my voice. "Not enough, though. I have to admit, I'm with Allison. As much as I wanted to help at the orphanage, I want to go home even more."

"Now you're making sense," Max says.

You hear those flapping sounds overhead? Yep. It must be those flying pigs again. No dissent between Mr. Magnificent and Andi-ana Jones.

But I'm too drained to think about it.

Unfortunately, it's going to be some time before I can catch that nap I want so much. We're not the only tourists in this tiny town, this stop at the intersection of various rocky, craggy trails through the Himalayas.

Remember Delia, her mother, and grandmother? Oh yeah. Their party's here too. Turns out, this is where they stopped on the way up and now back from their encounter with the guru. And guess what? That little gathering took place just west of Soomjam.

Maybe I need sleep a whole lot more than even I think.

Either that, or I'm getting a wee bit paranoid. Weren't these folks in Srinagar at the same time we were there? Now they've spent a couple of days not so far from—you got it—where we were.

See the pattern?

Oh, okay. I can't see Delia, her mother, or her diamond-demented grandmother killing anyone. The two men with them, Delia's dad and granddad, probably, don't look any more threatening than the women do. But, then again, I can't see me killing anyone either.

And I'm the authorities' prime suspect right about now.

Go figure.

But there's still only one reality. There are two dead bodies; I don't think Robert killed Farooq, and I know he couldn't have killed Xheng Xhi—he's been in jail all this time.

Lord? Can you give me a clue here? Or am I really as clue-less—in every way—as Glory says? What have I missed?

Something's up; I don't believe in coincidence. I just have to figure out what's what. My life might depend on it.

Those soldiers? They're not playing cops and robbers with their guns.

"That old fool was full of hooey!" Delia's grandfather, Mr. Russell, says at dinner. "And charges too much to dish it out."

"But Grandpa! Didn't you find your inner gem?"

My ears perk up. Dinner table talk about some fake religious leader out to separate people from their cash doesn't snag my attention. But gems? Oh yeah.

"What do you mean, Delia?" I ask. "What's that about an inner gem?"

Too late to do anything about it, her smug smile reminds me I'm dealing with a teen. She takes a deep, dramatic breath and, once she's sure she holds center stage, gives me her goofy answer.

"Swami Devamundi's Eternal Growth gatherings teach you to, like, know yourself, how you're a gem deep inside. You know?"

I shake my head.

She scoffs—she's a teen, all right.

"You should come with us to the next gathering, Andie. You'd, like, learn so much from the swami. He's too cool. He'll teach you to find that gem inside plus the good Karma, and then you, like, have the key to keep growing. The best part is, you can keep coming back to more gatherings and learn to grow even more. After a bunch of gatherings, you become a realized soul, and you can get to Nirvana. Isn't that totally awesome?"

No. That kind of semi-spiritual gobbledygook gives me the creeps. But the gem part . . . ? "I don't get the gem deal. What does a gem have to do with the whole Nirvana thing?"

Max smothers—sorta—a laugh. I kick him under the table.

He grunts but keeps on eating, a grin working its way back onto his face.

"All I know," Mr. Russell says, "is that I agreed to foot the bill for this trip because I wanted to see the Himalayas. I'm not about to pay that phony another penny to hear him tell everyone to meditate on the gem in their soul. Who's got a ruby, emerald, or sapphire in their soul? Who knows what anyone has in their soul?"

The glare Mrs. Russell gives her husband would strip the nacre off your best Tahitian pearl. "Thanks to the swami, some of us do know. And since we're in Kashmir, I'd like to think of my inner gem as a sapphire."

Ding, ding, ding, ding! "Sapphire, huh?"

"Me too," Delia says. "Me too."

I wonder if anybody else around the table feels like the crowd around the emperor when he sported his new duds.

"I think sapphire blue's the perfect color for our souls," Delia adds. "So I want a whole new wardrobe. The swami says we should show others our inner gem. Daddy's cool with buying me some new clothes, not the whole wardrobe, but he won't buy me a sapphire ring."

Does this sound creepier to you by the second? It might to Delia's daddy too, since he shakes his head and takes another helping of red *roganjosh*, a spicy mutton curry.

It also seems to sound funny to Max, who's trying—without much luck—to keep his laughter down at the mild-chuckle level.

All righty, then. I might as well do my gem-show host thing, and maybe that'll bring the silly swami-talk to a close. "I guess it's not so strange to like to wear clothes in a color that's special to you. And lots of people want a sapphire ring. We can sell you a nice one from the S.T.U.D. collection. Why don't you watch my show once I'm back in Kentucky?"

"See?" Delia's mother tells her husband. "It's not so strange." She turns to me—oh, joy. "Tell me, Andrea, did you pick up much Kashmir sapphire while you visited the mines?"

Hmm . . . "How'd you know we visited the mines?"

At her side, Aunt Weeby tsk-tsks. "Why, sugarplum, we told the Russells where we'd been when we first met up with them this afternoon. Don't you remember?"

Since visions of Kashmiri jails have been dancing in my head, yeah, okay. I might have forgotten a thing or two. Especially when it comes to loony Americans looking for faith in all the wrong places.

"So did you?" Delia's mother prods, her eyes glued to the S.T.U.D.'s stud.

"No, ma'am," Max answers. "We didn't come to Kashmir on a buying trip. We came to help at an orphanage that just happens to be located near the old, played-out sapphire mines. Last I checked, the S.T.U.D. has no Kashmir sapphire. But we might have some nice Burmese stones left."

"Too bad," she says. "I'd really like a Kashmiri stone. Like my daughter said, our dear swami encourages his followers to reflect their inner selves—their inner gem—in what they wear. My mother, Delia, and I have agreed that in honor of this wonderful land, we'd like to reflect the pretty blue of its sapphires. Could you at least tell me where I can buy one?"

I'd better take over the gemological conversation. Who knows what Mr. Magnificent might come up with? "It's virtually impossible to buy Kashmir sapphire these days," I say. "The mines haven't been seriously worked in almost seventy years."

She props her elbows on the table, glances toward me, but then beams back at Max. Good grief!

Then she says, "That doesn't mean there aren't any Kashmir sapphires out there somewhere, does it?"

I stare, and that forces her to pay attention to what I say. "That's right. Private collectors and museums own Kashmiri stones. The largest collection is supposed to be owned by the local government. I doubt the private owners are willing to part with their gems, but I've heard rumors that the government is thinking of selling some of their stash. So far, though, no stones have come on the market."

She looks at the two men in her party, seated side by side, more than likely for strength and solidarity. "I'm sure," she says, her voice thoughtful and calculating, "they'd sell if the price was right."

I laugh. "Okay, fine. Go for it. The latest auction at Christie's brought about one hundred and thirty-five thousand dollars per carat for a twenty-two-and-a-half-carat, hundred-plus-year-old Kashmir sapphire. Do the math. You'll need three million sixty-some thousand bucks for your own stone of that kind."

Stunned silence follows my words.

Then Grandpa Russell bursts into loud guffaws. "I owe you one, young lady. That's so crazy even these three can't imagine that kind of dough. That'll get 'em off my back—at least for the rings."

"But Mo-om!" Delia whines. "Don't you remember what the swami said? He said there are new mines and new, less expensive stones here in Kashmir—"

That's when things turn ugly. The armed soldiers march over to our table, and in seconds, we're all sent off to our separate rooms. By the time I collapse on my sleeping bag, I'm shaking from head to toe.

So the rumors are true.

New sapphire veins have been found in the mountains of Kashmir. Understandably, the government wants to control what happens. Just to know for sure rocks me with shock waves. The thought of more exquisite Kashmir sapphires makes the gemologist in me drool in anticipation. The thought of how close we came to seeing new mining activity disappoints the TV show host in me.

The prime suspect in one, maybe two, Kashmiri citizens' deaths? My thoughts are all about that certain hinky feeling I'm getting right about now. You know what I mean?

It's got to do with connecting those dots.

The rest of our trip to Srinagar, all six-plus days of it, passes in almost complete silence. Each time any of us tries to talk about anything other than the mules, the time of day, the weather, or "pleases" and "thank-yous," the soldiers wave their weapons to remind us we're not on a guided tour of the countryside anymore.

What I do learn during these six days is that those who attend the swami's gatherings can and do wander from his compound to meditate. What if a "participant" wanders off to dig not for inner gems but for—you got it—sapphires?

Rumors of new mines and possible sales by the Kashmiri government aren't the only ones that have buzzed around for years now. Some have suggested that as much as billions of dollars' worth of gemstones are smuggled out of the country each year.

Yeah. At one hundred thirty-five thousand dollars a carat, those billions add up fast, so we're not talking huge production numbers here. A couple of stones here, a couple of stones there are pretty easy to smuggle for those who lean that way.

I've also heard that some of the more unfortunate smugglers are sharing an address these days—adjacent cells in some deep, dark prison at an undisclosed location. Dunno about you, but I don't think it's ever a beautiful day in that neighborhood.

Don't want to move there, *capisce*?

Finally, we reach Srinagar. Because we're such a large flock of Americans, and because of the potential international conflict and embarrassment, the embassy has been alerted to our arrival. They send someone to meet us, a Mr. Smith, who then drives us straight to a new hotel—no houseboat, which is fine by me and my bad memories. Room assignments are handed out—each room comes with an armed guard outside the door—while authorities from both countries sort out details of the upcoming interrogations.

What fun.

"Great," I grumble as I close the door to the room Aunt Weeby and I will share. "Now our own government's helping these people hold us hostage."

"Now, now, sugarplum," Aunt Weeby says, her voice serious, unusually serious. "They're just trying to protect us. Would you rather stay here at a nice, clean hotel or go back to that dirty, stinky jail?"

I drop onto the nearest bed. There's no question which of those two choices I prefer. Still . . .

"I'd rather be on an airplane on my way back home."

So much for Andi-ana Jones's spirit of adventure.

$11\underline{^{00}}$

By the time the authorities—American, Indian, and Kashmiri—are done grilling me the next day, I know I've had a close encounter of the smoldering barbecue briquette kind. Just call me Shish Kebab.

Mr. Smith from the U.S. embassy escorts me back to the hotel, by myself, and says little aside from letting me know I'm in for more of the same the next day. I'm not surprised.

"I realize it's early yet," he adds, "but would you care for dinner?"

I want to relax. "Thanks, but I should meet up with the rest of the folks from the S.T.U.D. Network in a little while. I'd like to go to my room first."

He shrugs, then leads me to the elevator, walks me down the hall, greets the cop by the door, and waits until I'm inside before saying goodbye. I'm sure he thinks I'm the rudest life form around, but there's just so much a girl can take.

Once he's gone and I close the door, I collapse against the solid slab.

"You're back!" Aunt Weeby cries, relief in her voice and on her pretty face.

"Of course, I'm back." I drag my stress-sore, drained carcass farther into the room and make myself smile. "You couldn't have been worried they'd keep me. You know I didn't hurt Xheng Xhi."

She opens her arms.

I walk into the hug.

She sighs and holds me tight. "I know you, sugarplum, but they don't, and I've told you that before. It was nasty, wasn't it?"

Tears fill my eyes, and I can't find the strength to pull away from my aunt. "Yeah," I mumble into her slender shoulder. "It was pretty bad. Worse than what happened last year after the ruby vendor died. That time, a whole TV audience was watching me right when the man got killed."

"But you were all alone the other day at the wrong time."

"I was all alone the other day at the wrong time."

She looks confused. "That's where you discombobulate me, sugarplum. Weren't you supposed to be with Glory?"

The blush rushes all the way to the crown of my head—at least, that's how it feels. "Uh . . . we split up once we got to the farmhouse."

Aunt Weeby pulls back to look me in the eye. "Whaddaya mean, you split up? Where'd she go? And why'd you girls forget all about the buddy system? It still works real good, you know."

Groan. "I took her gear bag to our room and decided I wanted some alone time. I went for a walk, and that's when I met up with Max and his golf gear, oh . . . about ten minutes later."

My aunt's no dummy. She gives me the evil eye. "What you hiding from me, Andrea Autumn Adams? If you don't have a hankering to go rot in that there dirty, stinky jail a' theirs, you'd best be talking 'bout what all you did and didn't do."

I gust out a breath. "It's embarrassing, okay? We had a disagreement." That's the nice way to put it. "She said something I didn't like, and so we . . . ah . . . came to a parting of the ways."

"Now don't you go playing me for some stump-dumb fool. Out with it, girl! What'd she say?"

I rub my hand over my face. When my fingers hit my lips, I murmur, "Shssstawskoolessss."

"Say what?"

"You heard me. She said I was"—I lower my voice—"koolessss."

"What kind of dirty word is that there koolessss? I never heard such a thing in all my born days."

I roll my eyes. "All right, already. She said I was clueless, and she said Xheng Xhi had a crush on me."

She clucks her disappointment. "Izzat it? That all she said?"

"You wanted more?"

"Well, sugarplum, she didn't say nothing much new." She walks to the dresser to check her updo in the mirror above. "Y'always have been kinda spacey, and that poor man did take hisself some shine to ya. Why, he followed you everywhere you went. What's the big deal with that? You went and got your knickers in a twist for nothing much at all."

"*I'm* kinda spacey?" There's that pot and kettle thing again, but it won't do me any good to bring it up.

She nods without noting the heavy dose of sarcasm.

Don't ask why I feel such a need to defend myself. "I'm just a serious gemologist. I like what I do, and I spend a lot of time studying."

Her nose tips up. "Much too much, I'm thinking."

"But work's not my whole life. I do go to church, and I hang out with Peg. I just don't go around thinking about what men think of me every time I meet one of them."

Aunt Weeby shakes her head, snags her handbag, and heads for the door. "Suppertime."

I groan. "I'm beat. Can't you give me a little while?"

"C'mon now, Andie. I'm so hungry my belly button's been tickling my backbone for a while now."

My grumble gets me nowhere.

She goes on. "And it just might be time for you to start thinking about those men who might just be thinking about you."

"They're just not that important to me—"

"They better get to getting important and all. You're not getting any younger, you hear?"

I snag my backpack—my favorite Coach bag is now evidence—and follow her to the door. "As far as I'm concerned, when the good Lord's ready for me to find a man, I will, and that's all I have to say about it."

"So now we know why you and Glory went and split up."

Just when I thought she'd forgotten about it.

She opens the door and tsk-tsks again. "Your temper plumb got the best of you, didn't it? Again. And it's all about Max."

Before I'm forced to answer, I'm glad we do a face-to-face with our forbidding guard.

Aunt Weeby, however, is a woman on a mission. "Food." She mimes fork-to-mouth. "I'm hungry, son. I'm going down to eat. And don't you go getting no bright ideas here." She jabs a thumb over her shoulder in my direction. "She's coming with me."

I don't know if the man understands a word, but I'm sure he gets every bit of the determination in her voice and her face. He lets us by, then follows us not more than two steps behind. In the dining room, he has the decency to sit, not with us, but at the nearest table to our right.

Miss Mona walks in as my butt hits the chair. "There you are! I was going stir-crazy all by myself in that room. At least the two of you have each other."

"I'm so totally glad to see you." I pull out a chair for her. "Since you're here, and you've been all locked up, I bet you're just as hungry as we are."

She winks. "I could eat me one of those yaks."

In the end, we don't eat yak, but we do have a nice lamb dinner. Every few minutes, I check the doorway, expecting Allison, Glory, and Max to join us. But none of them show up.

Finally, when my nosiness quotient gets the better of me, I ask, "Where's the rest of our crew?"

Miss Mona looks surprised. "Didn't Livvy tell you?"

I look at my aunt. "What did you not tell me?"

Aunt Weeby gives me one of her vague waves. "The cops reckoned he didn't have nothing to do with nothing much, so they told Max he could go. He took hisself an early flight home."

I can't have heard what I think I've heard. I stick a pinky in my right ear, wiggle good, and try again. "What was that I know Aunt Weeby *didn't* say?"

165

"She just told you, Andie," my boss says. "Max was sent home. Farooq died in Glory and Allison's room, and Xheng Xhi was head over heels over you. I wouldn't leave you for the world, and Livvy . . . well, honey. Livvy's Livvy."

I don't know what's worse: the sense of betrayal or the rage I feel. I let the rage take over, since I can't deal with the other emotion right now.

"That louse!" I really am madder than mad. "That rotten, lousy, miserable rat! How could he just up and go home while I'm still here?"

Miss Mona slants me a look. "Would you stay if they said you could go?"

I hesitate the teensiest fraction of a second. "Yes! Yes, I would." I feel oh, so virtuous. "I wouldn't leave friends behind." I really wouldn't.

Would I?

Miss Mona arches an elegant brow. "I'm not so sure you're being honest with yourself. Or fair to Max."

I slump and look away. Why does she have to know me so well? Maybe better than I know myself. And that's something I don't expect. At all.

"Well," I say a couple of uncomfortable minutes later. "That's that." I take a sip of water, count to ten. I turn to Aunt Weeby. "So what did the cops tell you?"

"Tell me?" she says. "They didn't tell me much. They did all the asking, and I did all the telling. They wanted to know what I heard the night that Farooq boy died. But when I told 'em I sleep with them earplugs a' mine, they lost all interest in what all I had to say."

Believe it or not, she looks offended. I should be so lucky.

166

"How about you, Miss Mona? Did you find out anything from anyone?"

"About what? I don't know what you wanted me to find out. They're the ones who want to get to the bottom of what happened."

What's wrong with this picture? "Me too! I want to know what happened." I blow on the loose strand of hair tickling my nose. "That's what I want to find out. If you've forgotten already, they think I killed one or maybe even two people. I want to know who did the killing, and why."

That's when the Russells walk in, none of them looking happy, their cop as serious as ours.

"Hi, y'all!" Aunt Weeby calls out. "Let's pull up another table, be hospitable and all."

Once the Russells join us, the conversation turns to less intense topics. Eventually, though, we come back to the matter at hand.

"I've never been investigated before," Delia says. "It was *fierce!*"

"Oh, I agree," Aunt Weeby says. "They're tigers, those cops. They chew and chew and chew at you with more questions than a body can stand."

I roll my eyes. "I don't think she means fierce the way you mean fierce."

Delia sniffs. "Fierce is fierce. Wicked cool. What's so hard about that?"

I'm not prepared to explain the generation gap and communication issues to her. "What did they say about the crimes?"

"Crimes?" Delia's mom asks. "There's more than one?"

Miss Mona shakes her head.

Aunt Weeby tsk-tsks. "Toldja you weren't supposed to flap your trap."

"Miss Andie?" the older Mr. Russell says. "I like you, and I don't think you killed that man. So I'm going to tell you what I got from my interview. The officers were awfully interested in the swami and his men. I told them I wouldn't trust that fake one bit."

"Oh, Grandpa!" Delia cries. "That's so not fair. The swami's way cool."

"It was his guys who followed us almost all the way back to town," her grandfather counters. "What kind of religious men spend all their time following followers? And with serious guns strapped on their backs!"

I suck in a breath. "Do you mean the terrorists were part of the swami's cult?"

"Terrorists?" Delia looks thrilled.

"Terrorists?" Her grandfather looks horrified.

"Well . . . yeah. The ones with the beards and the turbans and the guns. They look a whole lot like the ones on the evening news back home, don't you think?"

Delia's grandmother gives me a pitying look—I might have just lost a major customer for the S.T.U.D. "Those were the swami's guards. They're not terrorists, Andrea."

I scratch my head, run my fingers through my hair. "Why would a swami need armed guards?"

Mr. Russell shakes his head. "Why would they follow us?"

"Did you say anything to Mr. Smith about the guards?" Miss Mona asks. "He might make more sense than the Kashmiri cops."

He shrugs. "The man sat in on my interview, and I asked him what was going on, but he didn't have much to say."

The conversation's going nowhere, and my eyelids start to droop. "Well, folks," I say. "I'm in for another dose of grilling tomorrow, and I'm ready to turn in now. I don't want to be rude, but I'm heading to bed."

Aunt Weeby stands. "Me too, sugarplum. Let's go."

Our cop joins us, and the three of us ride the elevator in silence. Once she and I are alone in the room again, I turn to my aunt. "Something doesn't smell right to me."

Aunt Weeby starts pulling pins from her updo. "I was thinking the hotel kitchen uses way too much a' that curry stuff too. I'm so glad you agree. It can't do a body good. Why, I'm thinking it's about time to break out Great-Grandma Willetta's cod liver oil."

No way! Anything *but* Great-Great-Grandma Willetta's tonic. "I love the curry!"

"*Pffft!* I can't wait to get back to real food. First thing I'm fixing to do when I get home is buy me a Whopper and fries."

She's of the same persuasion as Xheng Xhi. Which brings me back to my original point. I seriously doubt she didn't get what I meant. She does this dizzy-ditz bit when it suits her oddball purposes. I wouldn't normally try to get her back on track, but this matters.

"Come on, Aunt Weeby. Something really strange is going on. Where does Farooq come into the picture? What's his connection to Xheng Xhi? How about Robert? And who are the Russells, really?"

"Ooooh, Andie!" She claps. "I just knew it! You're gonna do some more of that investigating you did last year. But this time, sugarplum, I hope you don't go digging through ladies' purses." She wags a finger at me. "We get a mite tetchy 'bout our bags, you know."

I shudder at the memory. The day I decided to play Pink Panther, thanks to Aunt Weeby's urging, mind you, I proved just that subtle, especially when I went digging in a retired army veteran's diaper bag.

Not something you want to do. Trust me.

"No handbags will be harmed in this operation. Not by me, at any rate."

Something's still tickling my mind, but I really don't want to go there. Not with Aunt Weeby. Her nutty imagination needs no encouragement. But what choice do I have? She really is a sharp cookie, even though she does enjoy her nuttier side—and keeping everyone on their toes.

I do know to pray for courage in the face of Aunt Weebiness. "What's the one element all these strange things have in common?"

She gives her long, champagne blond hair—at her age, bottle blond, of course—a final go with her brush, then points the bristles at me. "You."

"That wasn't the answer I was going for."

"I know, sugarplum, but that's the one that fits."

She might have a point. Remember, she's sharp, if a bit wacky. "Why don't you tell me exactly what you mean?"

"Well, Andie, my girl. It's simple. You're our team leader." She ticks a finger with her brush. "You're the one what knows all about them Kashmir sapphires." Another finger. "You're the one what knew about them mines." A third digit goes up. "You're the one l'il Miss Delia recognized, and you're the one Xheng Xhi liked."

A full-hand waggle makes her point.

Time for me to make mine. "There's something else that ties it all together."

170

"I didn't want to say nothing 'bout it."

"How come?"

"On account of you might say I was letting my imagination run wild."

I laugh. "So when'd you start worrying about things like that?"

She doesn't even crack a smile. "Since last year and your awful trip to Burma."

"Myanmar."

"Doesn't make no never mind, and you know it too. It's all the same, sugarplum. You say something don't smell right to you, and I say it's all about sin and greed and those pretty blue stones."

That's the little tickle in the back of my mind. "Sapphire smugglers."

"Sounds just about right to me."

Strange. Aunt Weeby doesn't sound so wacky anymore.

After another day of questions, I return to the hotel and Aunt Weeby. We call Miss Mona and head down to the restaurant.

"I haven't seen Allison or Glory since day before yesterday," I comment. "Are they okay?"

Miss Mona unfurls her napkin and sets it on her lap. "Allison's on her way down. She doesn't want room service tonight."

I'm not crazy about having dinner with my brunette nemesis, but I can't not ask. "How about Glory?"

My boss stares down at her empty plate. "She went home."

I must not have heard right. "Say what?"

She sighs, and when her eyes meet mine, I read sympathy in their depths. "Yes, dear. She gave the embassy her address, her fingerprints, answered all the questions everybody asked her, and they said she could leave. She's gone home."

Her answer launches an internal battle, but I don't know which side's going to win. On the one hand, I'm so mad, I see red. On the other, the green-eyed monster's leapt to life again. Mix 'em together, and the colors make brown, the same shade of mud I'm trying to see my way through these days.

"Did someone forget she was sharing the room where Farooq was killed with Allison? How come she gets to go home, but Allison and I don't?"

"Hi, Andie," Allison says as she pulls out a chair to join us at the table. "Glory got to go home because Farooq had his hand in my stuff. The police don't think she would care enough about my wallet to kill the guy. As if I would kill for twenty bucks."

She looks about as worn as the saddle on the mule I rode. Come to think of it, that's pretty close to how I've begun to feel.

I scan the room and notice another absence. "Don't tell me they let the Russells go home too."

"The Russells didn't get to go home." Miss Mona takes a long drink of green tea. "They're being held over for another day. The police want them to look at some pictures tomorrow."

Am I surprised? "And would those pictures include bearded, turbaned terrorists pretending to guard some phony-baloney guru?"

She smiles. "I think they might."

I try to inject some humor into the situation. "Hey! I wanna look at pictures and go home too!" Lame, lame, lame. "Seriously, though. How's anybody going to identify those men? Put a beard and a turban on the next Kashmiri guy, and who can tell what he looked like before? It's the perfect disguise, you know."

Allison leans forward, lowers her voice. "I can see those scary men killing Xheng Xhi."

No joke. "I can see them stealing rough from the mines."

"But, sugarplum, why'd they want to kill that nice Xheng Xhi or Farooq?"

It's time to try out my looniest theory so far. "What if Xheng Xhi and Farooq were part of the smuggling ring?"

Miss Mona chokes on her water.

Allison drops her fork.

Aunt Weeby "oooohs!"

I go on. "What if the terrorists gave the stones to Xheng Xhi to get them down the mountain? What if Xheng Xhi gave them to Farooq to pass along?"

A look around the table tells me everyone's on board. I nod. "That gorgeous houseboat sees a whole lot of foreign traffic. Anyone can play tourist and take the stones out of Kashmir."

My auntie coos again. "You're so good, sugarplum. You've solved the crimes. The smugglers must've had themselves some kinda nasty fight, and then, *poof!* The guys with the turbans killed the other two. Case closed."

Just because Aunt Weeby likes my theory doesn't mean it flies. "What do you think, Miss Mona?"

"It makes a lot of sense, Andie, my dear." She takes another minute to think things through. "I suspect we all just happened to be in that age-ol' wrong place at the wrong time."

"Even the Russells," Aunt Weeby says.

I slant her a look. "I detect a touch of disappointment."

She waves. "Don't pay me no never mind. My ol' imagination plumb loves the idea of international intrigue and Interpol and the FBI. You know. So exciting. Like last—"

"Don't go there! That was *not* exciting. It was awful. It's way better to solve the problem right here in the Kashmiris' backyard. Now I just have to convince the cops to let me go."

That's exactly what I do the next day. By noon, Mr. Smith brings me back to the hotel, I grab my backpack, my great-aunt, my boss, my makeup artist, and my Coach bag. An hour later, the four of us walk into the airport, rush the airline counter, and flash ID in relief.

"The nightmare's really over," I say on my way down the airliner's aisle. "We're going home."

But you know it isn't that easy. At the insistence of the Kashmiri authorities, I sign a sworn affidavit affirming my understanding that, should they deem it necessary, I will return for prosecution. If I try to dodge, Interpol will come chase me down. To arrest me, you understand.

I'm still a wanted woman.

$12\underline{00}$

The trip home is a blur of airports and airplanes. Everyone sleeps on the flights; everyone, that is, but me. I'd hoped to let the exhaustion take over, and my body's more than willing, but my mind refuses to get with the program.

I'm glad I'm no longer under the spotlight that shines on the prime suspect in a pair of murders, but I am the prime suspect in a case of self-deception.

My emotional response to Max's flight makes me face truths I'd rather avoid. I don't just find him attractive. He's not just good-looking. And he doesn't just drive me nuts because he's dumb, since he's really not so dumb at all.

It's all about those "justs." If I *just* found him attractive; if he were *just* good-looking; if he *just* irritated me, then I'd have no problem.

My problem is that I find him attractive, appealing, intriguing, and even charming—at times. He's good-looking, decent, determined, and hardworking—not just at sports. And he drives me nuts because . . . well, just because he does. You see, I'm really and truly falling for the surfer boy.

Who'd a thunk?

My not-so-cool jealousy toward Glory springs from my feelings for Max, especially because I'm so scared of getting hurt again. I've avoided dating for years, ever since a disastrous experience in college. Back then I thought my boyfriend felt the same way I did. It turns out, my knack for science and math meant more to his grades than I did to his heart. My inability to tell the difference before I let my heart get in too deep is what scares me most.

No one wants to be used. Been there, done that. Not going there again.

What does all this have to do with Max? Max wants to work at the S.T.U.D. And that's the thing. Would he go so far as to romance me to keep his job?

That's what I don't want to face.

How mature of me!

Am I ready to . . . fall in love? *Could* I fall in love with Max?

Yes. And yes.

A better question might be whether this is the Lord's plan for my life or not. I have to believe God's brought us together for a reason. Coincidence isn't something I buy into.

I'm scared to put my heart on the line. Is my faith strong enough to let go of my jokes and snipes and superficial and totally false sense of control? Do I trust God enough to let him work in my heart? And Max's?

Do I trust him enough to catch me and patch me up again if Max breaks my heart?

And here I thought I'd faced the trust thing awhile back.

Lord? When am I going to grow up for real? I left the

baby-Christian stage behind years ago, at least that's what I thought. But now . . . this Max thing has shown me some nasty bits I haven't dealt with. Is this what it means to run the long "race" you want us to run? I guess growing up is a process that goes on forever, not something a person achieves one day.

I try—again—to find a comfortable fit in my uncomfortable airplane seat. Coming home to Kentucky hasn't turned out the way I expected. I figured I was heading for a simpler life, not so many demands, and fewer challenges. Instead, my life's more complicated than ever, and God continues to make me face things I would much rather continue to dodge for the rest of my life.

Then, while still deep in my serious thoughts, I'm back! Back in Louisville again.

Davina, the S.T.U.D. Network's limo driver, meets us at the Louisville International Airport. The girl's well over six feet, and I have to stretch up on tippy-toe to do it, but I hug her like there's no tomorrow.

"Get a grip," she says . . . minutes later. "You and your trips. You need a life, woman."

Groan! "Not you too! I traded New York for Louisville *to* get a life. What's wrong with this picture?"

Davina shakes her head. "Don't you get it? Stay home. It's all about those crazy countries."

I'm stunned. That's the most I've heard Davina say in almost a year. I suppose she does have a point. My bad experiences have all come when I've traveled to exotic places. Well, most of them. There was that horrible day when I found the vendor who was killed in the S.T.U.D. vault last year. But why quibble?

I give her a crooked grin. "How about I wait for gemstones to come to me rather than try and hunt 'em down in their native habitat?"

Davina grins.

Miss Mona cheers.

"Oh, phooey!" Aunt Weeby gripes. "What fun izzat?"

"Fun?" I wail. "How can you call it fun? I didn't have fun! Not while I was grilled like a plucked chicken over two dead guys I didn't even know. Maybe *you* should—"

Horror shuts me up. I'd almost told my crazy aunt she should try what she has just labeled fun. Can you imagine the international havoc the wacky woman could wreak?

I'm beginning to believe silence might truly be golden. "Um-hum-huh-hum-hum-humm . . ."

The others take my toneless music-making for what it is: a change of topic. On our way home, the talk turns local. Davina catches us up with what's gone on at the network during our trip. Nothing's changed, which makes me happy.

I can stand a whole lot of same-old, same-old right about now.

Since it's Sunday, and comfort, warmth, and welcome rank way high in what I want, Sunday evening's praise and worship hour at church is right up my alley. Aunt Weeby comes with me.

The familiar building, familiar songs, familiar faces, even the familiar structure of the service, soothes my dented nerves. By the time we're ready to head home, I feel almost back to normal.

Almost.

We get in my new Honda, and I drive home, a soothing Brahms CD in the player.

178

But before we've gone more than three blocks, the strident wails of a fire truck ravage the peace of the night. *Wee-uh, wee-uh, wee-uh!* Flashing lights approach in my rearview mirror, and I pull over to the shoulder to wait for the truck to pass.

Aunt Weeby reaches out and takes my hand. "Let's pray."

My aunt's typical response to someone else's distress adds to my sense of rightness. We pray for the rescue workers, the victims, everyone affected by the emergency. Once they're gone, I get back on the road.

At the house, I make a beeline for my room. Aunt Weeby, however, hits the kitchen and makes a pot of her trademark cocoa. The scent draws me back downstairs.

"It's always helped ease the ouchies away," I tell her after I take my first sip. "And you know when I need it the most."

"What makes you think you're the one what needs the cocoa?" Aunt Weeby shakes her head. "I do confess, I had me a big ol' scare in that there Kashmir hotel. I didn't know if those cops would ever let you go."

The events of the past few days have hit her hard. I put down my mug and wrap my arms around her. To my amazement, I feel her sobs under my hands. "Aunt Weeby! Don't cry. Everything's okay."

She nods, but the sobs and tremors continue. I hold her until they're gone.

With a quick swipe at her eyes, she puts on her regular, beaming smile. "Oh, don't go paying this ol' lady no never mind, sugarplum. I can't believe I doubted the good Lord for even one smidgen of a minute." She takes a shaky breath, then squares her shoulders and nods. "I confess I did. I didn't know if he'd answer my prayers for you. I'm ashamed."

Arms open wide, I stand back. "You're human. That's why the Lord forgives. And see? I'm fine! In my Tweety Bird jammies too. Nothing's wrong with our world." Let's not mention that affidavit back in Srinagar I never told her I had to sign.

"I know you're fine now, Andie, my girl. But I didn't in that there hotel in Shrin . . . Shree . . . oh, who cares what that place is called? We're home in Kentucky, and that's what matters most."

When she drains the last dregs of cocoa from her mug, I take hers and mine to the dishwasher. "What we both need most of all is a solid, long, good night's sleep. We haven't had any of that since we left home."

"You're right. I'm off to bed. God bless you, sugar-plum."

"See you in the morning!"

After a brief prayer, I fall into the deepest, most restful slumber I've known in days.

I wake up in the dark, unable to breathe from the elephant-sized weight on my chest. Another try for a breath of air brings no results.

Fear doesn't help. My heart pounds harder with every gasp. The acrid stench of smoke stings my nostrils, and I want to know what idiot has decided to light up in Aunt Weeby's house. Don't they know . . .

Doesn't the smoker know he's risking . . .

I can't breathe!

Where am I? Fool smoker's risking the wrath of Aunt—

"Smoker?" My eyes fly open, and even in the dark I see the smoke billows above me. Unless he's a chimney in humanoid form, this is no smoker's fault.

I drop off the bed, roll to the bedroom door, touch it, find it cool enough to open, and then bellow at the top of my agonized lungs. "FIRE!"

Aunt Weeby echoes my scream.

Seconds later, I've dragged myself to her room. We make our way to the window, throw it open, and suck in gulps of fresh summer air.

"Hurry!" I urge. "It's a blessing we're right above the front porch. Let's go."

"Wait!" She crawls back, to my horrified wonder, and retrieves her cell phone. "Time to use those taxes I've paid all these years, Andie, girl."

She shoves the phone at me, and I dial 9-1-1. I throw a leg over the windowsill to crawl out onto the wide porch roof, and then help Aunt Weeby do the same.

When I notice the fear and tears on my aunt's face, I know I have to come up with something goofy, and fast. I slip an arm through hers and lead her to the side closest to the drive.

I sway. "Don't we make a pretty sight out here in the middle of the night? Did you ever think we'd get to do a soft-shoe duo on the roof of the porch? So much for peace and quiet back here in Louisville."

"I'm just glad we didn't pick up our darling little Rio yet. He's safe at Peggy's."

I shudder. Even though the bird's shrieks are deafening, I couldn't stand the thought of him getting hurt.

181

Minutes later, we hear the welcome *wee-uh, wee-uh, wee-uh* we'd heard earlier while on the road. I reach for Aunt Weeby's hand again. "Let's pray."

She squeezes my fingers. "I wonder if someone's heard the siren and is praying for us."

"I don't know how many people think the way you do, but I'd like to think someone's praying."

The firefighters screech to a stop before the house. A ladder rises. We clamber down—*fast*. Controlled chaos reigns for the next half hour.

Neighbors flood the street, curiosity leading the way. Hoses fill. Water shoots into the house. Then I remember. "My stones!"

Before anyone can stop me, I rush into the parlor, determined not to lose the collection I've worked on for the last fifteen years. The sight that greets me nearly sends me rushing back outside.

A wall of flames leaps out in the kitchen, licking the dining room doorway, scorching the wood, darkening the walls, filling the air with thick, dark smoke. I cough. My eyes burn and water from the dry heat.

But I'm determined, so I go on. My gems are stored in the dining room sideboard, and I refuse to let the collection go up in flames. I rush to the furniture piece, open the drawer with a hard tug, feel the scalding heat hard up against my face. I grab the gem trays, spin, and then run for the front door.

Behind me the furnace-heat grows greater, comes closer. And that's when it hits me. For real. How stupid of me, to run in, risk my life for . . . for things. "Lord, help me, please! I don't want to die because I'm too dumb to let things go."

The stench of burning fibers fills my nose. Heat follows me, my cheeks burning, my forehead hot, my neck seared.

"DOWN!" a firefighter yells the minute I step outside, grabs me, throws me to the ground, and rolls me from side to side. "Medic, please! I need a medic here."

"Hey!" I cry. "Get off me."

The rolling doesn't stop. "As soon as I make sure the red in that hair in the back's not from fire anymore."

Aaaaack! "Help!"

"I'm trying, lady. Let me do my job."

He moves my head again on the damp grass. Something sizzles as it goes out. "Oh! Oh-oh-oh-oh-oh-oh-oh! I'm really on fire."

The guy in the yellow slicker and hat gives me a disgusted look. "You're about ten seconds too late for that. You *were* on fire. You're not anymore."

I breathe a sigh of relief, but the first thing I register is the smell of my burnt hair. "Am I bald now?"

The firefighter's disgust knows no bounds. "Not by a long shot, and more important, you're still alive and well enough to be a pain."

The first thing I see when my rescuer splits is Aunt Weeby's ravaged face. Guilt tastes bitter. I've caused her anguish one more time. Sobs wrack me.

That's when I feel the stinging on the back of my neck. Little by little, it spreads.

An EMT rushes up and within seconds begins to swab my neck, ears, temples, and portions of my scalp with cooling, soothing cloths. I know sometime in my immediate future

I'm going to look into a mirror and freak. But right now, the only thing that matters is my aunt.

The minute the medic takes a break from swabbing goo on my smarting neck and ears, I scramble to my feet and run to her side.

"Get back here!" the EMT yells.

I ignore her; I'll be blistered but fine. "I'm so sorry, Aunt Weeby. I didn't mean to upset you. I never thought—"

"What else is new?" Max asks. "You never think."

"Where'd you come from?"

He gives me a disgusted glare. "You know my apartment's only three blocks away. I was on my way home from going out to dinner, heard the sirens, saw them head this way, knew where you and Aunt Weeby live, and came to check it out."

"Dinner? It's kinda late for dinner." *Unless he went out for scorched shish kebab*, my suspicious mind wants to know.

Could Max do something this horrible?

"It's not so late," he says. "It's only eleven thirty. We got to talking, and I lost track of time."

Okay. So maybe he didn't come burn us out of house and home. Then another question zips through my head. *Who'd you have dinner with?*

But I don't ask; I cross my arms and hold myself . . . but not my runaway mouth. "Chasing a fire truck was the perfect end to your evening?" I ask before I can stop myself. "I wouldn't have thought you were the kind who'd follow sirens for kicks."

He glares. "I'm going to do you a favor and chalk your rotten attitude to the trauma of the fire."

"Don't do me any favors—"

"But he can do one for me," Aunt Weeby says, her voice again as strong as ever. "He can give us a ride to Mona's. We can't stay here tonight."

Captain Roberts from the fire department approaches, a black smudge on his chin, helmet in his hand. "That's right, Miz Weeby. You sure can't stay here tonight. The PD's on its way to investigate, seeing as we found some strange marks we want checked out on the back of the house."

Despite the low-eighties temps, a chill ices my blood. "Do you mean you don't think the fire was an accident?"

The gaunt man shrugs. "I can't rightly say yet. First things first, and that's to put out the flames. But then after that . . . that's why I'm wanting the PD to look into some things. We'll let you know what we all find."

After we give the captain our contact info, Aunt Weeby and I take one last look at our beautiful family home, then turn to follow Max.

"Don't forget your precious bling," he bites off.

I wince. "It's not so precious, but I have spent years collecting the stones. I didn't want to lose them to a fire."

"Last I heard," he says, "rocks don't burn."

"Fire will ruin a lot of my gems, but that's not the point. I'm sorry. I didn't mean to upset anyone. I just acted on instinct."

"Then your instincts aren't so hot."

"Fine. My instincts stink. Are you going to help me pick up the stones?"

He gives me a woman-you're-nuts look. Then he shakes his head and runs a hand through his blond hair. "I suppose I won't be able to get your aunt to Miss Mona's house until you find every last amethyst, peridot, and citrine."

I glance at Aunt Weeby. The fear's left her face, and a smug smile now curves her lips. On the one hand, she's not crying anymore. On the other, I'm in a whole heap of another kind of trouble here.

The great matchmaker returns. *Great.*

"Please, Aunt Weeby. Don't do this. Not now." I turn to Max. "How about you take her to Miss Mona's?" I say. "I'll get Peg to take me over once I'm done picking up my stuff."

"Are you out of your mind? I can't leave you here on your own. For all I know, you'll decide to rush the flames again for . . . for—oh, sure! That dumb C bag of yours."

I don't have the energy to snap back. "I know what I did was dumb, Max. And I'm really sorry, especially because I scared Aunt Weeby. I won't do it again, that's for sure. I don't need a babysitter."

"Want to make a bet?"

"Children, children!" Aunt Weeby chirps. "Let's all of us get along, now. How 'bout we all take the time to find the gemstones, and then we can go to Mona's together. I'll bet she has some good ol' cocoa and milk. Every one of us can use a nice, hot cup once we're done here."

Max meets my gaze. "Hot cocoa?"

I give him a wobbly smile. "Aunt Weeby's cure-all. Most of the time it works."

He shakes his head. "You two are the looniest females I've ever met. But who am I to argue? Let's pick up the rocks so we can get to the cocoa."

While we scrabble around the blades of grass on the hunt for my gems, I can't dislodge one thought from my head. Who did Max have dinner with?

I never got my answer because I never got the guts to ask. But I do find the strength to control my sharp tongue. I thank Max once we get to Miss Mona's large, faboo home. It takes no effort to sound sincere, because I am.

When Max leaves, we get the chance to steal some sleep, but the sun's rays stab in through the curtains too soon for my taste. After I take a shower and dress in one of Miss Mona's—lime green, ouch!—jogging suits, I get on the phone to the fire department. I'm sure my back-pack and purse survived the blaze; they were up in my room, and the damage was to the kitchen and below. But unfortunately for me, the house is now wrapped in yellow crime tape.

"What exactly did you find?" I ask Captain Roberts.

"I'm sorry to say, Miss Andie, the basement window was broken in. We also found traces of accelerant—gasoline—in the basement, right under the kitchen. I'm afraid that part of the house is a total loss."

My knees give way, and I plop onto a delicate gilded French antique chair. "Are you sure?"

A pause lets me know he doesn't much care for my ques-tion. "Yes, ma'am. Quite sure."

I bite down hard to keep my teeth from chattering. "How soon can I pick up my backpack? I need my wallet for ID and cash. I can't get into the house, and I couldn't wear the smoked-out clothes even if I did make it inside. Since I'm scheduled to work, I'm going to need my credit cards to get clothes that don't stink."

He sighs. "I suppose the PD will have to handle that. Why

don't you call Chief Clark? I'm sure he'll tell you whatever you need to know."

Oh, goody. Chief Clark. The man who tried real hard to pin a murder on me last year. "Uh . . . thanks, Captain Roberts. I'll follow up with the PD."

It takes me awhile to quit shaking. Who would ever want to torch Aunt Weeby's house? With us inside? And why?

My burned ear hurts where I held the phone against it. Was it worse than just arson, as bad as that is? Was it an attempted double homicide?

If so, then why? Who'd want us dead?

Will Chief Clark tell me?

Maybe. Maybe not.

At least I know the chief's not stupid enough to try to tell me I tried to kill Aunt Weeby. No one's that dumb. Especially since I was still in the house. Even he's not likely to accuse me of having a death wish.

With a sigh and another shudder, I pick up the phone again and dial the PD. I need to know. And more, much more than just when I'll be able to pick up my stuff.

"Chief Clark?" I ask once I get through the layers of voice mail. "It's Andie Adams. I have a few questions for you."

13$\underline{^{00}}$

"Whaddaya mean, my backpack wasn't there?" I yell at Chief
Clark. Then I realize who I'm talking to.

Get a grip, woman!

"Ahem." I tug at the borrowed and very large lime green
warm-up suit jacket, then square my shoulders. "I took that
backpack upstairs. I put it on my bed, took off my travel
clothes, showered, dressed, and the backpack was still there. I
went to church, came home, and the backpack was still there.
I put on my PJs, dropped the backpack on the sage-green
chaise, crawled into bed, and didn't move it anywhere else.
Of course that backpack was there."

"Livvy," the chief says—yeah, I brought my aunt for moral
support. "I know your niece and I have had us our differ-
ences before, but would you please tell the girl here I ain't
lost my mind yet?"

Aunt Weeby arches a brow and smiles.

I glare. "Don't you go dragging my poor aunt into this
argument. Where'd your guys put my backpack?"

He sighs. "Miss Andie, *you're* the one who brought Livvy

189

to the station. I'm just hoping for some common sense here. My officers haven't touched your *missing* backpack."

"Okay. Fine. I did bring Aunt Weeby. But . . . how about the firefighters? The backpack didn't go missing until the firefighters and your officers went into the house."

"Now listen here, you two," Aunt Weeby says. "How come it's not hit neither one a' you that we have us some kinda problem here?" She makes a funny face, pats a finger to her temple, and then nods. "Oh, now, that's right. You're both a' you too busy blaming each other for this brand-new kerfuffle to see what's hanging right off the tips a' your snouts."

I gape.

The chief gulps.

Aunt Weeby smiles. "Now isn't this silence so much better? We can all of us hear ourselves think. Why, maybe we'll make some sense a' what's really going on, don'tcha think?"

Ideas *bing-bing-bing-ba-bing* in my head—and they have nothing to do with Aunt Weeby and snouts. "Maybe—"

"So now we've gotten all that other *hoo-hah* outta the way," my dearest relative and best friend in the whole world goes on, "don't you go making me wrassle a real answer outta you, Donald, dear." She wags the back of four fingers at the chief. "Go on. Talk to her. It'll go much better for us all."

Sputters and coughs are the chief's response.

My smile might just remind you of a smirk.

"My, my, my, sugarplum! That look doesn't do a thing for you," Aunt Weeby says. "And you know what I always say, Andie. A girl's gotta look her best at all times. You never know when you're gonna meet the right man. And you only get yourself one chance to make a good first impression."

The chief's burst of laughter makes me blush. "Okay, Aunt Weeby. You win. You've had your fun."

"You always did have you a mean ol' streak, Livvy."

She stands, claps imaginary dust from her hands, and heads for the great outdoors. "My work here's done. The both a' you have some talking to do, so do it. And don't you go wasting any more time trying to win some silly ol' spitting contest while you're at it, either."

The slam of the door *boings* from wall to wall.

After a handful of awkward, silent minutes, the chief says, "Miss Andie. I promise you, no one here saw any backpack at Livvy's house."

"And I promise you, sir, the backpack was there when Aunt Weeby and I crawled out the window onto the roof of her front porch."

He sits at his desk. "Then I have me another job to do. I have to figure out who took that there backpack outta that burned-out house, and why."

His words make me think a minute . . . two. "You don't think . . . ?"

The chief steeples his hands. "Go on."

I shake my head. "It's too dumb."

"Give it a whirl. I'll be right happy to tell you just how dumb it is."

I give him an Aunt Weeby–arched brow. "How's this for dumb? D'you think someone could have torched the house for the sake of a stupid old backpack?"

He narrows his eyes. "Depends on what you had in that stupid ol' backpack of yours."

"It's not like I hid a brand-new pair of Manolo's in it."

The chief looks—is—clueless.

191

I roll my eyes. "Designer shoes, okay? And I was kidding."

"Let's get serious here."

"You're right." I think back to my crazy cramming and shoving version of packing back in Kashmir. "I had a clean change of undies—never know what the gorillas at the airlines'll do with your luggage. I put my purse inside so I could carry just one thing from flight to flight. Of course, I always have my toothbrush and toothpaste with me, my Bible, and I don't think I ever threw away the magazine I bought on the way to Kashmir, so it's probably still in the pack. I can't imagine who would want any of that."

He slaps his desk. "I have to agree—no offense meant. So I'll get to getting on a backpack theft."

"I suppose that'll have to do. I just hate having to jump through hoops to get all new stuff again. You know. My driver's license, checkbook and bank accounts, my credit cards . . ."

"Can't say I envy you."

We shake hands and I head out.

"*Pssst!* I'm here, sugarplum."

I hurry over to my aunt. "That was not a nice thing you did in there, leaving me with that cop-friend of yours."

"Got the two of you to quit honking and bleating and beating around the bush, didn't I?"

Honking and bleating. *Swell.* "But you didn't have to be so . . . so—" I quit while I'm ahead. Besides, she's not listening.

She's smoothing the skirt of the new dress she bought with Miss Mona while I slept, and starts walking down the hall. "Now that we've got that straight, let's go have us some fun, sugarplum."

The woman who thought an interrogation at the hands of Kashmiri police was fun wants to have *more* fun? *Oh, my!* "What do you have in mind?"

She puts her hand to her upswept champagne blond hair, sleeks a loose hair or two, and then says, "You know perfectly well we can't just go back to that house, sugarplum. We need to go house hunting to solve our little dilemma." She runs—well, trots—down the PD steps to the sidewalk. "Ooooh! I'm so excited. It's going to be such fun."

Fat chance. "What's going to be such fun?"

"Why, I can't wait to call a realtor and go look at darling little cottages. Kinda like on HGTV, you know. *House Hunters?* The show where they look at three places, and then they choose the one they wanna buy?"

I know the show, but she's lost me. For real.

I chase after her. "Aunt Weeby! You don't mean you're really buying a new house, do you? We just need to get the old one fixed. Insurance will take care of that."

She waits by the passenger door to my new car. "Why, sugarplum, nobody said nothing 'bout not fixing the old house. But it's gonna take a whole bunch of time and work to make that place right again."

I'm feeling queasy all of a sudden—Aunt Weeby's adventures do that to me. "And you're going to buy a temporary house?"

"Not a whole house, Andie. Just a bitty l'il ol' cottage. I told you that already. Lissen up, girl."

She's still not making sense. "Why are you buying this temporary cottage? Why not just rent an apartment?" See why I know I've wandered into a brave new universe? "Better yet. Why don't you just stay with Miss Mona? I'll

. . . I'll—oh, I don't know what I'll do yet, but I'll figure something out."

"Oh, I suppose I could stay with Mona. That's what she wants." Aunt Weeby looks like she's just bit into an overripe egg. "But this is for the best. Besides, the cottage isn't really gonna be for me."

I click my electronic door lock, and we open our doors. "I'm confused," I say as I slide into the driver's seat. "Who's the cottage for, if not for you?"

She clicks on her seat belt. "Why, Andie, girl. I love you more'n I can say, but it's long past time you grew up, graduated from crazy girl to grown-up lady. You're all of thirty years old, and still living at home. The cottage is for you, sugarplum. The down payment's my graduation gift."

"But I graduated college eight years ago!"

"*Pshaw!* This is a different kind of graduation. I'm talking about when you graduate from girl to woman, sugarplum. It's more'n time you get around to doing that, you know. Time to grow up came awhile ago, and you have to get to getting."

Knock me over with a feather. Aunt Weeby strikes again. Now what do I do?

No matter how many times I tell her I don't want to live alone again, Aunt Weeby digs in her heels. "I won't hear another word, Andrea Autumn Adams. And I even talked to your daddy and mama about this. We all agree. You need your own place."

"When I lived in New York," I say, "I realized I didn't like living alone. Even a cat didn't cut it. I came back to my family home. That's what I really like."

She puts on that look of hers. Come to think of it, it looks a whole lot like the one on the mule I rode in the Himalayas. I'm afraid nothing I say or do is going to change her mind. As usual.

Should I start looking for that sinking ship?

"Well, sugarplum," she says. "If you like family living so much, then it's fine time you quit being chicken and find yourself the man what'll give you that there family you say you want. And I know you won't be bothering yourself to do that while you're bunking down with me. Besides, I like to have my . . . umm . . ." She brings her brows together, thinks. "That's it! I like my *space*."

I start the car, but before I put it in drive, her cell phone rings. "Good morning. Olivia Adams Miller here."

A woman's voice crackles over the connection, but I can't make out the words. Trust me. I try.

"Oh no!" Aunt Weeby says. "You don't say."

More crackle. Then, "That's awful, Mona. Did you call Donald yet? A' course, we'll be right there. We're in the car already, Andie's got the engine cranking, and it won't take us but a shake of a puppy dog's tail to get there."

She closes her phone and holds it between both her hands, eyes shut as tight as the phone while she prays.

Curiosity nails me again. When she opens her eyes, I burst out, "Well? Aren't you going to tell me?"

"Tell you what?"

"Aunt Weeby! Miss Mona just called. You said something was awful, that she should call the chief, and that we'd be right there. Start at the beginning and go right through to where I'm supposed to drive us."

"I'm sorry, dear. It's just so strange . . ."

195

Turns out, there's been trouble at the S.T.U.D. Someone broke in, tossed the place, and the security company is there. Miss Mona and the rest of the S.T.U.D.'s employees are going through their offices or dressing rooms and desks to see what, if anything, was taken. I need to do the same.

A fire and a break-in.

Coincidence? Yeah, right.

While I don't normally have what you might call a lead foot, I'm afraid I would've wound up with a speeding ticket had a PD cruiser been anywhere in my vicinity. I made it to the studio in what felt like seconds.

My footsteps echo down the deserted halls. After a quick check, I'm pretty sure nothing's missing from my dressing room, but the same can't be said about Glory's cubbyhole. Every scrap of film she shot in Kashmir is gone.

"Why?" she asks.

No one can—or will—say. We don't know. For sure.

Yet.

Then there's the really weird one. Allison comes marching down the hall, two red spots on her fair cheekbones, anger in her blue eyes. "My makeup bag's gone! Who'd want to steal that? Even with all the jams, jellies, and potions I keep in there, it's not worth much."

"Trust me," I tell her. "Whoever took your bag didn't want the war paint."

She seems fascinated by something just over my brow line. "Uh . . . Andie? Have you looked in a mirror yet? You really have to do something about that . . . hair."

Ouch! I'd done everything possible *not* to look in the mirror after my shower. "It must be bad, if you noticed it after all"—I wave—"this."

"It's bad."

I clutch my head, pat around, and realize I have fewer clumps than I did this morning when I got up. "It didn't look too bad after my shower."

Allison turns me around. "It's really bad in the back. It must have been plastered to your head while it was still wet." She bends over to pick something up off the floor. "Look."

A Brillo-pad look-alike sits in the palm of her hand, the color somewhere between aged copper and scorched mac'n'cheese. I've scorched a batch or two in my day, so I know.

Swallow me earth! "Oh. My. Goodness. I gotta get to a salon. How much longer are we going to have to stay here?"

Chief Clark—you knew I'd have to face him again here, didn't you?—steps out of the call-in center down the hall. "You can go get yourself fixed, Miss Andie. You need all the help you can get."

I look from side to side, waiting for Max's snort of laughter, but he's nowhere to be found. And even though I'd rather not, I have to ask. "Anybody seen Max?"

"He was here when we opened up this morning," Miss Mona says. "I'll have Ruth Marie page him. Hang on a second."

Even though he's said I could leave, I hang around to listen to everybody give the chief a rundown of where they were overnight. Nothing sounds too interesting, since everyone says they were in bed. But that's what you'd expect, right?

Still, can you imagine Allison ripping off her own makeup bag, then tearing the place apart?

Neither can I.

By the time everyone's done, Mr. Magnificent is still conspicuously absent. "No Max yet," I point out.

The chief glances down the hall both ways and then pulls out his cell. "I'll be needing to check his dressing room, then. But let me ask one of my officers out there by them studio gates. He'll know if Mr. Matthews went off somewhere."

From Chief Clark's end of the conversation, I figure out it's a no. No one's seen my cohost. And I'm beginning to worry. Could he be the one who trashed this place? Is he the one who stole the Kashmir film? Allison's bag? My backpack?

Do I go back as far as the dead Kashmiri men?

He's conveniently been everywhere that matters.

I'm glad I'm not a cat—curiosity's got a chokehold on me. And worry too. I don't like to think I might've fallen for a creep. While the chief thanks his officer, I start walking. "I'll check his dressing room."

Before the chief can stop me, I'm down the hall. Max's door is open, and I walk right in, then stop. Oh yeah. He's there, all right. I scream and scream and scream.

Sprawled on the floor, Max lays flat on his back, his forehead split open by a two-inch gash. Blood muddies his blond hair, and his blue eyes are closed.

My stomach turns. My temples pound. My eyes well up. "He can't be dead," I yell at God. "He can't be. You can't do this—"

"You're giving me a headache, Andi-ana Jones," Max mumbles. "Why're you screaming?"

"Because you're dead—Whoa! You're not dead." I fly to his side. "What happened? How'd you split your head?"

He blinks. "I split my head? You mean, it's not your screaming that's making it hurt like nobody's business?" When he goes to sit, he moans and falls back again.

"Don't do that!" I hold him down. "Somebody call an ambulance!"

Allison runs in and to my side. "They're on their way. I dialed when I heard your first scream. I know I screamed like that when I found the houseboy in my room."

"God's been good this time," I say. "Max is going to be fine."

"There you go, folks. Dr. Instant-Diagnosis-Adams has it all figured out." He winces, but goes on. "Like you said, I'm still among the living. How about you let me speak for myself?"

The chief joins us. "So why don't you speak awhile, son? Tell me what happened."

Max rubs his forehead, his fingers gentle over the wide cut, then grimaces. "I'm not sure. I came to check my dressing room, and while I was going through my desk, someone walked in. I turned, but before I could see who it was, I went down, man. All I know is, it hurts."

Chief Clark takes notes. "You don't remember anything else after that?"

"How could he?" I ask. "He was still out when I walked in. Why don't you quit badgering him?"

An ambulance gurney follows a sharp rap at the door. While a pair of EMTs secure Max for his trip to the hospital, the rest of us stand back to give the professionals room to work.

On their way out, one of the medics gestures for the chief.

Okay. So it isn't the smoothest move on my part, but I have to know what's going on. I slink over, inch by silent inch, and perk up my ears.

"His pockets are ripped almost all the way out," the middle-aged woman says. "There's nothing in them."

"Aw, no!" Max moans. "They took my wallet?"

The chief gives the torn-apart room another good look. "I don't see a wallet anywhere in this mess, but I suppose it could be buried. Not likely, you understand. And Debra's right about them pants of yours. The pockets are shot."

I'm ready to go out on a pretty big, sturdy limb here. I'm willing to bet whoever's been attacking us is after a sapphire or two. From Kashmir.

No joke.

But am I ready to take prisoners out on my limb? Am I ready to embarrass myself? I'm sure I'm on the right track. Too much has happened, and it all points to those new mine sites and the smuggling that's been rumored about for years.

It's a long way from what I know to what I'm willing to share. For once, I don't blurt out my every thought. I follow the gurney down the hall, a prayer of thanksgiving in my heart. I may have my suspicions about Max, but I also have other feelings for him. I don't wish him any harm. I'm glad he's going to be fine. The sight of him makes my stupid heart go pitter-patter. And that response only grows as time goes by.

When I get to the front door, Miss Mona comes up from behind and puts an arm around my waist. "You're worried about him, aren't you?"

"Depends on what you mean by worried."

She looks confused—just a tad. "Worry is worry, Andie, dear. Max's injury looks bad, but I'm sure they'll stitch him up good. I'm more concerned about a concussion than that gash."

200

And I'm more worried about a snake in the grass . . . one that's wriggled his way into my heart.

My worry—and feelings for Max—is not something I'm ready to share with our boss, either. "A concussion's no fun."

Miss Mona makes me face her. She stares long enough that I'm sure she can see my feelings for Max. I blush. But I have nothing to say, not around the lump in my throat.

"Neither's that dreadful hair, dear." She pats my cheek. "You really have to do something about it."

"I had other things on my mind today."

"I understand." She reaches into her pocket. "Here's the studio card. Please go treat yourself. Get your hair done, buy yourself an outfit or two, shoes, a purse, some nice lotion, and makeup. You've had more than enough stress in the last few weeks than any ten women should have. And I don't want you going on-screen looking like that."

I'm tempted, really tempted. "But I drove Aunt Weeby—"

"Don't worry about her. Davina will drive us home."

Had this offer of the seemingly bottomless credit card come about a year ago, Miss Mona wouldn't have had to tell me twice. But too many things have happened since I came home. I've changed. My focus has broadened, and fashion and my looks don't take such a big chunk of my attention. The realization stuns me. Wow!

"I suppose . . . if I'm going to work anytime soon, I do have to do something about my head."

"Didn't I just say that, child?" my boss asks. "Now don't waste another minute. Go take care of yourself."

I give her a quick hug and kiss, and then head outside.

The sun's high in the sky, blazing hot, like any good Kentucky summer day. My sleek silver Honda Accord sparkles like a gleaming silver pendant.

"Like my new wheels?" I ask the off-duty police officer Miss Mona's hired to do security, as he checks out my car.

He shrugs. "Nice car. But I'm checking them all. The chief asked me to make sure nothing was taken from any of them. I noticed your door wasn't closed all the way." He reaches out. "See?"

"Strange. I know I slammed it shut"—I was pretty mad about the break-ins, both at the studio and Aunt Weeby's house—"and clicked the key chain lock. Maybe there's something wrong with this gizmo." I press the button.

BOOM!

Pieces of silver and tongues of fire fill the sky.

The earth shakes.

I stumble, scream.

Everything goes black.

14

White. Everything is blinding white. A strange buzz shimmies through my head. As if from a great distance, I hear muffled voices.

"She's waking up."

"Let's pray."

I blink, but all I see is more of the same white.

"Andie! Can you hear me?"

"Ye—" The gurgle dies in my sore throat. It hurts too much to try and push it out, so I shake my head. *Moan.*

Bad, bad idea. I know exactly how Max felt—

"Max!" The word scratches out of my dry lips. "Is he okay?"

"Isn't that sweet, Mona?" Aunt Weeby says. "She's asking about Max. I told you and told you there's more than snarling going on. Why, I'd bet you we'll be hearing wedding bells soon."

Someone chokes.

In spite of the pain, and while exiled to this weird, white

never-never land I'm in, I know when trouble strikes. Aunt Weeby's nothing if not trouble. And then some.

"No," I whisper. "No bells. Alarms don't chime."

"Aw, look." Miss Mona's voice rings with sympathy. "Poor thing's still knocked silly. She's not making any sense."

"What's so strange about that?" Max says. "Andie never makes sense."

My eyes pop open wide. "Max! You're s'posed to be hurt."

Even though my ears are ringing, and even though my head's pounding, and, yes, even though my throat and lips sting like bad sunburns, I fight for a toehold on conscious-ness. My struggle brings results, and I prop myself on my elbows.

"Hi," I say. "Why's everyone here?"

Aunt Weeby and Miss Mona rush my bed—yes, I'm in bed, and all the whiteness comes from staring straight at the ceiling above. I'm not so loopy I can't figure out I'm in the hospital.

"Don't fight so hard," Miss Mona says. "The doctors say you're going to be fine, but the explosion didn't do you any favors."

"Oh no!" I groan. "Did I lose the rest of my hair?"

"Yes, ladies and gentlemen," Max says. "She's going to be fine."

"My new car's gone, isn't it?"

"'Fraid so, Miss Andie," Chief Clark says from the foot of the bed. "It looks like my men found them an explosive rigged to go off when you used that there electronic lock."

A memory of the last thing I saw before my world blew up flies through my head. The cop next to my car . . . his hand reaching for my door . . .

"Is your officer . . ." I can't make myself put my fear into words.

Chief Clark winces in obvious pain. "He's alive. Barely."

I collapse back onto the bed. The impact pulses through every inch of my body, but I know my pain is nothing compared to what that poor man's going through. "And all because I unlocked my car . . ."

"Oh no, Andie!" Aunt Weeby places a cool hand against my hot cheek. "None of this is your fault, so don't go picking up any burdens that aren't yours to haul around."

"But—"

"She's right, Miss Andie," the chief says. "Fault lies with the animal who rigged up your new car. I know I've had to come down hard on you a time or two myself, but this time, you're all the way out in the clear. I don't think you'd blow yourself up."

His vote of conditional confidence doesn't make me feel any better. "It was still my car. He said the door wasn't closed right and went to show me . . . I clicked the lock, thinking it wasn't working right."

"That electronic lock is the most common trick to blast a car with," Chief Clark says. "And it doesn't take long to wire the thing. Where'd you park it overnight?"

I give him a crooked smile. "Out on Miss Mona's driveway. Max insisted on driving Aunt Weeby. I don't know why. By the time we left, I wasn't shaking anymore. I could have driven us over. But whoever did it had plenty of time to set it up."

From the corner of my eye, I see Max run a finger over the fat, white bandage on his head. "There's too much going on for my liking." He turns to the chief. "What have you found out?"

205

"Not a whole lot, I'm afraid." Chief Clark sends me a look. "But there's plenty I'm thinking right about now."

I raise my head again. "My backpack . . . ?"

He nods. "Seems to me, all this violent stuff is all about you."

"Hey! That's not fair—"

"Lissen me out here, Miss Andie." When I reluctantly nod, he goes on. "Nothing much happens normal-like, and then you take off to traipse through some other weird land, and *bam!*"—he slams a fist into his other palm—"we have us a truckload of destruction following you around."

"But you just said it wasn't my fault."

The chief rubs his stubby nose. "I'm not so sure it rightly is. But sure as I'm standing here, looking at you and Mr. Matthews all banged up, this is all about that there trip of yours. While you were out there, did you go messing with foreign folks' jewelry again?"

I shake my head. "No—"

Max nods. "Yes!"

"Now, Max, dear," Miss Mona says. "Andie didn't have any contact with any gemstones on this last trip. All she did was go film some empty ol' mines. I don't think that's messing with much of anything, do you?"

"I just thought of something," my cohost says. "What if she had Glory film something she shouldn't have filmed? The chief said the film's about all that's missing from the studio."

With a wriggle, I ease up again. "Allison's makeup bag's gone too."

Chief Clark reaches for the nape of his neck, looks down at the floor, and "uh-huhs." Then he pins me with another of his looks. "What else happened out in that there Kashmir?"

Max crosses his arms. "Yes, Andie. What else did happen while we were out in Kashmir? Are you going to tell the chief about Farooq and Xheng Xhi? Or do I have to do it all?"

The chief's expression turns suspicious—a familiar turn I've seen before. "What's a Far—ook or a Shen . . . Cheng . . . whatever you're talking about?"

"Why, Donald, dear," Aunt Weeby offers. "They're the saddest thing. I'm afraid they're a couple Kashmir boys gone bad. Seems they got theirselves all caught up in crime. Smuggling, I really think. Then something must've gone all catawampus between them and the rest of the thieves—you know how that goes."

She's at my side, nodding, an all-knowing expression on her face. *Oooh-oh-oh-oh!* I don't know about this. Do I cheer or do I cry?

On the one hand, the leashed, fifty-pound gorilla of suspicion is about to be sprung. On the other, Chief Clark is about to come after me again like he did before.

When Aunt Weeby doesn't say another word, the chief loses his patience. "Livvy! Get on with it, woman. What? Are you wanting me to play twenty questions on this? Or do you expect me to read that there wacky mind of yours? Tell me what you're trying to say, and tell it to me straight. And I don't want no more of them little word games of yours, either, you hear?"

She sniffs. "I've never known you to playact so dense before, Donald Clark. I'm sure you've figured it all out by now. You know perfectly well those two wayward boys got theirselves killed."

"Aha!" he cries. "I knew it. I knew there was more to this than a firebug and a coupla thieves. So which one of you's the one what smuggled out the goods?"

Not a word.

No one speaks.

No one has to say a word.

Now it all makes sense.

We didn't smuggle anything out. We didn't have to.

One of us was an involuntary mule.

Who?

". . . And Father? We really need a good shaken measure of your strength down here," Aunt Weeby says. "We're none of us a part of this here mess, but it's all come to roost on us like some sick chicken. Give Donald wisdom—goodness knows, he's got a mighty need right now—and heal Max's and Andie's hurts . . ."

"Lord Jesus," I murmur, "we thank you for your protection in all that's happened, but please bring your healing touch to that poor cop too. He had even less to do with . . . all this, and he's the one hurt the worst . . ."

"It wouldn't hurt if you provided us with some really good gemstone vendors, Lord," Max adds. "That way Andie won't have to get any more ideas for field trips."

I'm outraged. "What kind of mean-spirited prayer is that?"

"One you really need," he counters. "All your trips have done is get us a handful of good gems and a truckful of bad grief. Stay home, okay?"

"I'm not going anywhere. I'm stuck in a hospital bed. How about you? How many midnight dinner parties are you going to go to?"

"You're delirious."

"No, I'm not. Where were you—*really*—when our house went up in flames? Who eats dinner at eleven at night?"

He sputters.

"Seriously. You've been right there every time something happened. And then, just when our house looked like a Baked Alaska dessert, you showed up with some goofy story about a dinner that ran late. I think you can put our minds at ease—shouldn't be too hard. Please."

Silence stuffs the room—again.

"Well?" I ask. "Is there a good reason you can't answer my questions?"

Mr. Not-So-Magnificent-at-the-Moment seethes.

Aunt Weeby gasps. "Andrea Autumn Adams! What is *wrong* with you, sugarplum? A good ol' knock on the noggin doesn't normally knock all common sense right out a body's ear like that. Apologize to Max. Right away too."

Miss Mona lays a hand on Max's forearm. "I know she can get pretty strange at times, and her questions were awfully offensive, but Max? If I'd been burnt out of my home and had my brand-new car blown to bits too, I'd be likely to want to know where you were when the house went up in flames."

Max's cheeks turn red and he looks out the window. "I met Glory and Allison for dinner when they finished work."

"That's the big secret?" I ask. "I don't get it. Not for one minute. That's too normal. Why wouldn't you just tell us? What's the big deal? I can ask both of them, and you know they'll tell."

The red goes redder. "That's it. We went to dinner, talked for a while. Allison went home about nine or so, and Glory and I stayed at the restaurant for a while longer. We talked about the trip, working at the S.T.U.D., *you* and your fixation on rocks . . ." He shrugs. "We talked—that's it—and before I knew it, it was late. We said good night, and I went home."

Good thing I didn't let anyone know I've fallen for him. He and Glory have something going already. That's just what I've been afraid might happen. The knowledge brings on a flare of the green-eyed nasties, but I make myself tamp it down.

"As long as Allison, Glory, and the restaurant all back you up," I say, in an abundance of magnanimity, "then I have no problem apologizing for my accusation."

"Well, then," he says, his voice . . . umm . . . sarcastic—and who can blame him, *if* he's as innocent as I really hope he is, in spite of the Glory part. "Then I have no problem wishing you well and getting my sorry behind home again. I suppose you won't object to my doing that, right?"

I blush. "Just go."

As he makes for the door, the telephone on the ugly, hospital-issue nightstand rings. Aunt Weeby answers, listens, then holds it out to me. "You won't believe who's calling you, sugarplum."

My eyes still glued to Max—who's standing by the door, his back to me, hand on the knob—I reach for the receiver. "Hello?"

"Andrea!" A voice from my past bursts with exaggerated cheer. "I'm happy to hear the rumors of your death aren't true after all."

"Roger?" Is it really my old boss? The one convicted of grand theft? The one who's supposed to be rotting in jail? "Where are you?"

He takes a moment's pause. "Where do you think I am? I still have three years to serve on my sentence."

This is too weird. "And you're calling *me*?"

210

A new silence lengthens.

Max, still by the door, turns and crosses his arms.

I keep my peace.

Roger sighs. "I've always thought the world of you, Andie. You know that. I heard you were killed when your car blew up, and, well . . . I didn't want to believe it. I called the PD in that little town where you're living these days, and they gave me the number to the hospital's switchboard."

Did he call to make sure I lived? Or did he call to find out where to have me finished off? I wouldn't put anything past Roger now that I know what he and his murder-one-convicted wife are capable of doing. Freaky. Way freaky.

"As you can see—hear—I'm fine, Roger. Bruised and criss-crossed with scrapes, sure, but I'll be okay." What do you say to someone who used you and your knowledge to his illegal benefit? "How are you?"

Yuck.

He lets out a nervous laugh. "Fine, fine. Better now that I know you weren't hurt."

The false enthusiasm sets off more alarms. "I'm surprised you even heard about my car. It only just happened, and I didn't think you'd have much access to—"

I stop. What *do* you say to a con?

"I'm not in solitary, Andie. I have access to a phone. Tiffany's the one at a high-security facility. Don't forget. I never killed anyone."

"True." His trophy wife's the one who took care of that.

He forces a couple of chuckles. "I hear you've been traveling again."

Hmm . . . might we finally be getting to the reason for his call? "Aunt Weeby, Miss Mona, a couple of studio employees, and I went on a short-term mission trip to help at an orphanage in Kashmir."

"Bet you couldn't resist a visit to the mines."

I roll my eyes. Everything's getting clearer by the minute. "We shot some film of the holes in the rocks. Played-out mines don't make for exciting footage."

"But the new ones do."

There you have it. "Are you buying in to a bunch of rumors?"

"I don't think anyone gets much in the underground market for rumors these days. New Mine Kashmir sapphires? That's another story."

I've been accused, interrogated, burned, blasted, and hurt, all because of those stupid blue stones. I don't have the time or the patience for Roger's game. "If you're interested in smuggled goods, which I wouldn't be if I were sitting where you are, I can't help you. I didn't visit any new mines, real or rumored, and I don't have any Kashmiri stones. Not legal ones, and no way would I get within a continent of the illegal ones."

"Andrea!" His indignation doesn't ring true. "Where would you get such an idea?"

From your track record; you're not in jail for nothing.

I sigh. "What do you really want, Roger?"

The clock ticks about thirty seconds before he speaks. "Okay. I'm going to level with you. I hear a pair of magnificent Kashmir stones have been making the rounds. Underground, of course. Any idea how good they really are? And where they might be?"

"Even if I did, which I don't, what good would it do you to know?"

He hems and haws, coughs and clears his throat. "None.

I just . . . like to keep up with the good old gem trade. I'm not going to be here forever, and hope to set up shop again someday."

Not in this lifetime. Who'd buy a pebble from this con?

"That, Roger, sounds about as real as your ex-wife—the second one. The bleached and siliconed one who killed for a parcel of rubies and the bucks they'd bring."

"No. Really. I'm just curious. Wondered if you knew where they'd gone. But I guess you don't, do you?"

My head throbs, and I've had enough. "Goodbye, Roger. And good luck. Sounds like you don't learn the easy way."

When I cut him off, I realize that Max, Aunt Weeby, and Miss Mona are all staring. Before any of them gets a chance to speak, I say, "You heard. I don't want to talk about it. And you're all welcome to come to whatever conclusion you like best. I'm going to sleep."

I roll over on my left side, which takes some doing, since that's where they have me leashed to the IV pole but also where I'm less scraped, close my eyes, and pray for rest. "Goodbye, gang. Don't come back for a couple of hours. I love you all, but right now, I love sleep more."

The only thing I hear is the *click-click* of high heels against the hard hospital floor, followed by the soft slap of the closing door.

Peace. At last.

15$\underline{00}$

I'm the victim of a conspiracy.

Fine. You can tell me I've lost my mind. Conspiracies are the stuff of lunatics. Or so they say. But I know better.

Don't laugh. It's true. The forces of torture have come together to keep me from getting any decent sleep. Someone, and never the same someone, wakes me up every time I try.

See? Conspiracy.

How are they conspiring, you ask? Let me tell ya. About forty minutes after I kick out the Terrible Trio, a torture specialist disguised as a nurse wakes me up to take my vitals. Then, when she decides she's done poking and prodding, she offers me—get this—a sleeping pill.

"Is there any chance," I ask, "that you could let me sleep when I'm sleeping? I mean, that's not when I need a sleeping pill."

"Yu do vat I say, and I do my yob," she shoots back.

"Oh-kay. How soon can I get out of here?"

"Ask dock-torr."

My first instinct—and they're not nearly as rotten as Max says—is to pick up the phone, call this prison's business office, and threaten to cancel my health insurance company's payments if they don't spring me *now*.

But then, with my luck, they'd stick me with the minor fortune this little spree through the health care system is sure to cost. Goodness knows I can't pay it on my own. Especially not now that I have to replace my brand-new car.

I'm going to have to scrabble down deep to find any patience to exercise. The "dock-torrrrrrrrr" will do rounds at least once tomorrow. That's when I'll make my move. A move out of here, of course.

I have a creep, if not more than one, to track down.

The fire and the break-ins—plural, since I know my backpack, like the Kashmir footage, was stolen—could have been carried out by more than one perp.

Who they might be, I don't know. But I'm going to find out.

Then I sleep again, only to wake up to the "dock-torrrr" and Nurse Evil-Eye discussing my case. "Hey! I'm here. Please wake me up the next time you stop by to talk about me."

Nurse Evil-Eye gives me a know-it-all glare. "Yu said to leaf you sleep next time."

I blush. "Well, yes. I did. But you knew I wanted to speak with the dock—" I stop, catch myself before she can accuse me of making fun of her, which I really don't want to do, no matter how smart-mouthed I tend to be.

"Dr. . . ." I read his name tag. "Dr. Billings, aside from my ruined hair and a couple of burns and scrapes, I'm really okay. I'd like to sign myself out."

We waste the next nine or so minutes arguing, during

which he flashes the equivalent of a laser beam into my poor eyes, but in the end I remind both medical professionals that the law allows me to accept responsibility for my health.

The doctor sighs. "Very well, Miss Adams. I'll have the paperwork prepared. But from what I hear, you no longer have a car, and you're in no condition to drive even if you did, so you will need to call for transportation."

"Thank you. I'll call my aunt."

Aunt Weeby, of course, is aghast. She tries to talk me out of my "lunacy," but I'm determined. There's not much I can do in the hospital but steam and stew. That won't get me anywhere but into a permanent state of migraine. Dr. Billings does give me a prescription for horse-pill-sized painkillers. I'm grateful and I let him know.

In the end, it's Davina who comes to pick me up, chauffeurs me to Miss Mona's mini-mansion, and helps haul me to bed.

But before I crawl under the fluffy duvet and lay my head on the cloudlike pillows, I kneel on the superplush carpet to hook into my Andie-to-God line. I thank him for my life, for the home Miss Mona's happy to share, for the blessings I still have.

I also ask for his help in deciphering this sapphire mess.

With every instinct screaming against it, but with every scratch, bruise, and burn begging for it, I pop one of the pain pills, and in a blink or so, I zonk out.

By the time I wake up with a clear head, since I've finally rested, I know what I have to do. I grab the bedside phone and call the salon for an appointment. Clumpy, Bozo the Clown hair went out of style a long time ago.

And I need a measure of normalcy to carry on.

Think about it. We go on a missions' trip. But somewhere along the way, Miss Mona changes it to a business trip, one where we plan to film legendary mines. Who shows up?

Yep. Max does.

Two Kashmiri smugglers get snuffed out. Why?

Because there are Kashmir sapphires involved.

Who leaves the scene of the crime, so to speak, the minute he can flee the scrutiny and the heat?

You got it: Max.

Who's lurking in the fire's background? Max.

Who's on-site for the burglaries? Max.

All right. You have a point. I don't know that I believe he bashed his own head. But let's not get hung up on that detail, since there's also the bombed car. And who was on-site for that too? Max again.

You do see the light at the end of my California gem-dunce surfer boy nightmare tunnel, don't you? I'll finally get to ditch the gemologically uninformed cohost. Yeah, the one cozying up to Glory at late-night dinners.

Once he's gone, the pain pills better work on heartache.

Garbed in another of Miss Mona's warm-up suits, this one lilac with fuchsia racing stripes down the sides of the legs—*shudder*—I hit the salon and leave the rest of my home-fried frizz on the cutting floor. To my surprise, the short-short cut looks over-the-top chic.

My next stop is Macy's—a girl needs something to wear other than a senior citizen's workout wear. Forty-five minutes later, in a pair of tailored, soft-gray linen slacks and a pale gold silk top, I begin to feel more like myself. I'm happy to recognize—again—how much confidence nice clothes can give you.

217

Then I head to Miss Mona's to use the phone—my cell's with whomever pinched my backpack. No one should be at the Latimer home right now, so I won't have to worry about sneaky eavesdroppers. The Daunting Duo decided at breakfast that, in order to feel themselves again, they have to—*have* to—hit the flea-market circuit for the day. How junking can possibly help, I'll never know. But, since it works well into my plans, I can't complain.

You see, I'm about to dance the fine line between creative evasion and perjury. Why, you ask? To investigate Max's past once and for all.

Armed with the gem-dunce's bio and a brand-new yellow legal pad, I call the police department in Podunk-in-the-middle-of-nowhere, Missouri, where Max used to read the weather for the local TV station.

I launch my spiel. "Hi. This is Autumn Adams with the S.T.U.D. Network. Because of a number of unfortunate events, we're investigating the backgrounds of all our current and former employees. I need a copy of Mr. Maxwell Matthews' criminal record—arrests of any sort, complaints filed. You know the drill."

The silence on the other end makes me wonder what kind of blunder I've made. "I'm new at this," I add. "So if I need to fax something to you, please let me know."

"We don't normally do things this way, but since I remember Mr. Matthews from when he reported our weather here, and I know he has no record, I don't have a problem telling you that over the phone."

"Oh." I can't stop the disappointment from leaking into my voice. "I see. No record? No speeding tickets? No parking violations? No murder convictions?"

The answer is a very final click.

After four more tries with the same results, I come to a reluctant realization. Unless our Max has assumed the identity of the über-law-abiding and ultra-boooooooring real Max Matthews, the guy's clean as the proverbial whistle. Four police departments; no issues.

I get nothing on him. Zero. Zip. Zilch.

If past performance predicts future action, then Max isn't our perp.

The half of me that feels a heart tug every time I see him rejoices. The half of me that's desperate to find the creep who's terrorizing us groans. I have to dig deeper, cast a wider net to come up with other potential smugglers-cum-arsonists-cum-vandals-cum-killers and bombers as well.

I'm starting to believe I'm not going to find them within the S.T.U.D. family. So who, if not one of ours? The Russells? If I remember correctly, they're from somewhere out west. I can't see one of them zipping cross-country to wreak havoc in our lives . . .

Now that I have to consider that, I'm not thrilled to note it's time for me to head in to the studio. I have to get together with—who else?—Max so we can plan our first post-Kashmir show.

First, though, I'll have to call for a rental car. I do need wheels, even to hit the car dealerships as soon as my insurance claim is approved. Isn't it awesome when car-rental companies pick you up wherever you're stuck?

After I drop off my rescuer back at his office and while there, sign the million papers for the rental contract, I head to the S.T.U.D., where my new hair creates a sensation.

Allison's eyes go huge. "Oooh, Andie! I love it. Of course,

we're going to have to play around with your makeup to make the most of your cheekbones. You're going to look faboo!"

"The camera's going to love you." Hannah, my usual camerawoman, narrows her eyes and tilts her head to get a better look. "Oh, yes. This is nice. You should have cut it sooner."

"Sure thing, Hannah." I wink. "Next time you think I need a makeover I'll call the local arsonist and have him do his thing. Just for you."

Hannah laughs. "That's not what I meant, and you know it, you brat."

"Okay. I'm a brat. But I'm a live brat." Memories of the fire and the bombed car will take time to fade. "One that thanks the Lord for his mercies, but also one that has to get to work. Anybody know where I might find Max?"

"I saw him wandering the halls earlier," Marcie, our kitchen specialty host, says. "But that was hours ago. You'll have to look for him. I think his SUV's still in the lot."

Figures I'd have to hunt him down. "See ya!"

I run into my dressing room, turn a blind eye to the mess still strewn where the vandal threw it, drop my purse—a beautiful new, plain-leather non-Coach one—on my desk, and walk back out. As I head down the hall, I hear a too-familiar *craack* coming from the direction of Mr. Magnificent's dressing room.

The door's not fully closed. I go in. "Hey! We're supposed to plan a show, not whack golf balls. Miss Mona's gonna just love it if you blast out one of your fancy-schmancy sound-proof windows."

His eyes bug out. "Andie? Is that really you?"

I roll my eyes. "Who else would I be? Do I look like an alien life force who dropped down onto your poor banged-up head?"

He touches his bandage. "That pain might not be so bad. I'm sure the alien wouldn't have such a smart mouth."

"I'm not going there."

But neither is he going to work. Instead of joining me so we can check inventory, he drops another golf ball on his Astroturf putting thingamajig, fixated on his game.

He does his foot-to-foot-to-foot pre-swing wiggle, taking his time to aim.

"Didn't you hear me?" I ask. "We have a show to plan. Not Tiger Woods to beat."

"You don't know when to stop, do you?" he says, his words crisp and short, his tone controlled. "Give me a minute. I only have another two balls, and then I'll go with you to the vault."

"Don't you think that after all that's happened, we might have a bunch of other things to do after we plan the show? You know—things to do, places to go, problems to solve? You lost your wallet too, so we both have to take care of that. Maybe we can hit the license bureau together—"

WHAMMO! He lets loose with more oomph than he should have. The ball misses the contraption rigged up to simulate the hole in the green, but hits his desk with a sickening *thud*, leaves a dent in the wood, and then bounces back to roll to a stop at my feet.

"Good work," I murmur.

"I'd like to see you do better, especially with a pest buzzing at your ears."

"I don't have time for games."

He crosses his arms and gives me a head-to-toe stare. "I bet you can't hit the ball if you try."

I slam my fists on my hips. "Is that a dare, Matthews?"

"Take it any way you like, Andi-ana Jones."

Something tells me I'm asking for trouble, but I've yet to make myself let a dare go unchallenged. "Give me the stupid club. How hard can it be to hit a dumb ball with a steel stick so it plunks into a hole in the ground? Little kids play golf all the time. I've seen them when I drive by the course."

"Go for it. After all, it's only child's play." He laughs. "But if you can't hit the cup, then you owe me."

Whoa! That didn't figure into my calculations. "What exactly do I owe you?"

"A snipe-free work environment would suit me just fine."

I suck in a toe-deep hard breath. It's not that I don't want to pay up should I lose; it's more a matter of whether I *can* control my tongue should he win.

God? Are you behind Max's dare? I never thought you'd use a dare to get a point across . . . and we both know I have major issues with my outta-control mouth.

I've known God to use the oddest means to get my attention in the past. *Gulp.*

That's when Max seals my fate. He sticks his hands in his armpits, flaps his elbows, does a bent-knee waddle, and clucks. "Not up to the challenge, I see."

His superior tone and the outrageous chicken taunt are more than I can take. "Give me that club."

"Gladly."

Club in hand—it weighs a whole lot more than I expect it to—dread swirls into my gut. It's not the swinging part or the hitting part that scares me. It's the getting-the-ball-in-the-hole part that inspires sudden respect.

But it's too late to back off. "Here goes," I say in my chirpiest, perkiest voice.

I swing the thing back and forth a little, just to get an idea of how it works. Then, because I haven't seen a golfer who doesn't do the pre-whack wiggle, I step from one foot to the other a couple of times. Once I think I've got the hang of the club and the wiggle, I look at the hole ten feet away, at the ball, at the flat end of the metal stick, and back at the hole.

Golf's all about aim, I realize. And coordination. Aim, I think I can handle. Coordination should be a cinch; I've never been a klutz.

So with a quick plea for heavenly help, I swing the club over my shoulder and haul off with all my strength.

"NO!" Max yells. "That's too hard—"

Bing! Bing-bing-bing! Bing. Bing. Bing—whomp.

To my horror, the ball, after ricocheting from every possible wall, ends its voyage with a spectacular death. It cracks right down the middle, and the two halves thump to the floor. I don't dare look at the holes I'm sure I've put in Max's dressing room walls. A couple of hours' worth of puttying, sanding, and painting are in my future thanks to my pride.

"I'm sorry, Max."

He looks ceiling-ward and shakes his head. Then he laughs. "No more snotty comments, okay? You lost. Fair and square."

I swallow. *This isn't going to be easy, Lord. I'm going to have to take the time to think before I open my mouth. Come to think of it, that's what I'm supposed to do, isn't it? Every time. Oh, help me, Father. I'm supposed to be an adult, after all . . .*

An adult who put a bunch of holes in a bunch of walls. Plus one busted golf ball. Time to clean up. Literally.

I go pick up the ball, but before my hand makes contact with the rubber pieces, I catch sight of something wonderful. Something horrible. Something so unexpected, that I freeze.

"Max?" I whisper.

"What's the matter now? Losing's that hard for you?"

"You're not going to believe this. Come here."

When he reaches my side, I point.

"What's that?" He reaches for the foreign objects embedded in each half of the ball's innards.

"Don't!" I grab his hand. "*That* is what it's all been about."

His eyes meet mine. We stare at each other. His hand turns and clasps mine. He shakes his head.

I nod.

We both look down again, hold our breaths for a second . . . ten. Then, slowly but deliberately, he nods too. "That's what it's all about."

I squeeze his fingers then drop back to sit on my heels, my eyes never leaving the remains of the ball. The long breath I take doesn't do much to calm my nerves, but I do know what we have to do.

"Call the cops."

16<u>00</u>

"Guilty!" I belt out the minute he hangs up. "I knew it. You're the one."

"What?" he asks, confused. "Are you nuts? What are you talking about?"

My heart cries, *"No, no, no! He can't be."* The evidence makes my head say . . . maybe? "That, Max Matthews, in case you choose to pretend you don't know, is a pair of fifty-plus-carat sapphires, and since we were in Kashmir, then I'd say that's where they're from. That's also your golf ball. True, it's no longer much of a ball, split down the middle, but what you see is what you get."

He runs a hand through his hair. "That bomb that took out your car must have turned your brain into scrambled eggs. Do you think I'm that dumb? Do you seriously think I'd risk playing with a golf ball stuffed with world-class sapphires?"

I've got to press him, see if guilt does make him crack—even though I hope he doesn't. "Who knows? You could have mistaken it for an innocent ball. Then, when it cracked down the Kashmir-sapphire-in-the-golf-ball middle, you realized you goofed, and now want to backpedal for all you're worth."

"You're crazier than I thought." He gusts out a breath. "I'm getting Miss Mona, your aunt, Allison, and Glory in here. They were all there, in Kashmir, for every minute of the trip, with us. They'll vouch for me. I never had the time to stuff a ball with anything."

I cross my arms, tap my toe against the floor, and tamp down the fear. What if I am right? "Go ahead. Call them. The evidence speaks for itself. I'm waiting for the chief."

One call each, and Allison runs into the dressing room. "I'm here," she gasps for breath. "What's going on?"

"Look," I say, pointing to the ball. "There's the cause of all our grief."

She looks from Max to me. "A golf ball? What's up with that?"

"That," Max says, "is Andie having a breakdown. She took a whack at the ball with my golf club, broke it, and found sapphires stuck inside."

Allison drops to her knees. "Those dingy things are sapphires? No way! If they are, they're the ugliest sapphires I've ever seen."

"That's because they're all smeared with glue," I say. "And I'm not having a breakdown." I point. "That, Allison, is Max's golf ball."

"I know. He's the only golfer—besides Tanya—around here. But how'd the sapphires get inside the ball?"

I give them a smug smile. "That's the multi-multimillion-dollar question, isn't it?"

Allison looks from my cohost to me. "Oh. I see what you mean. His ball, his . . . sapphires?"

"Well, it's his ball, but I suspect the sapphires belong to the government of Kashmir."

"The sapphires those men died for."

"Um-hmm . . ."

Max looks scared—for the first time ever. "Where's Miss Mona? Aunt Weeby? They won't believe this garbage. They know me better than that. I didn't have time to get involved in some kind of international smuggling ring while I was in Kashmir. They'll vouch for me."

"They went junking." Which might be for the best, since they're both crazy about Max. "And you wouldn't have had to get involved in international smuggling while you were in Kashmir. You would have done that here, before you set foot on a plane. Besides, I don't know if I'd trust Aunt Weeby's and Miss Mona's judgment when it comes to you. Older women are known to fall for"—if he's guilty, this'll be the breaking point—"younger con men."

"I'm not a con man!"

His indignation looks pretty real to me—thankfully.

"Why'n't you tell me all about that there con man bidness, son?" Chief Clark drawls, suspicion in his gaze. "What's going on here? Why'd all y'all call this time?"

"Look!" I point. "Remember how you and I agreed the fire, the break-ins, and the bomb were all about Kashmir? There's the proof and the reason for everything that's happened."

Chief Clark, guilty of a less than razor-sharp image, saunters over to the busted golf ball, goes down on one knee, stares, then scratches his chin. "You'll have to excuse me, Miss Andie, but I can't rightly say I understand. What's a bad golf ball got to do with murder and all the rest?"

Max squats down at the chief's side. "Those things in the middle of the ball are—"

"Those are sapphires," I say. "Ridiculously big and valuable Kashmir sapphires."

The chief loosens his tie, then shakes his head. "If them ugly things are sapphires, then I sure as sure don't get what all the trouble's been for."

"The trouble's been about the money these stones will bring when sold," I say. "Trust me, they're beautiful stones. What you see is the glue the thieves used to hold the two halves together with the stones inside. That much glue is overkill. It spread all over the stones. That's what makes them look so bad. Once they're cleaned up . . ."

He shakes his head. "I'm going to have to take your word for it, 'cause I'm not seeing no beautiful stones. All's I'm seeing is some dirty lumps in there. And you're saying Mr. Matthews here put them sapphire rocks in the ball?" He swings to stare at Max.

I glance at my cohost, wince at the anger in his expression. I'm coming to the certainty that he's innocent, but I have to know the truth, and he did have control of the contraband. "I don't know for sure if he put them inside the ball or if he just picked up the ball to smuggle the sapphires out of Kashmir."

Allison comes over for a closer look. After she's stared at the remains of the golf ball, she says, "You know? I don't think Max is responsible for this. Wouldn't it have been just as easy for someone to slip the 'fixed' ball into his gear? So that someone here in the U.S. could pick them up—you know, like in a movie. Max didn't exactly hide his sports stuff during the trip."

228

"That," Max says, his voice bright with relief, "is what happened. It's obvious."

Chief Clark shakes his head. "Not to me, it ain't so obvious."

Impatience flashes across Max's face, but I have to give him credit. He smothers it right away.

He answers in a controlled voice. "The native guide who was murdered spent hours asking me about football and golf and a whole lot of other American stuff—you know, McDonald's and Wal-Mart. Well, those two, he asked Andie, but he wanted to know everything I could tell him about sports. I taught him to toss a football and loaned him my club and balls. It's not as if I kept my gear in hand every minute I spent in Kashmir."

The chief scratches his chin. "So you're telling me you made friends with a man who was killed because of them sapphires." He shakes his head. "I can see where Miss Andie's coming from."

Max clenches his fists. "You have to know that the man only came over to me after 'Miss Andie' sent him. He started out asking her his questions—he had a huge crush on her—and she got tired of answering. That's how I wound up as the guy's expert on all things American."

"So he liked her and he liked your toys," Chief Clark says. "I don't see no sapphires in that picture."

Mr. Magnificent glares at me. "Maybe Andie's the one who wanted the sapphires. She collects gemstones, you know. Maybe she and the guy agreed to stash the stones in my things so she could get them here without being the one to smuggle them out."

Huh? "But—"

"Yes, Miss Andie." The chief swings toward me. "How 'bout that? You've been the target of all the trouble what's followed you here from that there Kashmir place, more'n Mr. Matthews. Maybe all your smuggler friends want to take you out so's they can keep the dough they get from them stones for themselves."

I snort. "Oh, right. I want the stones, but I call you the minute they show up, right? Like you like me all that much, and believe every word I say. Wouldn't I have—oh, I don't know—conked Max with his club and run off with the stones?"

Max slaps his thighs and laughs. "There you have it, Andie. Wouldn't *I* have conked *you* with the club and run off with the stones? Your logic just fell apart."

"I would never hit you with a golf club."

"And I'd hit you?" he asks. "Don't you think I'd have bopped you with a club before this if I were going to do it at all? You've done nothing but shovel grief my way since I walked into this place. Of course, I'm innocent. You just proved it."

Allison heads for the door. "I'm done. I wish you two would quit arguing. It's boring and it doesn't help. I don't think either one of you has the sense to steal the stones in the first place, much less become smugglers—successful ones. You're too busy thinking up ways to outdo each other."

The chief pulls a plastic bag from his pocket, grabs the golf-ball halves, and stands. He sighs. "I hafta agree with her. You're both too busy bashing each other to have the brainpower left to think something like this out. I'm thinking you're neither one of ya guilty. Ya don't have the sense of a flea on a dog's behind."

He leaves.

Max and I hem and haw, and a few seconds later, I clear my throat. "You . . . ah . . . and Chief Clark might have a point. Since I didn't do it, and I didn't try to snuff you out, and you didn't try to snuff me out when you had me all alone in your office . . ."

To my surprise, he laughs. "Don't ever let anyone accuse you of being logical. You're seriously lacking in that department."

"Hey! I thought you wanted a snipe-free work environment."

He crosses his arms. "I believe the agreement was for *you* to watch your mouth. There was nothing about me and mine."

"Oh, now that's a noble attitude. Hogtie my mouth, and give yours free rein."

His smile spreads from ear to ear.

Easy, Andie, easy. He's been on the receiving end for a long time. "That's sooooo mature, Matthews. But I will rise above it all. I will focus on what really matters. Who smuggled those sapphires to the S.T.U.D.?"

"It wasn't me, and I'm going to give you the benefit of the doubt, so I'll say it wasn't you."

"You know it wasn't Miss Mona or Aunt Weeby, either."

"You didn't have to say it." He laughs. "Who'd ever imagine them as international thieves?"

We both laugh—surprise, surprise!

He goes on. "There's nothing to suggest Allison had anything to do with it, and the same goes for Glory. She hasn't even been around. She'd scheduled her vacation before we left, and she's only come by the studio to drop off the film— that got stolen. I can't see anyone smuggling a fortune in jewels and then dumping them."

231

I shrug. "That makes about as much sense as suspecting me."

"Agreed." He taps his fingers on the top of his desk. "So where do we go from here? Who slipped the ball into my gear? Who had the opportunity? And who would have a chance to pick up the goods on this end?"

Thoughts buzz through my head. "If we do the TV-cop thing and check out means and opportunity, then we do have some other possible culprits."

"Who?"

"I know it's a little far-fetched, but the Russells went everywhere we did during the whole trip. And you heard Delia, her mother, and grandmother. They all want sapphires."

"True." He doesn't sound convinced. "Which one do you think might have done it?"

I study my cuticles. "Truthfully? None of them."

He sighs. "So why'd you bring them up?"

"Because it doesn't matter whether I think they did it. What matters is whether they did or not."

"And how do you plan to find out? Do you even know where they live? Is there any way they can pick up the stones here? Or are you saying they have a connection with someone who could?"

At least he reached the same conclusion on his own. He can't accuse me of leading him there. "That might be the link."

But then he hits the same snag I do. "Who's the contact?"

"What? Do I have to figure it all out by myself?"

"No, but you at least have to try to stay on the side of logic. As a start, let's figure out where the Russells live. That might help."

"How do we do that?"

He chuckles. "Are you trying to tell me this is your first time at this?" His voice has a hint of taunt to it. "Don't you remember last year? The FBI and Interpol came to call when you were involved—"

"Hey! You weren't exactly a distant bystander, either."

A shrug. "Fine. *We* were involved in another international gem heist. Don't you think Chief Clark's already called in the big guns?"

I have a lightbulb moment. "Oh! I don't think I ever told the chief about the Russells."

"No time like the present."

When I get through, the chief confirms Max's thought. "I been on the horn with the Bureau, Miss Andie. You'll be hearing from 'em and maybe others," he says. "The agent I spoke to seemed to know about them Russells but didn't give 'em much importance. They're from Oregon somewhere. Not likely they'll be heading this way to pick up the loot, ya know?"

Figures. The West Coast's notorious for woo-woo faith, and the Russell women fit the bill. But they are too far, as the chief says, to pick up the loot. "They might have a local contact . . . Oh, well. I'll wait for the call."

Max walks to his window, stares out, humming a toneless drone of sound.

"Okay," I say minutes later when it gets on my nerves. "Spit out whatever you're stewing in that head of yours."

He turns, and I immediately read the excitement in his gaze. "Something occurred to me when you said you'd be waiting for a call. I suppose the chief meant from the FBI or some other government group, but it made me think of another phone call. One I don't know if you remember."

"The car bomb didn't give me amnesia."

"Never said it did, but you did get hit pretty hard by the fire and the bomb. You also had a good brew of meds in you, and I wouldn't be surprised if your memory's not at its best."

I think back through the events of the past few days. The fire . . . the burglaries . . . the bomb . . . the hospital—

"Roger!"

"You got it."

My mind goes into overdrive. "He did everything but tweeze out of me what I knew about smuggled Kashmir sapphires."

He raises his brows but only says, "That's what I got from your end of the call."

"Do you think that idiot's still trying to wheel and deal from behind bars?"

Max shrugs. "Wouldn't be the first time it happens. Mafia types do it all the time."

I snort. "Don't go giving Roger more credit than he's worth."

"He might not be the mastermind, and he didn't steal anything himself, but he's crooked enough and connected enough that he might be involved. Maybe he was the message go-between for the mastermind and the boots-on-the-ground thief."

Anger simmers in my gut. "This is personal now. First, he takes advantage of me for years, then he and his bimbo wife set me up to take the fall for stolen rubies and a murder, now I'm sure he set this sapphire gig up too."

"So call the feds. They need to know."

"Forget the feds. I'm going to New York."

"You're going to New York? But he's not work—"

"No, Max. You don't get it, do you? I need to look him in the eye. I'm going to visit Roger in jail."

"You're not going alone."

"Fine." I sit at his desk, boot up his PC. "Do you want a window or an aisle?"

By ten o'clock the next morning, we're pulling into the parking lot of the correction facility where my former boss has lived since he was picked up for grand theft not quite a year ago.

Max and I go through embarrassing pat-downs; we answer six million questions about our reason for visiting—I ask a few of my own, but get nowhere—and eventually, when all the powers-that-be decide neither Max nor I are going to slip Roger a file or anything, they let us through to a visiting room.

The twenty minutes that follow are nothing if not the definition of surreal. The visiting room is outfitted with the glass window panel of movie fame. Roger shuffles in, led by a guard and dressed in the ubiquitous prison-orange jumpsuit. He sits in the metal chair on his side, and I wait for the canned music to swell in the background. It doesn't.

"I'm surprised to see you," Roger says.

"Don't think this is a social visit. I have questions for you." I lean forward, prop my elbows on the counter. "What's the deal with the sapphires?"

"What deal?" His voice strikes me as a bit tight and too innocent. "What sapphires?"

"Come on, Roger. I'm no fool. You might think I am, since I trusted you for years, but I don't anymore. They didn't stick you in here for being a Boy Scout." I draw a deep breath.

"Who's supposed to pick up the smuggled sapphires? And why have they been terrorizing my family and me?"

He blinks, and if I weren't watching him so closely, I might have missed the slight tremor that shakes his hands. "I'm supposed to know this? I'm in jail, Andie. I don't have the kind of contacts I once had—"

"Stop!" My yell yanks the guard to his feet. He gives me a look full of menace. *Oooops!* "Sorry, sir."

I turn back to Roger. "I haven't forgotten your call to the hospital. You wanted to know all about a pair of spectacular sapphires—smuggled goods. Well, they've been found, and they're in the hands of the authorities. So go ahead and tell me you don't have contacts."

Roger does the backpedal better than most. But I no longer buy the act.

"Well," he says, his voice booming and—too—jovial, "I do have friends, but I don't know anything about any smuggled sapphires, not beyond what I said. I heard there were stones making the rounds of the underground gemstone market." His chair squeaks as he leans back. "So you 'found' them. How can you try and say I had anything to do with them when you're the one who knows all about them?"

I glare. "The ring-around-the-rosy of the underground gemstone market, huh? Is that how come they arrowed straight from Srinagar to the U.S. without any detours?"

This kind of thing goes on for the rest of our time with Roger. Even Max can't get a thing out of the liar.

Finally, frustrated beyond belief, and well aware of the time of our return flight, I stand. "I know you're not so disposed, but I hope you decide to tell the truth pretty soon. A spotlight will hit this theft any day now, and I don't think you'll look too good when it catches you in the thick of things. I doubt you want anyone adding more time to your sentence."

He blinks, and that's when I know he knows. But that's when I also know I won't get another thing out of him. "Have a great life, Roger. Enjoy the luxury. It is your choice."

Max and I head back outside, and the sunlight nearly blinds us. He turns to me. "You were right. The light will shine on this mess. If I were Roger, I wouldn't want it on me and my sins."

I sigh. "There's nothing more for us here. Ready?"

"Sure. But I don't know what for."

"For whatever comes next. Any ideas?"

17<u>00</u>

Hours later, once we've landed in Louisville and are in Max's SUV on the way to Miss Mona's house, I turn in my seat. "There must be something in the film."

"It doesn't matter, now, does it?" He clicks on his right turn signal. "It's gone."

The master of the obvious. But I don't say a thing—there's that dare I lost . . . and the memory of Max doing his chicken dare. Instead, I stick to the sapphires. "Do you think Glory might remember something . . . oh, I don't know, odd in those clips?"

He lets out a bark of a laugh. "Tell me what about that trip wasn't 'odd'?"

I chuckle too. "Okay. You're right, but I think it can't hurt to talk to Glory. Maybe if we all put our heads together, we can figure this out."

"Go ahead. You have a phone. Ask her to meet us at Miss Mona's house."

Glory agrees to join us in a half hour, certain she doesn't re-member anything more than barren landscape and rocks.

Then my dentist's drill of a mind goes back to my un-answered questions. "Shouldn't we make sure the Russells aren't anywhere around here? Just because they're from Oregon doesn't mean one of them isn't waiting here for the stones. They were hanging out with that nutcase swami and his friendly goons. I can see them all in the thick of the sap-phire smuggling scheme."

"And just how do we go about checking them out?"

"*Bingo!* I hate not having the right to ask for answers I want!"

He howls. "This is one of your most honest moments ever, Andi-ana Jones. But I think you can start by siccing the chief on that. I'm sure he'll be happy to connect you to potential perps."

"That's what I mean. I'm not official or anything like that."

"Go ahead. Call him. Remind him of the family connec-tion. Get your answer, or else you'll keep us going in circles until our boogeyman leaps up from the shadows and really takes you out."

I snort and dial. "Wouldn't you just love that? You'd be done with my smart mouth."

Chief Clark takes my question and suggestion to track down the swami-silly Russells as he does anything I say: first with skeptical silence, then reluctant acceptance.

"Fine, Miss Andie. I'll have them feds check out the flights from JFK to Portland and Louisville too. But if they ain't there, they ain't there. And if they're in Portland, they're there. Ya hear?"

"I hear."

After I hang up, the silence in the car thickens, grows

heavy, uncomfortable. Max turns a corner six blocks from Miss Mona's, and then shoots me a serious look. "I wouldn't want anything to happen to you, Andie. Not even when you're being your brattiest-pest self."

His voice rings with sincerity, even the swipe. I look at him, and the glowing light of the sunset outlines his profile. His good looks take my breath away, but what really hits me hard is his rich voice, what he says.

He glances my way and catches me staring. "I know you put up this tough-cookie smart-mouth front whenever you're scared or when things come too close to make a difference, but I've also seen beyond that. I've seen your love for Aunt Weeby and Miss Mona, the kids in Kashmir, and you do love the Lord. There's more to you than the mouth and attitude, and I want to get to know it better. I mean it, Andie. I'd do anything to keep you safe."

"Th–thanks." No smart-mouth answers this time, and I still can't look away. He, however, does, and fixes his gaze on the road.

"You do know we have to talk," he adds. "For real. After all this craziness is over."

"Mm-hmm . . ." Yep. He got it right back in his office; I'm chicken. I don't dare say more, but I know I'll have to. I owe him that much. But he's also right; this isn't the time. We have a puzzle to solve. And I can't handle the intensity of the moment under these circumstances.

What to do? What to say? Oh. Well, sure! There's this minor matter . . .

"Hey, Max. I just remembered I left my rental at the S.T.U.D. parking lot. I have to get it, or I won't have wheels for tomorrow."

"It's seven o'clock. I don't think anyone's there."

I'd lost track of time. By now, not only had Tanya's show finished, but the studio had also started up the prerecorded programs with the auto-order phone system. "I don't need anyone to be at the studio. I just want to pick up my car from the parking lot."

"Oh, all right." Talk about dragging your feet! "We'll detour. Go ahead and call Miss Mona. I don't want her and your aunt to worry when we're later than they expect."

He does have all those redeeming moments, you know.

I call, and then, as a courtesy, give Glory a heads-up too. Plus, because it makes sense, I give Allison a ring. I tell her about the Kashmir trip postmortem we're having and ask her to join us. "Who knows who'll remember what when we all get together? But give Max and me about twenty minutes to get to Miss Mona's. He's taking me to pick up my car at the S.T.U.D. first."

When I click my phone shut, an awkward silence fills the car. Once he pulls into the parking lot, I jump out. "See ya at Miss Mona's."

"Drive carefully. No one's going to care if you're a minute or two late."

"Oh, don't worry. I'll be fine."

I hop into my little rented Saturn, turn the key, and flick on the AC. It's hot in Louisville in late August, folks.

Max honks and waves as he turns out of the parking lot. I pull up to the stop sign right behind him, then wait for a plumbing rooter van that zips past me and pulls up behind Max. I follow, but get caught by the first red light.

A couple of blocks later, as I turn onto the semi-rural road that leads out to Miss Mona's new subdevelopment, I glance in my rearview mirror. The black Hummer framed by my back window first showed up at that initial red light. Ten minutes later, it's still with me. Unease makes the little hairs on the back of my neck pop right up.

I hit the gas.

The Hummer does the same.

I slow down, edge over to the right to give the guy a chance to pass, but to my horror, he speeds up.

"NO!" I hit the gas again, but it's too late.

He rams the rear of my rental with his huge fender. My little car bounces on the shoulder. The rumble strips rattle my teeth.

I fumble for my phone, but my bag's on the floor, and I don't get a good grip before the Hummer hits me again. This time I smack my head against the steering wheel. The momentary daze rattles me good.

I need help.

But there's nothing on this stretch of road.

My only hope is in the rented Saturn's maneuverability versus the Hummer's deadly mass. So I accelerate, but this time I swerve the wheel from side to side, zigging each time the Hummer zags.

Then he beats me at my game. I zag, he zigs, then rams his mountainlike front into the rear of my rental. The Saturn goes airborne into the weeds, shrubs, and young trees on the side of the road.

"Lord Jesus, I love you! Take care of Aunt Wee—"

CRASH!

What seems like a lifetime later, my door opens, and a voice calls my name. "Let's go," she says. "Out of the car."

I shake my head. Blink a couple of times. I think all my

pieces and parts are still connected, but a few of the critical ones aren't in full working order yet. Like my legs.

"Now!" she demands.

"Okay, okay." *Give me a break, lady. I just killed another car.* "I'm not so sure my legs want to hold me up."

"They better."

Something cold touches my temple. This is no rescue.

I turn, and the barrel of the pistol winds up against the bridge of my nose. "Hey! What's the deal? You hit me."

"You really are stupid," Glory says. "Get out of the car. We're going to get the sapphires. Now."

Glory? *Glory?* My camerawoman? "Huh?"

"You heard me. We're going to find your stupid cop friend, you're going to come up with some stupid excuse to take the stones with you—you can tell him you want to clean them, study them—I don't care. Just get the stones."

A series of images *click, click, click* into place in my head. I remember her schmoozing Max during the trip. Her support of his sports breaks had made me crazy, but I'd seen it as a way to gain his attention. The jealousy must have blinded me to any weird signals she might have given off.

It must've been a cinch for her to slip him the doctored ball.

The missing film? I'm sure it shows something interesting, if not incriminating. And finally, her vanishing act the minute she got home was no fluke. I'll bet she had planned to fade into the sunset—with the sapphires—the minute she and Max hit U.S. soil. But somewhere along the line, things didn't go Miss Glory's way.

I take a deep breath. "Tell me. What went wrong?"

243

"Don't yap. That mouth of yours is going to get you killed."

No. You're the one who's going to kill me. "So what if I do talk? Your gun tells me I'm not making it out of your escapade alive."

"True, but you don't need to drive me nuts these last few minutes, either."

What I need is my phone. "Okay. You have the gun. What do you want me to do?"

"You might be dumb, but not that dumb. Get out of the car."

I reach down for my purse. "Where are you taking me?"

"Don't!" The gun presses deeper. "Drop that thing back where it was. You're not giving me a faceful of mace or pepper spray."

My grubby paws hang on tighter. "Wow! That would have been a great idea. Too bad I don't have any of either."

"Drop it, Andie. Don't mess with me. I have the gun."

"Whoop-dee-doo, Glory. The chief has the sapphires. You snuff me out for the sapphires, and you have nothing left. What are you going to tell your 'friends' then?"

That's when I realize she's desperate. Desperate people rarely think clearly. I should know. I've been desperate a time or two.

But Glory isn't there yet. She leaves no space between her gun and my skin. "Not so cute," she says. "Let's go. And I'll take your purse, since you want it so much."

As we do the handover, I snag the snap on the outside flap of the bag with my pinky, and my slender phone slides onto my lap. I sigh with more oomph than necessary, cross my right leg over my left, hide the phone between my thighs, and pretend to try to slide out of the mangled car.

"Ouch!" I cry, without any need of pretense. I do hurt.

"You're going to 'ouch' a lot more if you don't hurry up."

"Okay, okay. I don't know why you're in such a rush. The chief's not going to give me the stones. He probably doesn't even have them anymore. The feds are involved, and probably a bunch of international agencies too."

Glory grabs my arm. "I've had it with you." She drags me out with surprising strength. "We're doing this my way, and you're getting those stones. If I have to let you go to Miss Mona's because it's going to take the cop time to get the sapphires back, then so be it. But if you even think of blabbing, to him or anybody else, it's goodbye Aunt Weeby."

I gasp. "She's done nothing to you. As scummy as you are, do you really want things to get worse? Why would you hurt an innocent old lady?"

Her smile looks more like a sneer. "Because you care. That's how I know you'll do what you have to do."

With everything in me, I fight the trembling her words set off. "Fine. I'll give it a try, but I doubt it'll work. Chief Clark might not be Einstein, but he's not Cro-Magnon man either." Since it looks as though I have nothing to lose, I add, "Just for kicks, you may as well tell me what your deal's all about."

She pulls on me again. "Life takes money. That's what it's all about. And your Miss Mona doesn't even begin to pay what I'm worth. A girl's got needs."

I stumble. *My need for help is a big one right now.* "How'd you get from running a camera to stealing stones?"

"I know a friend of a friend of a friend. She hooked me

up with the job opening here. We knew there was a fortune just sitting around in the studio's vault."

A friend of a friend of a friend. A super-hazy, vague memory flits through my head. And then it comes to me. The first time I saw Glory wasn't when she first started her job. It was the day a murder took place at the S.T.U.D. about a year ago. She'd said she'd come for a job interview.

Coincidence? I don't think so. I venture a guess. "Your friend wouldn't happen to be vacationing behind bars in New York, would he . . . or she?"

"That's none of your business."

But her answer comes too late. I notice the flare of her nostrils, the widening of her eyes. "You've got problems, girl," I say with a chuckle. "Roger and Tiffany can't do a thing for you from behind bars. He can't fence the stones. And she never could do anything but kill."

"Who said anything about Roger?" She laughs. "He had his uses, but you're right. There's none now that he's locked up. The guy sure does know a lot of people, though."

People? What people? "Tiffany's in worse shape than he is. She doesn't have the cash to help you with your 'needs,' and it sure won't help her 'needs' for you to wind up with all the ill-gotten gain for yourself. When's she going to share in the bounty? She's doing time for murder one. Looooots of time behind bars."

As I bide my time, I let Glory drag me through the rough weeds to the driver's side of the Hummer. I climb up into the awkward vehicle, my phone clutched in the hand I hold to my side as though injured.

"You want me to drive?" I ask, surprised.

"No. I want you to scoot over into your seat. Did you

think I was going to leave you to do your thing while I run around the car?"

She's not so dumb, after all. Not that thieves are mental whizzes, either. But . . . "Don't know what I can do without a key, Glory."

She leaps up and ignores my comment.

My rampant curiosity makes me try again. "So how does Roger connect to the guys at the Kashmir mines?"

"Roger doesn't," she says between her teeth. "That's the friend-of-a-friend connection."

"And Xheng Xhi and Farooq?"

"They were just messengers, if that. Farooq was supposed to have given the stones to Robert in Srinagar, but something went wrong. And then I caught the slug trying to steal Allison's and my stuff."

A chill runs through me. "So you killed him."

"It was self-defense."

"Yeah, right. The guy's after your wallet, and you defended your cash."

"Something like that."

"So you got rid of Farooq and Robert."

"Robert wasn't supposed to wind up in jail." Frustration creeps into her voice. "He should have gone to the mines with you guys. He's much more capable than that clumsy Xheng Xhi. All he wanted was to follow *you* around."

"And you needed the stones."

"I still need the stones." She starts up the mechanical behemoth. As it roars away, she steers with only one hand. If I can somehow manage to distract her, I'm sure I can take the gun. After all, it's still pointed right at me. What's the difference between dying now while trying to

247

get away or a half hour later when she realizes I can't get the stones?

"How do you intend for me to get the sapphires from the authorities? They don't generally fork over evidence just because you ask."

"That's your business." Her voice is deadly cold. "You might want to give it some thought instead of talking me to death. After all, your sainted aunt's life depends on your success."

"How about you drive me to the PD? I spoke to Chief Clark a little while ago. I'm sure he's still there."

"You think I'm going to turn you down, right?" Her smile is one of the ugliest things I've ever seen. "Well, guess what? I know how much you love that aunt of yours. I'm not the one watching her—I'm here, watching you. I'm not alone in this gig. You blow it, and I make sure she gets blown up right where she is."

I suck in another harsh breath. "Let's get it over with."

To my amazement, she intends to walk into the cop shop with me. How much of a sucker does she think I am? I know Aunt Weeby's being watched, but if I can overpower Glory, she won't be able to alert her pal.

Then her accomplice's identity occurs to me. I feel sick. "Allison's waiting to hear from you, isn't she?"

"Allison? That religious nut? No way."

The relief makes me weak in the knees—weaker, at any rate. "Fine. Keep your secrets, but I know Miss Mona's not your pal, and at this point, I doubt Max has the crooked gene."

She pulls into the parking lot outside the headquarters. "Let's go."

I see my glimmer of hope—and I take it. "Which way do you want me to go? Are you going to shoot me just for opening my door? Or do you want me to climb into your lap to get out?"

She pauses a moment to consider her dilemma. Then she takes a deep breath. "I'll get out, but the gun's going to be on you the whole time."

As she slips out of the car, I flip open my phone and hit the speed-dial button I'd programmed for 911 the day I got the device. I slowly slide toward the door, and as soon as the dispatcher answers, I know I have to talk over her voice.

"You're going to have to help me, Glory. I hurt my legs and my arm when you crashed my car off the road."

"I'm not stupid. You're not going to make me put down my gun so you can jump me. Come on. I don't have all night."

"Honest. I can't get out by myself. And if you keep wasting time, a cop's going to walk out here sooner or later. We're in the PD parking lot, you know. That's who'll overpower you if you just stand there waiting with that gun in your hand."

"You really don't know when to shut up, do you?" She climbs back up onto the running board. "Here."

I grab the hand she holds out. "Thanks. I really do need the help. I did get hurt when you rammed my car off the road. You don't need to keep the gun on me the whole time. I'm not going anywhere on my own. What I need is a knight in shining armor to rescue me—911 isn't an option, since you're running this show with a gun."

A car's headlights illuminate the Hummer's cab, and I wince. "Ouch!" I click my phone shut, and hope my cry of pain covers the sound. "I think I might've wound up with a concussion from the crash. The lights hurt."

"I wouldn't worry about a concussion. You won't be feeling anything soon."

I gulp. "Let's get it over and done with."

As I slip out of the Hummer, I drop my phone onto the driver's seat. Hopefully, the 911 dispatcher who answered my call realized this wasn't a prank but a kidnapping in progress. A weird one, true, since we're at police headquarters, but a kidnapping no matter how you look at it.

We head for the entryway, and then I hear a voice that, while it brings me hope, also chills me to the bone.

"Andie!" Max cries out. "I swung back around when you never caught up with me, and I saw your car out in that field. How come you didn't call 911? How'd you get here—"

"Shut up, Max," Glory says. "One more stupid word from you, and she dies. Right here."

But despite the bravado she stuffs into her words, I realize that Mr. Magnificent has just given me my best shot to get us all out of this. Hopefully, alive.

"So which one of us are you going to take out first?" I ask her, playing for time. There is that dispatcher. I hope she's done her job, and someone's on the way to help. We're at the cop shop, for goodness' sake. Where are they when you need them?

I go on playing for precious seconds. "Look, Glory. You can't aim at us both, you can't shoot us both, and whichever one's left isn't going to let you get away with killing the other."

A shrewd gleam brightens her eyes. "You wanna make a bet? Just watch."

She presses the barrel tight against my head again. "Okay, Max. Either you leave like a good boy, or she bites the dust."

I hear Max's indrawn breath, feel his hesitation. "Don't listen to her, Max," I urge. "She can't kill us both, and she knows she'll have a swarm of cops out here if that thing goes off."

"Shows you how much you know," he counters. "That thick thing attached to the barrel's a silencer. They won't hear a thing."

"Hmm . . ." Glory says, edging me forward. "Not so dumb, are you, Max? Tell her to get in there and get the sapphires."

His eyes widen. "You're still after those stupid things? Now, when the authorities have them? Talk about dumb. And here I thought you were smarter than Andie. Seems you have less smarts than even she does. Bad news for a would-be international gem thief."

She falters. "I'm smarter than you think. So far, no one's got a thing on me—"

I duck, then dive for her knees. "Max—RUN!"

But he doesn't take direction well. He goes for Glory too.

The gun blasts off a shot with a muffled "hiss."

The three of us land in a tangle of arms and legs, roll around on the blacktop, and I never stop screaming at the top of my lungs.

I grab Glory's gun hand. And scream.

She fights back, flailing the arm with the gun. She's more dangerous now than when she'd aimed. I let out another scream.

Dirt grinds into my bare arms, my cheekbone.

She smashes Max's head with the gun.

He grunts.

I scream. My throat aches from the nonstop screaming, but I don't let up. Glory bangs my head against the ground.

251

Max thrashes his large body down between us and keeps wrestling her for the gun.

I scream some more.

Then, with my last ounce of strength, I launch myself over Max and land on top of Glory, use my body to pin her to the ground, fist my fingers in her sleek, dark hair, and hold on for dear life.

That's when the swarm of cops I'd predicted shows up. One officer picks me up as if I were no more than a fly. Another drops down next to Max, and minutes later, they've collared Glory. Silver flashes when handcuffs catch the glow of the streetlights nearby. Before I know it, the officer leads her into the building, those brand-new bracelets shackling Glory into submission.

I collapse. The cop kneels at my side. "Are you hurt? Did she shoot you?"

My teeth chatter, my throat tightens, my vocal cords refuse to work. I shake my head.

Max comes to my side. "It's okay," he murmurs, and then he does the most unexpected thing. He picks me up in those muscular arms of his, presses me tight against his chest, and whispers a prayer.

"Thank you, Father. She's still alive." He glances down and lets a smile curve his lips. "And she's finally shut up."

I shudder. "You . . . you—"

"See?" he tells the cop. "She's going to be fine. Lead the way. We have a ton of questions to answer, don't we?"

With both fists, I pummel my knight in gravel-encrusted summer-wear. The blows don't even begin to faze him. "Put me down, you great big jerk."

What does the great big jerk do? Put me down and help

me inside? No. Not Max. He stuns the breath out of me. Again.

He laughs. And then he kisses me.

Long and hard.

On the lips.

Oh, my . . .

Ginny Aiken, a former newspaper reporter, lives in Pennsylvania with her engineer husband and their three youngest sons—the oldest is married and has flown the coop. Born in Havana, Cuba, and raised in Valencia and Caracas, Venezuela, Ginny discovered books at an early age. She wrote her first novel at age fifteen while she trained with the Ballets de Caracas, later to be known as the Venezuelan National Ballet. She burned that tome when she turned a "mature" sixteen. An eclectic list of jobs—including stints as reporter, paralegal, choreographer, language teacher, retail salesperson, wife, mother of four boys, and herder of their numerous and assorted friends, including soccer teams and the 135 members of first the Crossmen and then the Bluecoats Drum and Bugle Corps—brought her back to books in search of her sanity. She is now the author of twenty-seven published works, but she hasn't caught up with that elusive sanity yet.

Stunning jewels, endless shopping, exotic travel—
what woman could resist?

The Shop-Til-U-Drop Collection

Stunning jewels,
endless shopping,
exotic travel—
what girl could resist?

Priced to Move

A Novel

Ginny Aiken

Don't miss book 1 in the Shop-Til-U-Drop series!

"Ginny Aiken's gift: masterful storytelling, witty dialogue, and characters you will never forget."

—Lori Copeland, author of *Simple Gifts*

 Revell
a division of Baker Publishing Group
www.GinnyAikenWrites.com

Available wherever books are sold